Jessica Huntley

# The Darkness Within Ourselves

JHuntley

Hope you enjoy it!

First published in 2021 by Amazon

This is a work of fiction. Unless otherwise indicated, all the names, characters, businesses, places, events and incidents in this book are either the product of the author's imagination or used in a fictitious manner. Any resemblance to actual persons, living or dead, or actual events is purely coincidental.

IBSN: 9798588513326
First edition
Website: www.jessicahuntleyauthor.com
Cover Design: More Visual Ltd
Edited and proofread by: Michelle Craker
Printed by Amazon KDP Print

# About Jessica Huntley

Jessica wrote her first book at age six. Between the ages of ten and eighteen she had written ten full-length fiction novels all over 100,000 words as a hobby in her spare time between school-work.

At age eighteen she left her hobby behind her and joined the Army as an Intelligence Analyst and spent the next four and a half years as a soldier. She attempted to write further novels, but was never able to finish them.

Jessica later left the Army and became a mature student at Southampton Solent University and studied Fitness and Personal Training, which later became her career. She still enjoys keeping fit and exercising on a daily basis.

She is now a wife and a stay at home mum to a crazy toddler and lives in Edinburgh. During the first UK lockdown she signed up on a whim to a novel writing course and the rest is history. Her love of writing came flooding back and she has managed to write and finish another novel: The Darkness Within Ourselves, inspired by her love of horror and thriller novels. She is now studying to get her Level 3 Diploma in Editing and Proofreading, as well as working on further novels.

# Acknowledgements

I would like to personally thank those who have stood by me and dedicated their time and effort into helping me make this book worthy of self-publishing.

To my twin sister Alice and my best friend Katie - who have always read my stories no matter how bad they might be!

To Lauren, Rachel and Lisa - who read this book during its early stages and helped with story lines and mistakes!

To my husband Scott - who has put up with me hiding myself away in the office for hours on end.

To my son Logan - you may be too young to understand this now, but thank you for just being you (even though you attempted to distract me at every opportunity!)

To my dad - who never stopped believing in me right from the start and always told me I was a writer.

# Prologue

Children: they really are weird and wonderful creatures. They can take the seemingly mundane and turn it into something amazing, their creativity is often a sight to behold. They build bonds and forge friendships with each other that sometimes last a lifetime.

Friendship: it is a fascinating, natural thing. As children, we are taught to make friends with each other, to fix any arguments that may occur and to treat our friends how we would wish to be treated ourselves. It really is that simple ... or is it? Not all friendships can endure, not all can withstand the challenges of life nor the secrets that may emerge.

Secrets: they are there to entice us, to help form those bonds with other people that we all crave, but they can also drive even the tightest of friendships apart. They can ruin lives, change us, divide us, torment us and cause living nightmares.

Nightmares: a group of childhood friends, who share a terrifying secret, could grow up with it forever ingrained in their subconscious, constantly plaguing their dreams. It could turn them into people they no longer recognise; mere shadows of their former selves.

# Chapter One

*Monday, 20th of July 1998*

Little did she know, but this was going to be the worst day of her life.

Amber, the quiet and smart one, smiled as she glanced around the circle of her closest group of friends. They were all laughing, bickering and playfully throwing punches at each other, enjoying the freedom of being outdoors on the first day of the summer holidays, away from their parents, school and all other confinements. Her bouncy, shoulder-length, brunette hair danced in the cool breeze, flapping around her face, but she did not attempt to restrain it. Instead, she enjoyed the sensation of it tickling her nose.

Amber was blissfully happy; her friends were the most important people in her life, outside of her close family, and being an only child intensified the bond she had with them. They had all been friends since before she could remember (officially since the age of six), always hanging out at school throughout the years. She couldn't even remember *how* they had become friends; it was just one of those things that had happened naturally, seemingly overnight. Amber and her friends were all congregated in a field which was overgrown, the grass wild and free. The field had been left to develop into a wildflower meadow; no sheep or cows allowed to munch through the tall growth. This area of the Lake District was a place of stunning beauty, surrounded by rolling hills, vast mountains, numerous lakes and steep ravines. Amber's home town of Cherry Hollow was miles away from anywhere but perfectly situated in Hope Valley between two mountains. It wasn't a large town, but it housed the necessities; a school, shops, businesses, hotels, pubs, restaurants and a small police station. Cherry Hollow was a place that if you left to live elsewhere then you never returned and if an outsider moved here, then they never left.

The hot sun was beaming down, already causing a slight red tinge to appear on Amber's fair skin. She took no notice; no doubt her mother would tell her off later as she rubbed after-sun lotion into her sore skin. The heat of the sun made her feel energised and alive; she would remember this summer for as long as she lived. It was the summer that she and her four friends would turn into teenagers, leaving their seemingly innocent childhoods behind. Each of them would be celebrating their birthdays only a few weeks, or sometimes days, apart.

Tyler was the oldest – a handsome boy. He was funny, but maybe slightly too crude at times, often using words that no nearly thirteen-year-old should be using in a normal conversation. He was one of those boys that everyone seemed to love, even if he treated them badly. Amber always thought, that deep down inside, Tyler was very sad. She could not put her finger on exactly why she thought this. She could sense it somehow, but he still laughed and joked and seemed to enjoy life, so if he was unhappy, he certainly didn't show it. She often wondered whether she should ask him if he was okay, but then he would say something hilarious and she would change her mind. He was tall, broad for his age and confident; a trait all the local young girls found attractive. Tyler was the popular one, the one all the girls wanted to go out with and all the boys wanted to be like, but to Amber, he was just Tyler; her friend.

'Man, I'm so bloody bored!'

Tyler's voice echoed around the group, instantly pulling Amber out of her daydream; she had been imagining what life would be like for them in twenty years time. Where would they all be? Who would they become? Amber's dream career was to become a doctor or a scientist, someone who could help people or could help to change the world in a positive way. She knew she was intelligent and that she wanted to do something important, but that would mean leaving Cherry Hollow and starting a new life somewhere else.

'Let's do something,' continued Tyler.

'Like what?' Kieran's question caused everyone else to stop bickering and listen.

Kieran was the youngest of the group, but only by a few weeks. Despite this, he was considered the troublemaker, always causing arguments. There was usually one like him in every group of friends. Amber thought of him as the outsider. He was the loose cannon. His dark blonde hair was always flapping around his forehead; he thought it made him look cool, the same went for his overly baggy clothes. He constantly wore a small blue watch, which had been a gift from his parents on his tenth birthday. There was nothing noticeable about the watch other than the fact it had been engraved on the back of the dial with a special message from his parents: *We will love you till the end of time.* In general, Kieran was a good kid, but there was always some unspoken tension between him and Tyler, like there was a competition between them to see who could be the best at everything. Games would usually end with one of them beating the other and gloating, causing an argument. Then, the next day, it would have all blown over, like it had never happened. Amber sometimes wondered if they really were friends, or if they only just *played along.*

'Let's play a game.' Tyler's suggestion was met by lots of nodding and approval.

*Here we go,* thought Amber.

The group often played games; football, truth or dare and most recently they had discovered drinking games. Once, Tyler and Kieran had started a drinking game which eventually turned into a competition. It had ended with Kieran in hospital having his stomach pumped. It had not gone down well with either of their parents.

'How about hide and seek?' This time it was Brooke who spoke, her voice soft and feminine, but confident in its projection.

Brooke's natural beauty lit up every room she entered. All the boys loved her, something she was very much aware of and would often use to her advantage. Her brilliant blue eyes sparkled, her bright blonde hair was radiant, her skin glowed with youth and possibly too much makeup for a girl of her age. Brooke was Amber's best female friend. They told each other everything, all the little details of their lives as they happened and all the best secrets. There was one secret Amber hadn't told her though, something that had happened a couple of days ago, but she wasn't ready to tell the rest of the group yet. There were some secrets that did not need to be told straight away. Those were the best kind of secrets. Brooke always made Amber feel better, even if it was just by giving her a hug, she was always there for her. Amber knew they would be best friends forever; nothing would ever come between them.

Tyler scoffed at her suggestion. 'That's for little kids. I say we play *I spy*, but let's make it more interesting.'

'How?' Jordan was the last to speak up.

Jordan was the nice boy, the type of boy any young girl would love to bring home to meet her parents; a real genuine, polite young man. He never swore and never raised his voice in anger. He was also Amber's best male friend. They had a special connection – a deep and meaningful friendship. Jordan's eyes were a beautiful dark brown, the kind of eyes you could lose yourself in. His hair was wavy and brown and as soft as velvet. Sometimes he would gently kiss Amber on her forehead and she always knew, in that instant, that everything was going to be okay. He made her feel safe, secure, loved.

Tyler jumped to his feet, sending grass and pollen into the air. Everyone's attention was drawn to his enthusiasm. 'I reckon we turn *I spy* into a dare game. How bout it?' He glanced around at the group, each one rolling their eyes or screwing up their nose in response. 'Just follow my lead. I spy with my little eye something beginning with G.'

Silence followed; no one understood what the *interesting* part was supposed to be. Amber glanced around at the confused frowns on her friends' faces.

'Grass?'

'Yep. Now I *dare* you to bring me a blade of grass.'

Amber rolled her eyes to the back of her head. Bright green grass surrounded her, the sweet scent wafted into her nostrils as she plucked a single blade of grass and handed it over.

Tyler took it. 'Now it's your turn, but this time make the dare dangerous – make it fun.'

Amber's understanding of Tyler's *interesting* twist on the game was now starting to become clear. Her sense of danger and adventure was awakened; her eyes twinkled mischievously. She was not usually one to break the rules or push boundaries, but this game seemed harmless enough and certainly would brighten up an otherwise average day.

'I spy with my little eye something beginning with L'.

She had spied a nearby oak tree, its oddly shaped leaves dancing in the soft breeze high above in the thick, ancient branches. It was the only tree in the field, growing almost directly in the middle, like a lone statue left to defend its territory. The group of adolescents glanced around, anxiously and excitedly searching for the illusive object, with the added bonus of a dangerous element ahead.

It was Jordan who made the discovery.

'Leaf!' His outstretched arm directed the attention of the group towards the leaves above.

'I dare you to climb that tree and bring me a leaf from as high up as possible.'

Amber felt pleased with herself; it was dangerous, but not *too* dangerous. They also climbed that particular tree all the time, knowing all of the best branches to use to enable them to climb higher. Jordan jumped to his feet as the crowd cheered him on, whooping and clapping.

The oak tree was old, its branches bore the scars of many years of being beaten by the wind, but they remained strong and rigid as Jordan climbed. Thousands of green prizes surrounded him, but to bring one of those would have been too easy. He was aiming for higher up where his weight put pressure on the branches to stay intact. Below, the cheering could still be heard; it was spurring him on and on.

'Go on Jordan! Higher!' shouted Tyler.

'Too easy!' shouted Kieran.

The boys seemed to be enjoying the element of danger, but deep down Amber was starting to sense a twinge of fear, her heart rate increasing in speed, her breath beginning to catch in her throat. Maybe this hadn't been such a good idea.

Jordan was now out of sight, the thick foliage blocking her view of him. She was just about to call him back down when he emerged through the leaves and jumped down directly in front of her, his eyes sparkling with a sense of achievement.

'Your leaf, my lady.' He presented the leaf on an open palm, sarcastically bowing to offer her the prize. She took it and gave him a playful slap across his head.

'Your turn, genius.' Jordan winked at her in his usual cheeky and flirtatious way.

The game had now officially begun. Each of them came up with a new dare every time, their imaginations running wild. Most of the dares were fairly harmless. Brooke climbed the barbed wire fence at the entrance to the field with her eyes closed. Kieran climbed through a nearby hedge full of brambles. Tyler ate an unknown leaf from a random plant. They laughed, joked and made fun of each other. Amber loved to hear her friends laugh. She took a moment, soaking up the happy atmosphere. It was then that Kieran decided to take the game to another level.

'Let's go for a walk to the ravine – see what else we can find. There's nothing else dangerous around here.' His suggestion was approved.

The group headed across the field, the grass gradually getting longer as they reached the edge. A barbed wire fence blocked their path; an old, mould-covered sign read *"DANGER – Beaker Ravine Ahead. KEEP OUT"*. Everyone knew about the ravine, but no one took any notice of the warning. The sign had been put there because a local child had got stuck at the bottom for nearly twenty-four hours a few years ago, which had caused everyone in the town to avoid the ravine from then on. Everyone, that was, apart from the local kids. A small dark cave was situated in the rocky sides and that was the perfect place to smoke weed or get drunk. It was like the ravine was a haven for the teenagers of Cherry Hollow, a secret place; no adults allowed.

'Come on Kieran, out with it!' Tyler was impatient; he wanted the danger, the excitement, something to distract him.

A broken beer bottle lay on the path ahead, possibly casually dropped there by the older gang of local kids who would often visit the ravine to drink and fool around. Tyler picked up the bottle and hurled it at an innocent nearby tree; hundreds of tiny glass fragments exploded and scattered across the ground. Amber jumped in shock, quietly annoyed that Tyler was being so inconsiderate.

'Be patient loser!' Kieran snapped.

The group soldiered on towards the ravine, getting further away from the town. It was at least four miles ahead in the distance, but they always came here. Their parents were used to their children being gone the majority of the day, coming back in time for dinner, usually covered in mud and scrapes, but with happy, tired smiles on their faces.

Finally, the expedition reached some thick trees that blocked the way to the ravine; a silent warning to any travellers not to go any further. The ravine was several miles long, but seemed to stretch out into the distance for eternity; its steep, rocky walls created over thousands of years of erosion. Landslides were regular, often occurring when no one was around so that when the next person laid their eyes on the ravine it looked different. Loose stones paved a very rough path down the opposite side, but it wasn't suitable for human access; maybe nifty-footed mountain sheep, which were plentiful in this area of the country. A shallow, clear river snaked its way across the bottom towards a larger expanse of water a few miles away; a large, black lake known as Lake Peace, so called because to sit by the waters was to sit in complete and utter solitude; a peaceful place that calmed the soul.

After battling the thick trees, the sharp branches and brambles, which caused several scratches to appear on their bare arms, the group came to a halt at the edge, panting slightly at the effort it had taken to arrive here. They had emerged at one of the steepest sides, almost a straight, sheer drop of nearly one-hundred feet down to the water and jagged rocks. A decrepit fallen tree had created a natural bridge across the expanse, caused by a recent landslide, its roots torn out of the earth too soon, now doomed to slowly rot and die.

'I spy with my little eye something beginning with S'.

Kieran had begun the game again.

The search started immediately. Tyler jumped up on the fallen tree roots and peered over the edge, his head swimming slightly at the height. He wanted another go at completing a dare so was determined to answer first.

'Stones?' he guessed. They were abundant in this area, ranging from the small pebbles to the large rocks adorning the ravine walls.

'I dare you to go and get a stone from the bottom of the ravine.'

Tyler backed away from the edge. 'Aww man! I knew you were going to say that. You know I don't like heights.' Tyler's fear of heights had arisen due to getting stuck on the roof of his house once while his parents had been out. He had sat up there for almost four hours before he had been rescued by his dad, who had scolded him for his stupidity of climbing up there in the first place. Tyler was not keen on this new element of risk.

'Aww, what's the matter dickhead, you chicken?' Kieran jeered.

'Yeah come on Tyler, this game was your idea,' added Jordan.

Tyler was silent for a moment, thoughts buzzing around his head. 'Fine.' Tyler wasn't going to be called chicken by anyone.

'Be careful Tyler.' Brooke's words of comfort did nothing to calm his rapid heartbeat, his throat suddenly as dry as a bone. Beads of sweat started dripping down his neck as he approached the edge of the ravine.

Slowly he began his descent. The cheers from above seemed like a hazy echo because all he could hear was the pounding of his heart. Small, loose stones made his footing unstable, large boulders blocked his way so he had to climb over or around them, clinging to their smooth surfaces as best as he could. He took his time, not wanting to rush and fall to his death. He was almost at the bottom, a mere few feet away, when suddenly his right foot slipped from underneath him, caused by a loose rock. His left arm shot out to grab whatever he could find, but there was nothing there.

The skin on his arm was ripped open by a sharp rock, warm blood started trickling down, causing his whole hand to become stained and slippery. A loud thud signified the end of his fall. He lay still for a moment, unsure whether he was alive or dead.

'Tyler!' He could hear his name being shouted from somewhere high above him, but he was in no position to answer yet. The wind had been knocked out of him; he was struggling to draw breath.

Amber was beside herself. She could see he was alive, but he was barely moving. 'We need to help him!' She had never felt fear like it. The ravine had never been a dangerous place before today, but she knew they were being reckless by climbing down into it at its steepest point.

'Na, leave him. He's fine – look he's moving.' Kieran pointed out.

Tyler's weak voice echoed up. 'I ... I'm okay.'

'See! He's fine.'

Relief washed over Amber like a wave, her heart was still thumping hard in her chest. This game had been a mistake; she knew that now, or at least coming to the ravine had been one. She watched apprehensively as Tyler gingerly got to his feet and began his slow ascent back to the top. He couldn't use his left arm very well, but he used it to balance himself, blood staining any stone outcrop he touched.

Finally, he emerged, panting and sweating as he approached Kieran, who had an annoying smirk across his face.

'Here's your damn stone.'

'Quit being a wimp Tyler. You only slipped a few feet.' It was like he didn't care that his friend could have plummeted to his death. His attitude made all his friends turn and stare at him, a look of horror on each of their faces.

'Stop it Kieran,' warned Amber. 'Tyler could have died if he had slipped and fallen from any higher up.'

'Yeah, right. Go on Tyler, it's your turn. I'll guess the correct answer and I'll do whatever dangerous thing you come up with and prove that you were just being a wimp.'

Tyler straightened up and attempted to make himself look bigger; an act of intimidation.

'Forget the guessing!' he spat angrily. 'I dare you to walk across that tree to the other side of the ravine and back again without using your hands to steady yourself.' Tyler's voice was an angry hiss. The game was forgotten, now it was about revenge and trying to prove who was the bigger man. Amber should have known this would happen – it always did.

'Pffft! Easy peasy!'

It was coming up to half past three in the

afternoon. The sun was high in the sky, blinding the group of friends as they watched Kieran approach the fallen tree. Amber shielded her eyes with her hand, feeling an uneasy wave of fear throughout her body. She was angry at Kieran for being so heartless towards Tyler, but also annoyed at Tyler for letting it get to him and start up a new and dangerous challenge. A part of her wanted to watch Kieran suffer for what he had said to Tyler. It seemed everyone felt the same way because no one attempted to stop him as he jumped onto the tree, its branches quivering at the sudden impact.

Amber quietly watched as Kieran crept along the makeshift bridge. He had a confident grin on his face as he pretended to wobble every now and then, causing Brooke to scream. He loved to tease her. Brooke had her eyes covered with her hands, barely able to watch. Amber was holding her breath. She felt like she was in a haze, as if time had slowed down and was doing so intentionally. There was something wrong – something missing. She could hear angry shouting, screaming, voices, but couldn't work out where they were coming from. Everything was fuzzy, like she was looking at this moment through dirty glass.

Suddenly, there was a loud thud, followed by a scream and then silence. One moment Kieran was standing on the tree, wobbling slightly and the next he was at the bottom of the ravine, his body mangled and torn apart by the explosion of force as he hit the rocks.

Amber's world instantly came into focus, her brain snapped out of the thick fog and returned to the real world. Her whole body was trembling, tears poured from her eyes, her heart rate at its highest. No one moved a muscle or made a sound; they were frozen in time. There was an eerie, yet peaceful silence. Amber knew it couldn't last forever, but she also knew that she didn't have the strength or the courage to speak first. Someone was going to have to take control of this situation.

Her life was about to change forever. This was the defining moment of her life, the one that caused her and her friends to disappear down different paths, to walk alone and to fear the unknown. There are moments in life that define you, that shape you into the person you are destined to become, but it was this one single moment that changed Amber and her friends into people they never wanted to be – strangers.

## Chapter Two

*Twenty years later.*

Amber crouched as low as possible behind a rickety chest of drawers, her only defence against The Creature that was hunting her. It had pursued her for years, its unwavering determination never faltering, always focused directly on her. Amber was not sure how much longer she could keep evading it. Her strength was beginning to fade, but she had to keep fighting. She had to stay alive for her daughter. She peered out from behind the drawers. It was dark, hard to make out anything clearly. However, she could see a shape in the doorway; a tall, gangly, black shape. It was The Creature. Long, claw-like hands reached out towards Amber, a raspy, breathless voice whispered her name, sending a cold shiver up her spine. This was the end. Ugly, dirty hands clenched around her throat, squeezing, the sharp nails digging into her pale skin, drawing crimson blood; her breath left her body. She was gone. The Creature had finally caught its prey.

Then she woke up. Her eyes were wide and red with veins, but the nightmare was not over yet. An invisible force was pinning her down, its vice-like grip still squeezing her throat, her arms, her legs. She couldn't scream, her own voice silenced by intense fear. The darkness engulfed her, surrounded her. The Creature continued to bear down from above, hovering over her like an invisible shadow. Amber prayed for it to be over soon. The sleep paralysis usually only lasted for a couple of minutes upon waking, but the seconds ticked by in slow motion, casually taking their time to pass, ensuring that she suffered for as long as possible. Amber had once used Google to search for the definition of sleep paralysis and it had casually said:

*Sleep paralysis is when you cannot move or speak upon waking up. It can be scary, but it is perfectly harmless, and most people will only experience it once or twice in their lifetime.*

Perfectly harmless? Once or twice in a lifetime? She wished it were true for her and as simple and harmless as Google made it out to be.

Amber was petrified. The worst part was the terrifying fact of not being able to move her body even though she was awake. People would often tell her that they knew exactly how she felt, that they would sometimes dream of being paralysed, but it was not the same. Unless someone had experienced this phenomenon for themselves no one could imagine the intense fear of being held down by something heavy and invisible – something evil. Sometimes Amber would see The Creature out of the corner of her eye, standing beside her bed as she was frozen in fear, but this morning it was invisible, but still just as terrifying.

Then, without any warning, the paralysis ended. Amber immediately gasped for a breath, gulping and coughing, trying to get her lungs to draw in that sweet oxygen. Sitting up in bed she scanned the dark bedroom for The Creature in case it was here. It was not. She was alone. Maybe it had never been there at all. She was never sure if it was genuinely real or a figment of her imagination, or even a hallucination caused by her insomnia, which was a common side effect of a lack of sleep. Amber considered herself lucky if she managed to get three to four hours and it was not constant sleep either; her sleep cycle never got a chance to finish before her body jerked itself awake.

The eerie green glow from her alarm clock on her bedside table read 03:31 a.m. The night was not over yet. The warm body of her husband was next to her, sleeping soundly. She envied Sean, wishing she could sleep as deeply and peacefully as he did. He didn't even stir as she rolled out of bed and crept into the en-suite, closed the door and switched on the night light.

In the mirror a tired-looking, pale, thin creature stared back at her, fresh bluish bruises on her throat and arms. She gently stroked the contusions on her neck, running her fingers over some small indentations; they looked like they had been made by sharp nails, or claws. Amber gently pushed her own fingernails from her right hand into the crescent shaped lines; they matched in certain places but not in others. A tiny amount of blood oozed out of the injury; she wiped it away. This should have shocked her, but it was an almost nightly occurrence now. It had slowly been getting worse over the past two decades, ever since *that* day. The Creature had first appeared to her three nights later, signalling the start of her real life nightmare —

*Amber had spent the last three days trying to understand how she had got herself into this situation. Three days ago her life had been perfect and she had been happy hanging out with her friends. Now one of those friends was dead and the rest had made no attempt to contact her; the phone on the wall had remained silent. Her days had been empty and lonely, but she had been unable to tell anyone why. She had been questioned very briefly by the police, a young sergeant named Graham Williams who said he was working on the case of Kieran's disappearance. He had asked her about Kieran, whether he had ever mentioned about running away. She had replied no. And that had been that – no further questions. It was at that moment the guilt had started, a severe itch somewhere deep down that she couldn't satisfy. Could a person die from guilt? It felt that way to her. Amber wished that she could free herself of the guilty feeling, but instead she swallowed it, buried it deep down and carried on as if nothing had happened.*

*The night after she had spoken to the police she had trouble falling asleep. She tossed and turned, her mind whirling with a thousand thoughts of nothing in particular, not even of Kieran – just emptiness. Amber had never experienced trouble falling asleep before. Usually, her parents would have to drag her out of bed in the mornings after sleeping deeply for over ten hours.*

*Amber sighed deeply, feeling frustrated. If only it were possible to switch her mind off, like a light switch, one simple movement of the finger and suddenly she was asleep. Amber closed her eyes, willing sleep to come. It didn't; it continued to elude her. She could hear the ticking of her bedroom wall clock, its constant passing of time taunting her with every second. That was when she heard it for the very first time; the raspy breathing. It was coming from somewhere in her room, but she couldn't pinpoint where. It seemed to emanate from everywhere, from all four corners. Her eyes sprung open, but in the dull light of the night she could not see very well. The moonlight shone through her thin curtains enough to illuminate random patches of her room. There was nothing there. The sound continued. Amber pulled her bed sheet further up until it was right under her chin; she felt like it was a barrier between her and whatever was in her room.*

*'Hello?' she called out quietly. 'Is someone there?'*

*There was no direct answer. She felt the room go ice cold, but she did not shiver because of it. The coldness encircled her, wrapped her in a tight hold, and caused her breathing to become shallow. Amber had never felt coldness like it. She could not understand why her body was not shivering.*

*Then, a dark, claw-like hand emerged at the bottom of her bed and gently grabbed hold of her bed sheet, the ugly fingers curling over the fabric, slowly dragging it off her. She was trying to scream out for her parents, but her voice had been stolen by fear itself. Fear. Amber had experienced fear before, most recently a few days ago when the incident had happened, but this fear was different. It did not emanate from within her mind and body. It was real; a real physical presence that she could see, hear and feel.*

*Then the claw disappeared out of sight, gradually sinking into the inky darkness.*

*Amber woke up. It had been a dream, or more precisely, a nightmare. There was something wrong; she couldn't move. Was she paralysed? She tried to wiggle her toes, but they were frozen solid. A heavy weight pushed down on her from above, directly in the middle of her chest and neck, squeezing the breath from her lungs. Fear began to rise up from within, moving up her body, her legs, hips, stomach, arms and finally to her head. It was still icy cold. She tried desperately to move a part of her body – any part. Her fingers were twitching, trying to grab at her bed sheet. Inside she was screaming over and over for help, but no one could hear her.*

*'Please help me! Help me!' she screamed silently. No one came, no one heard, no one cared. She was alone, or was she? Amber realised she could move her eyes. She shifted her gaze to look to the side of her bed and what she saw was truly horrifying. It was a Creature – a large, dark, living Creature with blood red eyes. It was standing next to her, breathing in and out slowly, causing a large, dark shadow to loom above her. It didn't harm her or try and touch her, but it was there and it spoke.*

*'I see you,' it whispered in a raspy voice.*

*Amber immediately realised that she could now*

*close her eyes. She squeezed them tight, never wanting to see that Creature ever again. It was at that moment that the weight released itself from her chest and she was able to breathe properly again. She gasped and coughed and abruptly sat up in bed, relieved to be able to move her body. She launched herself out of bed and ran to her parents' room crying. The Creature did not follow.*

Amber cleaned herself up as best as she could, wiping the light beads of sweat that had formed on her forehead. She had endured many encounters with The Creature over the years, but none terrified her more than that first meeting. It haunted her to this very day. She took one last look at herself in the mirror and then joined Sean back in bed. She knew she wouldn't sleep for the rest of the night and prepared herself for the remaining three hours of silence, darkness and fear as she waited for her alarm to sound, signalling the start of another day where she had to pretend like everything was okay and that she wasn't hiding a deep, dark secret. It was a secret so horrible that it made her insides ache. She needed a release, to be free of that ache, but she knew it would never come.

When Sean's 06:30 a.m. alarm sounded Amber was already up, showered and dressed. Today was Monday. She had her monthly appointment with Dr

Allan, her therapist, and then she would go into work afterwards.

Amber worked at a local coffee shop called The Bean Café. She wore a high-necked top, her attempt to cover her bruises and marks, but she expected it would look suspicious, especially because today was going to be a scorcher.

Sean joined her in the bathroom as she finished her makeup, his thick black hair sticking up in random directions, a sign that he had experienced a good sleep.

'Morning babe.'

He kissed her on her cheek, leaving a warm sensation throughout her body, the same ritual he did every morning of their ten year marriage. It was the only time he really showed her any affection, except when he wanted something more, but it was the way it had always been. Yes, there had been a time when they hadn't been able to keep their hands off each other; that was twelve years ago when they had first met. Amber had been twenty, he twenty-two; just kids. They married two years later and Bethany came along three years after that. Their marriage wasn't perfect, but they loved each other and that was all that mattered. Although *love* was a strong word. Yes, she did love him, but there was a small part of her that was no longer *in love* with him, and that scared her. That was another secret she kept from him – one of many.

'Good morning,' replied Amber. 'Did you sleep well?' She already knew he had but liked to ask him anyway. She attempted to ruffle his hair in a playful manner, but he ducked away, heading straight for the shower. She had always loved his hair, loved to run her fingers through it, especially when it got a bit too long, like it was now. He was a handsome man. He had a good body for someone who didn't go to the gym or eat particularly well; not too skinny, not too muscular. He wasn't that tall either; a mere five-foot-ten-inches, but since she was only five-foot-five-inches he was a good fit for her.

'Yeah, was good,' he answered. 'You?' There was an empty silence between them which seemed to last for a lot longer than the five seconds it actually lasted. 'Another episode?'

'Yeah.' Her voice quaked for a slight second, but she quickly brushed past it. 'But I slept until about half three so a better night than most.'

'That's good.'

Luckily, he didn't seem to notice that she was wearing a high-necked top – either that or he didn't care. He very rarely questioned her about her sleep paralysis. She had told him about a year into their relationship that she suffered from it but had not mentioned the reason *why*. It had been getting more and more difficult to hide it from him.

Amber also suffered from hypnagogic and hypnopompic hallucinations, which occurred before she fell asleep and after she woke up respectively. This was the official name of the hallucinations of The Creature from the many doctors and therapists she had seen over the years. *They are nothing more than your imagination and are not real* she had been told over and over again. *They cannot hurt you.* The doctors had told her at the start that they were caused by Post Traumatic Stress Disorder, something that had developed after the disappearance of one of her best friends. *It was normal,* they said. *It will pass with time.* But it never did.

Amber never spoke about the physical injuries she often sustained during her hallucinations. How would the doctors explain that? Maybe she was doing it to herself, choking herself in her sleep? Possibly. In the end, twenty years after she had first seen The Creature, she had stopped telling her therapist about it because it only caused a never-ending circle of discussion. The worst part was that she couldn't tell anyone the *real* reason why she was suffering from these visions and sleep issues. Dr Allan would ask her many times why she thought she had them and she would reply with *I don't know.* Of course, she knew, but it was a secret only her and three other people in the world knew.

Amber's seven-year-old daughter, Bethany, was already up and sitting at the breakfast table when she arrived downstairs. She loved how independent her daughter was, while simultaneously it made her feel sad because she was growing up so quickly, no longer a baby or a toddler, but a proper child who could do so many things by herself. Bethany had already got her bowl, spoon and cereal out and ready, but hadn't yet poured the milk as she usually spilled it everywhere, so she was waiting patiently for her mother.

Bethany grinned at Amber as she entered the room, instantly lifting her mood and making her forget her nightmares and troubles. Her daughter was pure light and happiness itself. Her blonde curls and blue eyes made her look like a living doll, her perfectly pure and smooth skin like porcelain. In a way she was too beautiful and perfect for her own good. Amber knew one day she would be a heart-breaker. Amber's only wish was that she would stay an innocent child forever, always protected by her mother. It ached in Amber's heart to think that one day Bethany would no longer need her, no longer ask for cuddles and fall asleep on her, no longer ask her to cut the crusts off her toast or ask her to wash her hair.

The morning sunshine beamed through the double patio doors which led out from the large kitchen/diner onto a massive patio area, instantly lighting up the whole of the downstairs. Amber always loved this room in the summer, the extra long days meant there was more daylight to enjoy. It sent happy vibes through her body rather than the gloomy darkness, which often brought fear and horrible hallucinations. This house was Amber's dream house; four bedrooms, two bathrooms, a large kitchen/diner, lounge, playroom and an office, which was mainly Sean's domain. The garden was big too, stretching out for the length of a football field towards the rolling countryside. Sean had built Bethany a tree house in the old oak tree at the bottom of the garden. Bethany would often run at full pelt to it after school and play inside for a while.

'Morning Munchkin.' Amber planted a kiss on the top of her child's head, her beautiful blonde hair soft to the touch; it seemed to glow in the morning sunshine.

'Morning Mummy. I've got my coco-pops out of the cupboard, but I need help pouring the milk.'

'Yes, of course. Give me a second.'

Amber switched on the expensive coffee machine; coffee was severely needed this morning. She poured her child's milk into her favourite bowl, a sparkly blue one covered in snowflakes. Bethany's love of the Disney film *Frozen* was apparent all over this house. She then set about the morning routine of simultaneously preparing toast for herself and Sean, as well as gathering the leftover toys and things around the kitchen/diner that had been left out overnight. Amber moved effortlessly around the kitchen, easily swapping from one job to the next without pausing as Bethany sat quietly and watched while munching on her coco-pops.

A few minutes later Sean walked into the kitchen and switched on the small television that was perched on the side of the worktop. They liked to have some background noise while they ate breakfast, a time they used to catch up on the daily news, or at weekends they would watch cartoons.

'Daddy, I had a dream last night.' Bethany often told her father about her dreams. It seemed to be regular ritual. One time she told him that she had dreamt she had transformed into a ladybird and was being chased by a bird who wanted to eat her as a snack.

'Did you? What was it about?'

'Mummy.'

'Oh.' Sean glanced at Amber out of the corner of his eye as he took a bite of his peanut butter on toast. Amber smiled as she continued with her morning chores; washing up, wiping counters – all while eating her breakfast and slurping her coffee. She did enjoy hearing about Bethany's dreams; they were always harmless and often quite amusing. She was relieved that Bethany had no trouble sleeping; she took after Sean in that area. Both of them could sleep through the loudest thunderstorm.

'Yes, Mummy had some friends round and they were all playing games with me.'

'That sounds nice. Which friends?'

Bethany paused for a moment. 'I haven't seen them before, but one was very scary and angry. I can't remember his name.'

Amber stopped mid-slurp and slowly lowered her coffee mug, gently placing it on the counter, her eyes focused.

Sean looked confused and frowned. 'But Mummy doesn't have any male friends.' He didn't want to add any further details – that she didn't have *any* friends. It was often a subject he brought up. Clearly, he wanted her to have friends and he couldn't understand why she didn't have any. She had grown up in this town after all. Surely everyone had childhood friends, but he had never heard her talk of any, nor did she have any grainy photographs of herself when she was younger around the house. Her childhood was a mystery to him.

'But he said he knew her from a long time ago —'

'Bethany please go and get dressed ready for school. This is the last week before the summer holidays so you don't want to be late.' Amber cut off the conversation before it could go any further; her voice quivering as she spoke.

'Yes Mummy.' Luckily, Bethany was at that age where she forgot about things fairly quickly if she had a suitable distraction.

Amber breathed a sigh of relief; her heart rate had speeded up, her mouth was dry. There was that *fear* again.

'What was that about?' Sean got up and put his dirty plate in the sink, leaving the washing up for his wife to complete. 'Do you have a male friend from a long time ago?'

'No, of course I don't.'

Amber had never told him about her life before *it* had happened. Those people no longer existed. They were a distant memory, one which she never recollected if she could help it. In fact, those memories were buried so far down in her subconscious that she wasn't even sure they were real or which parts were real, but today they had started to resurface. She had never spoken about *that* day, not to Sean, not to her therapist, not to anyone, as per their pact. It was close to fifteen years since she had spoken to any of them; the last person she had spoken to was Jordan, near her eighteenth birthday. Of course, they all still lived in the area so they saw one another from time to time, but they always pretended like they hadn't. They were strangers. It was a very awkward situation. Amber wished she would have moved away years ago.

The dream that Bethany had dreamt last night disturbed her. Could it be related to what had happened the other night?

Amber was vaguely aware of the background noise of the local news broadcast, but as it played, she became more and more gripped by the content:

'An old, broken watch has been found in the Beaker Ravine. Local kids found it while playing yesterday afternoon. It had splatters of dried blood on it, but otherwise was clean and in good condition. After further investigation it has been revealed that the blood and the watch belong to Kieran Jones, who was last seen nearly twenty years ago. The boy's parents have confirmed the watch belonged to their son due to the engraving found on the back. It is not known if he is still alive as a body has never been found. Detective Inspector Williams, who worked on the case previously, is considering reopening the case and urges anyone with information to come forward. However, without further evidence, it is likely the case will remain unsolved. Kieran Jones was last seen on the 20th of July 1998 by his parents.'

Amber stared at the screen in disbelief. Seeing *his* name in writing and an old picture of him posing on his bike sent shock waves through her body; her mind was whirling with thoughts and questions. She wasn't sure that she had actually heard the news presenter correctly, but she dare not draw attention to herself by asking Sean to turn the volume up. Her mind had played tricks on her before. She constantly had to ensure that she wasn't hallucinating, sometimes she didn't know what was real or not.

Sean appeared to have not noticed the fact that his wife had turned as white as a ghost, her tired, sullen face drained of what little colour it usually had.

'Wow, that's interesting,' said Sean, finishing his coffee. That was all he said. Amber didn't reply to her husband, but he didn't appear to care. 'Right, well, I'm off to work. See you tonight.' He planted a kiss on her cheek, but she didn't move a muscle; he may as well have kissed a stone statue.

Sean left the house, leaving Amber alone in the kitchen – alone, afraid and confused. Her mind began to wander back to *that* day, that fateful day when her whole life had changed. She couldn't remember much before Kieran fell, almost as if her mind was blocking her memory, but she did remember what happened directly afterwards —

*Amber realised that she had been holding her breath. She didn't know for how long, but suddenly she took in a great big gulp of air. It burned her lungs, her throat, her whole body. It felt poisonous, but she breathed the oxygen in anyway because if she didn't, she thought she might pass out. Why wasn't anyone speaking? Someone had to take control. The only thing Amber knew for sure was that Kieran was no longer on the fallen tree, but there hadn't been a scream – or had there? She couldn't remember hearing any sound at all from him, just a sudden thud, like a pumpkin had been dropped from the top of a house onto solid concrete.*

*Amber looked at Tyler who was also frozen in time. His eyes were wide – wider than normal, his teeth gritted. She could have sworn he looked angry, but then he noticed her staring at him.*

*Time unfroze at that moment.*

*'Follow me.' His voice quivered for a split second before he turned and headed for the rough path he had taken to the bottom only minutes ago.*

*Then Brooke and Jordan started shouting and screaming at once.*

*'Oh my God! Kieran!'*

*'What happened! Where is he?'*

*Amber couldn't speak, her voice had deserted her. Brooke was screaming, pulling her hair, falling to the ground, tears pouring from her eyes – she was falling apart. Jordan was shouting at Tyler, getting right up in his face. He shoved him hard in the chest, an action that was very out of character for him.*

*'What did you do!'*

*'Shut up and follow me!' Tyler snapped, his voice full of anger. Amber had never seen him so full of rage. Everyone stopped and watched as Tyler started making his way down the rocky path.*

*Brooke turned to Amber and grabbed her arm, squeezing and digging her nails in so hard Amber thought she may have drawn blood, but she didn't bother looking. She felt the sharp sting of long nails embedding into her skin, but the pain did not register in her mind. She was numb.*

*'Amber, do something!' she wailed.*

*'I-I don't ... I don't know —' she began.*

*'We should go and call the police.' Jordan had joined Brooke at Amber's side.*

*'Get fucking down here now!' Tyler's voice was so stern that all three jumped in fear and scurried after him, not daring to make any further suggestions – Tyler had taken charge.*

*The trip to the bottom of the ravine seemed to last an eternity, each step filled Amber with terror. What would they find at the bottom? She expected the worst – Kieran was dead. She was sure about that. There was no way a person could survive a fall from that height onto rocks. She couldn't think straight. It was as if she was drunk, not that she really knew what that felt like. She had only had a couple of alcopops at a party once. It had given her a small buzz, but this feeling she had now was much stronger, her mind fuzzy and blurry.*

*By the time she arrived at the bottom, Tyler was already standing next to the body. The body – Kieran's body. It was hardly a body anymore though. It was a mangled pile of blood, guts, bones and skin. Brooke immediately heaved and threw up. Jordan inhaled sharply. Amber's eyes filled with tears and bile rose in her throat; a sick, empty feeling flooded her entire body. It felt as if her soul had left her. She was floating above seeing the events unfold – surely this was not real.*

*The impact of the body hitting the rocks had completely smashed it apart. Bones were broken, blood was gushing, slowly trickling down into the river, being washed away, gone forever. Kieran had landed just up the bank onto a pile of sharp rocks.*

*Amber approached slowly, barely recognising the remains of her friend, but it was her friend. She had never seen anything so awful, so gruesome. It was like something you would expect to see in a horror movie.*

*'Right,' said Tyler. 'This is what we do ...'*

*Amber looked at him, studying his body*

*language as he spoke. While everyone else was falling apart, crying or in shock, Tyler was calm, controlled and stern, so she listened intently.*

Amber blinked and her kitchen came back into focus. It all came rushing back so vividly. Tears filled her eyes. *The watch* – his damn watch had been found. More memories came flooding back; how she had returned home that day, rushed upstairs and hidden from her parents. She had been hiding something ever since; a secret. No one could know, but now the secret was beginning to reveal itself ...

# Chapter Three

The small studio flat stank of stale smoke, dirty clothes and unwashed dishes that were piled high in the sink. The old crusty remains from previous meals clung to the cutlery and stained the worktops. Tyler meandered slowly into the kitchen area, which comprised of a tiny hob, a sink, a mini-fridge and an oven. A single shelf and cupboard contained some pots, pans, plates and cutlery, all of which were filthy and in desperate need of being thrown away. He found a semi-clean bowl, emptied the rest of a cereal packet into it and began to eat the dry, crunchy flakes using his hands. A half-empty bottle of Corona perched on the very edge of the worktop. Tyler grabbed it and chugged it down. It was flat and warm. He then tossed the bottle into the makeshift bin; a black bin bag tied to the only chair in the flat.

He had work today, building a wall in some rich old person's garden. He wished he didn't have to work. He would rather do nothing and sit in his flat all day, in his own filth. It was better than going out into the world and earning a living, if you could even call it that. Becoming a builder had come naturally to Tyler. He hadn't been to college, just learnt as he went along, and the town came to know him as the quiet handyman. He had a few builder buddies he spoke to sometimes and worked with on bigger jobs as an extra hand. The money he earned was barely enough to scrape by, most of it going on renting his dump of a flat.

Tyler had hit rock bottom a long time ago, his depression had caused him to lose the will to live on several occasions, but somehow, he just couldn't die. The Black Shadow kept pulling him back to the land of the living, hell-bent on making him miserable until he died of old age. The Black Shadow was what he called his depression, a sickness that had slowly taken hold over the past twenty years. It gnawed at him from the inside, slowly eating him alive, never leaving him alone for a second. Clinical depression was the official name for it; causing him to become disinterested in his life and making him think, feel and behave differently than usual. He had been told by doctors that it was normal after a life-changing event to experience depression symptoms, but this was no ordinary depression. This was a living, physical being that constantly sucked the life out of his body, something no doctor could help cure.

A grimy mirror hung on the wall. He stared into it, wishing it would pull him into its dreary depths. He saw himself, a worn out husk of a man with shaggy hair and a rough beard, deep-set eyes – sad eyes. He also saw The Black Shadow, a shape that hovered near him always, sapping his energy. It was his only companion. He had no one in his life. His parents had moved away a long time ago, unwilling to look after their pathetic excuse of a son any longer. Once he turned eighteen he had been of no more use to them. He did have female visitors from time to time, but they only stayed for an hour or so, just random hook-ups. They pretended to be attracted to him and did whatever he wanted, sometimes he just asked them to hold him and stroke his hair while he slept, just so he could feel the warmth of another body close by.

Tyler hadn't always been depressed and pathetic. He had changed ever since the disappearance of his friend two decades ago. Really, it was all *his* fault. If he had just kept his big mouth shut then none of this would have happened and Tyler wouldn't be spending every day, day in and day out, wishing he would die. The darkness kept pulling him under, further and further down. Therapists had tried to help him, doctors had prescribed him varieties of medications, but nothing helped him, nothing took away that dark feeling deep down inside. There was once a time when he seemed happy on the outside. He would put on a brave face and show the world that he was a good kid, happy and full of life, but inside it was a lie, a terrible lie that he told each and every day. Nowadays, he didn't care about putting a brave face on for the world. Fuck the world. This was his life now.

Tyler switched on his television, a mere eighteen-inch screen, its signal fluctuating. The morning news was on. He usually watched it until it was time to go to work.

'An old, broken watch has been found in the Beaker Ravine. Local kids found it while playing yesterday afternoon. It had splatters of dried blood on it, but otherwise was clean and in good condition. After further investigation it has been revealed that the blood and the watch belong to Kieran Jones, who was last seen nearly twenty years ago. The boy's parents have confirmed the watch belonged to their son due to the engraving found on the back. It is not known if he is still alive as a body has never been found. Detective Inspector Williams, who worked on the case previously, is considering reopening the case and urges anyone with information to come forward. However, without further evidence, it is likely the case will remain unsolved. Kieran Jones was last seen on the 20th of July 1998 by his parents.'

Tyler stared at the screen for a few seconds, unsure of what he had just heard. He looked over at the mirror; The Black Shadow slowly nodded – it was real. Sometimes the shadow helped him distinguish between reality and his own imagination. It would often help him make decisions or even make them for him. Sometimes it was easier that way.

'Fuck,' said Tyler out loud. Now what was he supposed to do? All his fears had suddenly come to life, taken shape and spoken to him through the television screen. This wasn't supposed to happen. He had been so careful and thorough – they all had. He didn't know what to do so he waited for The Black Shadow to make the next move, but it didn't. It remained dormant.

Tyler lowered himself onto the chair and sat completely still, thinking. His mind wandered back to that dark day, the day when his whole world changed and The Black Shadow was born —

*Tyler approached the remains, trying not to look straight at them. Kieran's eyes were bulging out of his head, staring at him, blaming him. At least he wouldn't spill his secret now. At least now he had stopped talking. It was over, but Tyler had a new problem, one that needed covering up. He waited while the others made their way down to the bottom of the ravine and gathered around.*

*'Right, this is what we do.' He had their attention. 'We are going to get rid of the body.'*

*There was a stunned silence. He could see they were all wrestling with this idea.*

*'And just how are we going to do that?' gasped Brooke. She had finally caught her breath after vomiting up her lunch.*

*'Here's a better plan,' interrupted Jordan. 'One of us goes back to town and informs the police. It's what any normal person would do in this situation. It's the right thing to do.'*

*'Don't be bloody stupid Jordan. We can't tell the police. It's our fault that he was on that tree over the ravine. We made him do it. We're responsible for his death. We're —'*

*'Don't say it!'*

*'— Murderers.' The word hung in the air like a bad stench. It echoed around the jagged walls of the ravine.*

*'You mean you're a murderer,' corrected Jordan. 'It's your fault.'*

*'I don't know what you're talking about.' Tyler refused to believe what Jordan was saying. Kieran was the one who had walked across the tree. He could have said no. If it wasn't for his own stubbornness he would still be alive.*

*Jordan shook his head. 'You've lost it mate. You're in denial.'*

*'We were all there when he fell. We're all*

*responsible.'*

*'But if we get rid of the body we are even more guilty! We would be covering up a crime!' cried Amber, finally adding to the conversation. She was usually the quiet one, but sometimes it was the quiet ones that you had to watch out for. Tyler always sensed that there was more to her than met the eye. Maybe there was a darkness inside her too. He could sense it and that was why she scared him sometimes.*

*'Tyler is right.' Brooke had composed herself and was now standing alongside him. 'It's our fault he's dead. We will all be blamed for his death for the rest of our lives.'*

*'Then we should take responsibility for our actions now. We can't run away from what we have done.'*

*'The hell we can! I don't want to spend the rest of my life in jail. You and Jordan had better get on board with my plan or else.'*

*'Or else what?' Jordan's voice was serious. He took a step towards Tyler, squaring up to him.*

*Tyler gritted his teeth and took a step forwards, his fists clenched at his side, ready for a fight. 'Or else ... I'll make you.' Tyler meant it. He was backed into a corner and needed his friends to agree with his plan. One loose thread could unravel everything.*

*'You'll make us? And how do you plan to make*

*us?' challenged Jordan.*

*Amber took up her place next to Jordan, while Tyler and Brooke stood side by side. Two against two, but Tyler expected Brooke was only on board with his plan because she was scared of him.*

*'Jordan, I swear to God if we tell people what happened we will all go to jail.'*

*'We're twelve Tyler, get a grip. We aren't criminals.'*

*'I'll kill you.'*

*'What?'*

*'You heard me. I'll kill you, but I'll kill Amber first and make you watch.'*

*Jordan looked at Amber, then back at Tyler. He knew he had him where he wanted him. It was only a matter of time before Jordan agreed. Brooke was crying softly beside him and Amber was inching herself further behind Jordan; she was terrified.*

*Jordan sighed heavily. 'Fine. You win Tyler. What's the plan?'*

*Tyler relaxed his fists and breathed a sigh of relief. He wasn't sure what he would have said or done if Jordan hadn't backed down. Would he have really killed his friends? He didn't know, but luckily it was not an issue that needed addressing anymore. Tyler was desperate. He would make everything better now. They would all soon see. They would thank him one day. He needed to think fast and make sure that everyone stuck to the plan – whatever it may be.*

*'Okay, let me think for a second.'*

*Tyler stepped away and paced up and down a few steps. The others watched in silence, glancing around nervously as if expecting some passer-by to suddenly notice them. Visitors to the ravine were few and far between, but they did happen. It was only a matter of time.*

*Tyler walked back to the trio.*

*'First, we strip down to our underwear so we don't get any blood and guts on our clothes. If we get any on our underwear then we take them off and burn them at home later.*

*'Next, we need to get rid of the body. We bury it under that fresh landslide over there. We'll have to dig with our hands. The rocks that are covered in blood we need to throw in the river, the water will wash them clean.*

*'Now, we all need to tell people the same story, so if anyone asks, and they probably will, we will be in the clear. We need to all stick to the same story, okay? We say to everyone that he never showed up and that we were in the field on the other side of town – the south side – the furthest from the ravine. No one needs to know we were near the ravine today. So as far as we are concerned, we never saw him today – he never*

*showed up. He'll be reported as a missing person. They may look for a body, but won't have any reason to look in the ravine.*

*'That landslide looks like it may collapse again from above, so if we can get the body under it before it falls it will be hidden. We never tell a soul about what happened here today. We have to swear. We'll make a blood oath so that we never ever can reveal the truth about what really happened. Kieran disappeared, that's all we know. If his body is ever discovered, then we won't be brought into question if we all say that we never saw him that day. Maybe he took a walk by himself, maybe he walked across that tree, maybe he fell, maybe he committed suicide, then a random landslide buried him. That's the truth.' Tyler finished talking, pausing for any questions – there were none. 'Agreed?'*

*Brooke immediately nodded. 'Agreed.' She had always been one to follow the leader.*

*Jordan reluctantly sighed. 'Yeah, agreed.'*

*Amber began to cry. 'This isn't right. I can't do it. We can't lie for the rest of our lives. The guilt will eat us all alive.'*

*'Yes we can and we will.'*

*'I can't!'*

*'Amber, I swear to God if you ruin this and tell the truth of what happened I'll kill you! Even if it's years*

*from now. I will kill you.' Tyler's anger reverberated up the steep walls of the ravine, his last two words echoing throughout the chasm. This time he really meant it. He couldn't have a weak link in the group. They all needed to remain strong or their lives were over. Amber still didn't answer. She just kept shaking her head.*

*'I'll kill any of you if you tell!' Tyler shouted, spitting his fury directly at her.*

*'Amber please,' begged Brooke, her eyes brimming with tears. 'We can do this. We have to do this. Please.'*

*Tyler could see the constant battle going on within Amber. This moment would make or break the plan, otherwise he would have two bodies to bury. Maybe he had been wrong about her. There was no darkness within Amber. She wasn't like him at all.*

*There was a silence at the bottom of the ravine that stretched out for what felt like forever, but Amber eventually succumbed and slowly nodded, tears pouring down her pale cheeks.*

*'Okay,' she whispered.*

*Jordan hugged her and gently kissed her forehead. 'It'll be okay,' he said softly.*

*Tyler clapped his hands together. 'Right, everyone take your clothes off and put them in a pile over there. We need to get to work.'*

Tyler watched as the morning news changed to the weather, confirming that today was going to be another hot day, but he didn't care about the weather – he didn't care about anything. Every day was torture. Every day was not worth living thanks to his reckless decision *that* day to hide the death of his friend, a death he had caused. What was worse was that he had forced his friends to help him cover it up, something he now bitterly regretted. He didn't know how they had all lived with the guilt. In fact, he hadn't spoken to any of them in years, since they were teenagers. Despite his best intentions he had lost his friends anyway, all because he had been too much of a coward to face up to the truth of his past. If he had only just been brave enough.

Maybe he could be brave now. Maybe there was a way he could undo all this suffering and torture. He could end it once and for all. The watch belonging to Kieran had been found, which meant that the town had a new hope, a new piece of evidence to cling on to, but what they really needed was the truth, and only he knew the *real* truth.

Tyler glanced over towards his bed. The sheets hadn't been changed in weeks, possibly months. It was a small double bed and had a flimsy metal frame, which squeaked badly whenever he rolled over. He got to his feet and walked slowly over to the bed, grabbed the frame and dragged it across the floor away from the sidewall, revealing a bare piece of wall covered in dust that had built up over years of neglect. He got down on his hands and knees and grabbed the nearest heavy object to him; a lamp. He began slamming it into the wall, which started to disintegrate straight away as it was only made of thin plasterboard. Over and over he chipped away at the wall until he had created a big enough hole to get his hand in and then he started pulling the plasterboard away from the support behind.

Finally, after a few minutes, he reached in and took hold of what he was looking for, dragged it out and swept the dust off the top. For thirteen years, ever since he had moved into this flat, this hidden item had been buried in the walls, never seeing daylight until today. His mind started to drift again as he remembered the events that had unfolded —

*Tyler started stripping down to his boxers, leading the way. Jordan and the girls eventually followed suit. He couldn't help but check out the girls as they undressed, but he knew this was neither the time nor the place to have such thoughts running through his head.*

*'Jordan, grab his feet and help me move him over there to the landslide. Girls, start shifting some of*

*those bloody rocks and chuck them in the river. Make sure they are washed clean.'*

*They all set to work. He watched as Jordan reluctantly approached the feet, sharp bones were sticking out of the side of each leg, splintered by the sudden impact. Between them they peeled the remains off the rocks and carried them over to the landslide, gently placing them down on the dirt.*

*'Let's shift some of this rubble and bury him as deep as we can and then pile the rocks back on top. That landslide above is ready to go any day now. It should ensure he's buried forever.'*

*This recent landslide had only been a small one, but there were still hundreds of tonnes worth of dirt and rock teetering above on the edge of the ravine. All it would take would be a massive downfall of rain to soften the earth and it would plummet, burying the body, as he said, possibly forever.*

*No one but Tyler spoke; they just obeyed his commands. Tyler and Jordan started moving the larger rocks from the mound and put them in a pile ready to place back on top once the body was buried. When the rocks from the landslide had been cleared they started digging a hole in the earth using their hands. It was tough work, especially with the heat of the sun beating down. Tyler's hands were blistered, cut and filthy within minutes, but he kept going, determined to see out his plan till the end. Once the body was gone – out of sight – it would all be okay.*

*Tyler stood for a moment, pausing to catch his breath. He glanced over to where the girls were working. Brooke was trying to wash a rock in the river. Amber was knelt down on the ground. He could not see what she was holding, but she was studying something in her hand intently. Jordan let out an exasperated sigh next to him which caused Tyler to turn his attention back to the digging.*

*After an hour they had finally dug a big enough hole with their bare hands in which to fit the body. All four of them lifted it and wedged it into the hole. The lifeless eyes of their friend stared up at them; cold, dull, bloodshot. Tyler tried to look away, but he couldn't. Those eyes kept drawing him in and felt like they were staring directly into his soul. Tyler shuddered.*

*They moved the loose dirt back into the makeshift grave, covering the corpse layer by layer until it was completely out of sight. Tyler felt sick but he kept going, ordering Brooke to gather up any other evidence; any scraps of material, random bits of broken bone or teeth that may have splintered from the body upon impact. The silence once they had completed the job was deafening. It had taken almost three hours from start to finish. They all stood next to each other, puffing, panting, covered in sweat, blood and remorse.*

*The impact site was now cleared of any evidence that a body had exploded there. It was the perfect cover up.*

*'Right, remember, as far as we're all concerned Kieran never showed up today. We were never at the ravine, nor the field nearby. We were in the field on the opposite side of town. We are late home because we all lost track of time. We all assumed Kieran had been kept home for some reason. We haven't spoken to him since yesterday. Got it?' Everyone nodded. 'Okay, now we need to do a blood oath, swearing that we will never reveal what happened today.'*

*'What exactly is a blood oath?' asked Brooke timidly.*

*'A blood oath is a solemn promise to keep an agreement no matter what. We must swear on our own lives that we will never break this oath. We must cut and draw blood on our right hand and we must all grasp each other's hand and let the blood mix, thereby sealing the oath.'*

*There was a long silence.*

*'What happens if one of us breaks the oath?' asked Amber.*

*Tyler glared at her in annoyance. 'You'll wish you were dead,' he growled.*

*'Seriously though Tyler ... what will happen if one of us breaks the oath?' Jordan spoke up.*

*'Bad things will happen. Trust me. A blood oath*

*should never be broken. The person who breaks a blood oath should kill themselves because it's the only way to be at peace. So unless you plan on committing suicide ... keep your fucking mouths shut.'*

*Tyler picked up a sharp rock from the ground at his feet and sliced his hand open, a small trickle of blood oozed out of the wound, mixing with Kieran's blood that had dried on his skin, causing it to stain. He handed the sharp rock to Jordan who quietly, and without hesitation, did the same. Brooke followed suit and finally Amber finished.*

*They formed a circle and all reached their right hands out in front of them, grasping one another's hands, one on top of the other. They squeezed and allowed the blood to flow. It was impossible to know where their own blood began and someone else's blood ended; they were all as one now, together forever to hide the truth from the world. The grip was difficult to hold on to because the blood made it slippery, but they continued to hold on tight.*

*'I, Tyler Jenkins, swear to never reveal the truth of what happened today. I seal my oath with my blood so that if I ever break this oath, I will take my own life.'*

*'I, Jordan Evans, swear to never reveal the truth of what happened today. I seal my oath with my blood so that if I ever break this oath, I will take my own life.'*

*'I, Brooke Willows, swear to never reveal the*

*truth of what happened today. I seal my oath with my blood so that if I ever break this oath, I will take my own life.'*

*'I, Amber Walker, swear to never reveal the truth of what happened today. I seal my oath with my blood so that if I ever break this oath, I will take my own life.'*

*Tyler looked from one of his friends to the another, absorbing the moment. The tension hung in the air, surrounding each of them. Tyler never wanted to let go. These were his friends, but what had he done? Would they ever be the same again?*

*Tyler finally released his grip, the others did the same. They then went to the river and washed away the blood, leaving red ribbons floating away downstream before eventually getting diluted by the amount of clear water. It was done.*

*All four friends stood side by side and watched the river wash away the evidence of their crime. Little did they know that this would be the last time they would all be together for twenty years.*

Tyler picked up the heavy wooden box he had freed from its prison behind the wall and laid it to rest on his bed. He felt his own heartbeat speeding up and a heavy weight on his chest, like someone was squeezing the life out of him. Panic started to rise from somewhere deep down. The Black Shadow loomed overhead, causing his surroundings to look dull and faded. It always made things look worse than they actually were. It had always been the case. That was depression. It caused everything to look bleak, like there was no way out, but Tyler reckoned he knew a way out now, a way he could be free. He had finally reached the end of his tether. The time had come to break the blood oath, but it wasn't as simple as just confessing to the truth. He couldn't just walk up to the police station and confess. The others would be in danger and he didn't want that. Breaking a blood oath required planning and more importantly ... help.

The first thing he needed to do was find his friends, although now they would be complete strangers. He didn't know where any of them lived now, except for Brooke, but she wasn't the person he needed to talk to first. He needed someone who was level headed, calm and decent and that certainly wasn't Jordan. He needed someone with a hidden darkness inside, like him. He may not have known where Amber lived now, but he did know where she worked and a large coffee was exactly what he needed.

It was time to get the gang back together.

# Chapter Four

Jordan had spent the night on the sofa, again. His neck was stiff and sore from the uncomfortable position he had woken up in and he was still wearing the same clothes as yesterday; faded jeans and a black t-shirt with a chequered shirt over the top. He raised himself up from the low, worn sofa and padded out barefoot to the small kitchen, flicking on the kettle. His wife, Eleanor, had already set up the breakfast things on the dining room table. She was sat at the table, her hands wrapped around a mug of steaming tea, staring aimlessly into it. Jordan joined her and lowered himself onto the empty chair opposite, not saying a word.

Breakfast was spent in silence, as it was spent most mornings. Tension hovered in the air. Jordan knew it was his fault; it was always his fault. He could see the dark shadows under her eyes, the fear in them was plain to see. He had made his own wife afraid of him, but it wasn't really him. It was The Bad Man. That's what he called it; the demonic-type, angry force that took over his body and did things, said things, that he couldn't remember doing or saying. As usual, his poor wife suffered the brunt of the abuse.

Jordan had changed. Gone was the nice boy that girls wanted to introduce to their parents. He had been replaced by an angry, hatred-fuelled machine. That's what he felt like; a machine – no longer in control of his body. The doctors and therapists had diagnosed it as Intermittent Explosive Disorder, characterised by sudden outbursts of anger, hostility and recurrent aggressive behaviour. They had said that the disorder could have arisen due to a traumatic event in his childhood, one of the more common causes. It was also possible that his brain chemistry was not quite right, either too much or too little serotonin. Jordan knew it was something else; someone else. Whenever he had these outbursts he would never remember them, waking up to a scene of utter chaos – just like he had done this morning. The doctors couldn't explain it; maybe he was lying, trying to use it as an excuse for his behaviour. He wasn't. The Bad Man was in control, not him. Yet the one and only time he had explained to a doctor that a different entity took over his body the doctor had looked at him like he was crazy. Maybe the doctor would have locked him up if he had continued along that path. In the end, his blackouts were explained as a side effect of his disorder and it was left at that. Medication had helped in the past, holding the anger episodes at bay, as had Cognitive Behavioural Therapy, but only for so long.

The Bad Man always found a way back into his life.

Jordan hadn't always been like this. He experienced his first real explosive episode at the age of thirteen, only a few weeks after the disappearance of his childhood friend. Back then, his doctor had put it down to Post Traumatic Stress Disorder and said he would recover over time, gave him some medication and said to check back within six weeks. His parents took him back six weeks later and explained that things were getting worse. Jordan was turning into a very troubled, angry young man. He wasn't their son; their perfect, polite son was gone.

About a year later Jordan had started working for his father at his plumbing business, Fix It All. It had helped pass the time out of school hours, helped focus his mind on other things. He had worked there ever since, finishing school with very few GCSE's. He met his future wife at age twenty-five, married her at twenty-seven and beat her senseless not long after that. Now, at thirty-two, he was stuck with a wife who hated him, a father who only barely put up with him, a mother who had left him and his father because she could not stand her son's abuse anymore, a job he hated and an anger disorder that was ruining his life.

Jordan watched as his wife slowly ate some buttered toast. There was no fire in her eyes like there had been when they had first met. Her hair was no longer blonde and shiny, but dull and lifeless. She had more wrinkles than the average woman of her age and her shoulders were constantly hunched over, as if she didn't have the energy to stand up straight. This was what he had done to her. Whereas he, on the other hand, looked and felt great. He visited a small gym at least five times a week; lifting heavy weights made him feel powerful, strong. He thought if he was strong physically, he could be strong mentally. However, that wasn't always the case. He may have acted strong and tough, but inside he was frail, weak, beaten. The Bad Man often reared his head and took his anger out on other people and it took its toll on Jordan too. He was tired of fighting.

'Look, I'm sorry about last night.' Jordan said, not even looking at his wife. 'Did I hit you?' Eleanor shook her head, no. 'Okay, well, good, sorry.'

It didn't sound sincere and, in a way, it wasn't. Jordan couldn't keep track of his feelings. Sometimes he felt guilty for how he treated her and other times he thought she deserved the ill treatment. He often wondered why she had agreed to marry him in the first place; silly woman. *Of course he knew why, but he didn't like to think about that specific reason*. She could up and leave any time she wanted. He wouldn't stop her. There was no love between them anymore, probably never had been. He had really only loved *one* woman. That was what had started the argument last night; he remembered that much —

*Jordan had been watching television and drinking a beer when his wife entered the room. He didn't glance up at her as she spoke; a tense, angry note to her voice. She was dressed in a tight blue dress, black heels and a black blazer. Eleanor was a private woman, preferring to stay in rather than go out, but her friends had finally convinced her to go for a drink. She needed to get out of the house, away from him. She used to dress up all the time, always went out partying, but those days were long gone. She felt drained of life, a woman changed due to her past and her present.*

*'I'm going out tonight with the girls. I don't know what time I'll be home, but I expect it'll be late. Dinner is in the oven ready to be heated up.' Jordan didn't answer her so she continued. 'I made your favourite – lasagne ... did you hear me?'*

*'Yeah, yeah, fuck off already so I can watch the football in peace.'*

*Eleanor sighed. 'Okay, well, love you.'*

*'No, you don't,' he answered almost immediately.*

*'Well, do you love me?' she asked, already knowing the answer.*

*'What do you want me to say? You want me to*

*say I love you more than anything, that you're the only woman for me, that there's never been anyone else? Well, guess what, there has always been someone else.'*

*'I know you cheat on me if that's what you're getting at,' she snapped angrily.*

*'That's not what I meant.'*

*'Then what did you mean?'*

*Jordan gritted his teeth in frustration and anger, wishing his wife would just leave instead of baiting him for an argument. He really didn't want to have to talk about the fact that he had once loved someone else, a long time ago. He had still loved her even when he first met Eleanor. He was still in love with her now, but he could not bring himself to say her name. It pained him to even think about her. Sometimes Jordan would see her working in the coffee shop over the road from his father's business – always watching her from afar as she grew into a woman – always wondering what her voice sounded like now.*

*'Just fuck off,' he said quietly, turning his attention back to the screen. His team were losing, making him even more on edge and annoyed.*

*'Tell me who she is!'*

*'No! Fuck off!' Jordan jumped to his feet and hurled the beer bottle he was holding across the room. It smashed just behind Eleanor, barely missing her*

*head, against the wall. That was all he could remember. After that, The Bad Man took over. He didn't even know if his wife had gone for her girls night out. He had woken up on the sofa.*

'I want a divorce.' Eleanor's words were blunt and cut the silence like a knife; she meant business.

Jordan nodded. 'That's what you said last time.'

'Well, I mean it now. Jordan, I'm not happy and neither are you. We would be better off without each other.'

'I agree.'

Jordan rose to his feet, put his empty plate in the sink and flicked the television on in the process. He always put the news on for Eleanor to watch before he went out. She left for work later than him. Eleanor didn't move an inch as he leaned down and kissed her on the cheek.

'I'm off to work.' And that would be the end of it. She was never serious about these things. This conversation had happened before, several times. Maybe she was just threatening him with divorce in the hope that he would change, but he never did – he couldn't. This was who he was and who he would continue to be forever.

Jordan went to grab his keys off the side and happened to notice a familiar face on the television screen as the news broadcast ran in the background. It was the picture that had been used when he had first disappeared.

'An old, broken watch has been found in the Beaker Ravine. Local kids found it while playing yesterday afternoon. It had splatters of dried blood on it, but otherwise was clean and in good condition. After further investigation it has been revealed that the blood and the watch belonged to Kieran Jones, who was last seen nearly twenty years ago. The boy's parents have confirmed the watch belonged to their son due to the engraving found on the back. It is not known if he is still alive as a body has never been found. Detective Inspector Williams, who worked on the case previously, is considering reopening the case and urges anyone with information to come forward. However, without further evidence, it is likely the case will remain unsolved. Kieran Jones was last seen on the 20th of July 1998 by his parents.'

The young twelve-year-old face of his former friend stared back at him. Those cheeky brown eyes, that smirk of a smile, full of life, with his whole future ahead of him. Jordan froze in place, his eyes glued to the screen, absorbing the information. Surely it couldn't be true. They had all scoured the area for hours, ensuring all the evidence was removed and buried. Where had the watch come from? Why had it suddenly appeared *now?* He couldn't understand it. Why did it look so ... *clean?*

The picture showed a small blue watch, cracked and broken, a smear of dried blood, but otherwise perfectly clean. Jordan frowned; surely it should have been filthy and faded after being at the bottom of a ravine for twenty years. There was a part of him that thought the news broadcast had been a clip of a movie or television show and maybe the kid in the picture had just resembled Kieran. The watch – it was definitely *his* watch. There was that engraving ...

All of a sudden he was aware that his wife was talking to him, her voice growing louder with concern.

'Babe, are you okay?' He ignored her question. 'Babe?' She touched his arm.

'Get the fuck off me!' he roared, wrenching his arm away from her as if he had been scalded.

She recoiled. 'I'm sorry but you were just staring into space muttering horrible words for ages.'

'What?' It was more of a demand then a question.

'You looked like you were under hypnosis or something.'

'Don't be so fucking stupid woman.'

'Is that Kieran boy on the news the same one you knew all those years ago?' He had forgotten that he'd mentioned his name to her once, years ago. *Trust her to have bloody remembered.* He had been drinking at the time and in a sleepy state. She had randomly asked him if he had any friends from his childhood because he had grown up in this town, yet had no friends that she knew about. Jordan had mumbled something incoherently and then said his name out loud for the first time in years. She had questioned him further, but he had fallen asleep, mumbling the name over and over as he dreamt.

'Will you just shut the fuck up and leave me the hell alone!'

Jordan grabbed his keys and his baseball cap and stormed out of the house, not pausing to reflect until he was seated in his black pick-up truck. He could feel The Bad Man wanting to take control again, but Jordan fought him back. Not today. Sometimes he could make The Bad Man not appear by concentrating really hard on something else.

He quickly searched the local radio stations for any further mention of the illusive watch, but it seemed that segment was over for now. He needed to focus on something else. Jordan leaned back into the headrest and closed his eyes, his mind racing back to *that* day and the aftermath of the incident —

*Jordan walked slowly back from the field towards his house, which was at the end of a long road at the crest of a hill. He had left the others behind so they could go their separate ways home. His mind was numb, his hand still stinging from the cut made from the sharp rock. He had heard about blood oaths before, but had never taken them seriously. It was just one of those things you said when you really meant something, a promise you would never break. This was different. This oath forced him to conceal a horrible truth forever – a truth he wished he didn't know. He despised Tyler in that moment, hated his guts for what he had forced him and the girls' to do. They had all been innocent children up until three hours ago. Now what were they? Liars. Murderers. Jordan swore to himself that he would make Tyler pay one day. He didn't know how or when, but one day he would make things right again.*

*It was nearly seven in the evening by the time Jordan returned home. He had promised his mother he would be home in time for dinner at six earlier on in the day, otherwise she would worry about him. Jordan very rarely broke a promise to his mother because he hated to make her worry. He had a very close relationship with her. He was always honest, could always trust her and appreciated all the little things she did for him every day.*

*Jordan slowly opened the front door to his house, peering through to see where his parents were. He could hear his mother in the kitchen. His father was probably watching television in the lounge as he could hear a faint hum coming from that direction. He needed to get upstairs and shower; he felt dirty, his hands still bearing the faint stain of blood and dirt, no matter how hard he had tried to remove it in the river.*

*'Is that you Jordan?' His mother rushed in to see him. 'Where have you been? You missed dinner. I was so worried. I'll heat it up for you.'*

*'Sorry Mum. Got carried away, lost track of time.' The first lie.*

*'Are you okay? You look a bit ... I don't know ... different. Your face ... Are you feeling okay?'*

*'I'm fine.' The second lie.*

*'Did you have a good time with your friends?'*

*'Yeah. It was fun.' The third lie.*

*Jordan had never lied to his mother. He was a good boy. Okay, maybe he had told a little white lie from time to time, but never to this extent. He felt ashamed because she didn't deserve this.*

*Maybe if he told her she would understand and help him to do the right thing. Then again, maybe not. She was very understanding, but probably not that understanding. He remembered the blood oath. Even if he wanted to tell her he knew he couldn't. They had sworn to take their own lives if they ever told the truth. What would happen if he told the truth and didn't kill himself? Would something bad happen? He didn't know and he certainly didn't want to find out what happened if you broke a blood oath. Tyler had warned that he would kill them if they told the truth.*

*His mother, Anne, was an attractive woman, slender, petite and at least a foot and a half shorter than him, even though he was only twelve. She often did a lot of community work, volunteered at the school, cooked dinners for neighbours and helped out at local gardening events. She was renowned in the town for being lovely, happy and approachable and her lovely son Jordan was such a wonderful boy, always smiling, helpful and polite too.*

*'Actually Mum, I'm not feeling that great. Too much sun maybe. I'm just going to have a shower and go to bed. Is that okay?'*

*'Of course. Are you sure you're okay? You're filthy.'*

*Jordan smiled faintly. 'Yes Mum, I'm fine. We were ... digging.' He felt his face flush with shame; that lie seemed so innocent. All young boys like to dig and play around in the dirt. The truth was a lot more sinister. His pulse quickened as he walked forwards and slowly wrapped his arms around her, squeezing tight, feeling the tears developing in his eyes. 'I'm sorry,' he whispered.*

*'For what darling?' Anne stroked her son's soft hair and hugged him back. She knew something was*

*wrong. She could always tell when her little boy was in pain.*

*'For being late back home and making you worry.'*

*'That's okay. Don't worry. You're home now safe and sound. I trust you completely.'*

*'Thanks Mum.' Her words cut him deeply, rubbing salt into an already open wound. He released her and began climbing the stairs slowly. 'Goodnight Mum.'*

*'Goodnight Jordan. I love you.'*

*'I love you too Mum.'*

*Jordan closed the door to his bedroom, leaned against it, sunk down to the floor in a heap and cried harder than he had ever cried before. He hardly made a sound to ensure his parents left him alone. The stress and emotions of the past few hours poured out of him – he couldn't control it. He let his emotions take over for only a few minutes before ordering himself to get to his feet, undress and take a shower. He threw all his clothes in the dirty hamper, except for his underwear which he stuffed under his bed for now; he would destroy them later.*

*In the shower, he scrubbed his skin so hard it went bright red, no matter how much he tried he could still smell death. The dirt and blood embedded in his hands finally disintegrated after lots of water and soap, but all the scrubbing opened up the cut on his hand. He quickly applied first aid on it once he was dry. He stared at himself in the bathroom mirror. A twelve-year-old boy with soft brown wavy hair stared back at him, but there was something different about him – his mother had been right. It was a presence he felt within his soul, like a dark creature was beginning to emerge, taking over his thoughts, feelings and actions. No longer was he Jordan Evans. Instead, a new identity was surfacing, one he didn't like nor recognise. He stared blankly at his reflection for what seemed like hours, fascinated by the change in his demeanour.*

*Jordan finally dragged his gaze away from his new identity and walked back to his bedroom, closing and locking the door. He crawled into bed, pulled the sheets over his head, praying that it had all been merely a bad dream and he would wake up tomorrow and not remember the fact that he had buried his friend at the bottom of a ravine. He was exhausted, both mentally and physically.*

*The next morning he awoke from a dreamless sleep and looked over at his wall clock which was in the shape of a pirate ship. It was nearly ten; he had been asleep for over fourteen hours, something that wasn't unusual for a growing boy, but seemed odd considering the trauma of yesterday. Surely a normal human being wouldn't be able to sleep knowing what they had done? A normal person would feel remorse, guilt ... terror.*

*Jordan quickly dressed and joined his mother downstairs in the kitchen. She was always in the kitchen, cooking, cleaning, preparing meals. She had made him his favourite breakfast: pancakes and bacon. She beamed a smile as he entered.*

*He managed a small smile back. 'Thanks, Mum.'*

*'Good morning darling. Are you feeling better today? Did you sleep well?'*

*'Yes, thank you.' He was still a polite boy. 'Please can you pass me the syrup?' he asked as he took a seat.*

*'Here you go.' She handed him the bottle and watched as he dug into the tall pile of pancakes. He was starving – digging for three hours and skipping dinner would do that to anyone.*

*'Are you going to see your friends today?'*

*Jordan paused with his fork halfway to his mouth. 'Um, I don't know. Why?' He continued stuffing his mouth.*

*'Well, I had a call from Mrs Jones early this morning. Kieran's mum. He never came home last night. Wasn't he with you yesterday?'*

*Jordan stopped chewing and lowered his knife and fork. This was it, the moment he had been dreading. 'Um no, he never showed up yesterday. I haven't seen him since the day before.'* Another lie. The big one. The one he had been ordered to say, the one he had rehearsed all the way home yesterday. At that moment, the guilt started to creep over him, covering him in a cold embrace.

'His mother said that he left early in the morning. He didn't go and hang out with you and the others?'

'No.'

'And you didn't think to mention it? You five always hang out together.'

'I didn't think it was important. I assumed he'd been kept home for some reason.'

His mother paused, thinking. 'She is very worried. Are you sure ... you —'

'I told you I don't know anything about it!' Jordan snapped at his mother for the very first time in his life.

Almost immediately he wished he could take it back, but it was too late. He felt a strange sensation come over him; it was more than anger. He had never been properly angry before. He had always controlled his emotions and used his words carefully, but today was different. Something had happened – something had changed him. He could see the look of shock on his mother's face. He hated to see her upset, especially when he had caused it, but the fury was still there. It *wasn't going away. He needed a release. He could feel the tension building and building and thought he might explode.*

*Without thinking he grabbed the nearest object on the table – a cup – and hurled it at the wall and watched as it smashed into pieces. The sound had been instant and loud. He and his mother sat in silence for a while, neither knowing what to say or do next. All Jordan knew was he suddenly felt a bit better, like the anger was subsiding.*

*His mother began to gather the broken pieces that had spread out across the floor. Jordan immediately started helping her.*

*'I'm so sorry Mum.'*

*'It's okay darling.'*

*'No Mum, it's not. I shouldn't have done that. I'm so sorry. I really don't know where Kieran is.'*

*'I believe you. I'll let Mrs Jones know that you haven't seen him since the day before yesterday.'*

*'Thank you.'*

*And that was that. Despite hating lying to her he was surprised at how easy it had been. Maybe he could keep up the lie for the rest of his life. At some point the police would give up the search for Kieran and it would all go away. He was certain of it. This feeling of guilt was only temporary.*

Jordan took a couple of deep breaths, breathing in through his nose and out through his mouth, taking each one as it came. The rage was subsiding, sinking back down to the depths of his subconscious where it belonged. The Bad Man was making a habit of returning more often recently. Years ago it had only been every few months, then it changed to weeks, and now it was days. This was all *his* fault. Not him - Tyler. That dickhead was responsible for all of this. Jordan would see him from time to time and it never ended well.

Once, he had punched him square in the face in the middle of the street. He should have done that twenty years ago, back at the bottom of the ravine. Jordan hated himself for not doing more back then. Maybe if he had acted differently things would have been better than they were today. Of course they would have been better. He would be with Amber for a start.

*Amber* – the true love of his life. God, he missed her. He missed her smile, her warmth, her kindness. He wondered if all these years later she still had those amazing character traits that made her so special. He knew she was married now, to some idiot named Sean and had a daughter with him. That could have been him and that could have been his kid. He would never get the chance to be a father now. He couldn't put himself through *that* again.

Jordan quickly put *that* thought out of his head, started up the truck and got on the road to work. He still worked at his dad's plumbing business. It was opposite the coffee shop where Amber worked. Maybe he would see her through the front window of the shop, smiling and greeting customers. The last time he had properly spoken to her was fifteen years ago. They had both been about to turn eighteen —

*Jordan had just finished a shift at his dad's business. He had lost his temper again at a stupid customer who complained because his plastic bag of screws had only come with forty-five and not the fifty mentioned on the label. Who the fuck cared? He had been able to finish the job with forty-five screws so what was his problem? Jordan had stormed out into the back room and his dad had told him to go home and cool off. So that's what he was doing now – cooling off. He decided to go for a walk before he headed home. He wandered up the street away from the main road and towards the quiet green area in the middle of town. That was when he spotted her – Amber. She was walking directly towards him and he didn't have time to duck out of sight before she spotted him. They both froze, unsure whether to stand and talk or turn and run away, like they usually did. Luckily, Amber made the first move.*

*'Hi, Jordan.'*

*'Uh, hi.' He really didn't want to talk to her. Damn, she looked sexy in her vest and shorts, but she looked tired, like she hadn't had a good night's sleep in years. Gone was the girl he once knew. She was on the verge of becoming a grown woman now; a mature woman.*

*'How are you?' she asked timidly. This was horrible; they didn't know how to be around each other anymore.*

*'Fine. You?'*

*'Tired, but otherwise okay. You doing anything for your eighteenth?'*

*'Getting wasted probably.'*

*'Cool,' she said, nodding. 'How is your mum?'*

*'Fucking great, thanks.' He knew that had been rude; he didn't care. He just wanted to get on and be alone, like always. It was better to be alone than around other people and risk The Bad Man making an appearance.*

*Amber looked taken aback by his tone of voice. 'I'm trying to be civil Jordan. There's no need to be rude. We've barely spoken in five years.'*

*'Yeah well, covering up your friend's murder and burying his body will do that to a friendship.'*

*Amber sighed and hung her head. 'I'm struggling with it too.'*

*'Yeah, I'm sure you are. We all are. Why can't we just throw Tyler under the bus and blame him. It's his fault after all. We're innocent.'*

*'You know what will happen if we tell the truth. I've tried.'*

*'You've tried?' Jordan stopped for a moment, confused. 'How?'*

*Amber looked embarrassed and flushed a deep shade of pink. 'I ... I tried to tell my parents. I couldn't take the guilt any longer. I told them that I had something serious to tell them. I said that I knew a secret ... and then ...' She stopped, unable to continue.*

*'Then what!' demanded Jordan.*

*'Then I fainted. I couldn't do it. I couldn't face what would possibly happen to me, to us, to all of us. Tyler was right. We can never break the blood oath. Our lives are at risk.' Amber took a deep breath and composed herself. 'Have you seen Tyler lately?' she asked casually.*

*'Nope. The less we see of him the better. He's a fucking fool.'*

*Amber folded her arms in a defensive manner. 'Well, it sounds like you've taken a leaf out of his book and turned into a rude, arrogant dickhead!'*

*Jordan couldn't help but smirk at her attempt at being aggressive. He had never heard her swear before – he found it cute, but he couldn't tell her that. Instead, he did the only thing he knew how to do. He turned without another word and walked away from her and that was the last time he properly saw her and spoke to her.*

# Chapter Five

Brooke sat on the old and worn leather sofa, her knees hunched up to her chest and her arms wrapped around her legs. This was her usual position – it felt safe. She was munching on some peanut butter and toast for breakfast, while listening to the morning news on the radio. She never watched the news on television. It was too terrifying to see the outside world. Despite the amazingly bright sunshine outside all the curtains in the lounge were drawn, blocking out the sun's rays and causing shadows to fall over everything in the room. This was how she liked it. Her parents ensured they drew the curtains before Brooke entered any room in the house to avoid any panic attacks or unnecessary fear.

Brooke was ghostly pale, her skin having never seen the sunshine for seventeen years. She was a sickly, stick-thin figure, twisted and controlled by The Fear, an invisible entity that forced her to stay inside at all times. If she stayed inside then she was safe.

Her severe agoraphobia diagnosis had been almost instant. The day after *it* had happened, she had been afraid to leave the safety of her parents' house, choosing to stay inside for weeks. A doctor had visited her and diagnosed her with her mental illness immediately and said it should pass in time, but if it did get progressively worse then to give him a call. It did get progressively worse, *much* worse. Brooke started getting severe panic attacks whenever she stepped outside. The panic would build up inside until it took over her entire body and she had no other choice but to return home. She imagined a creature called The Fear was hunting her in the outside world, a statement no doctor or therapist believed or understood. She was given strong medication, which controlled The Fear for a short while, enabling her to venture outside with her friend Amber once or twice, but not for long. The Fear would find her and chase her back inside. She had run as if her life depended on it. Now she couldn't even open the front door to the postman and all curtains had to be drawn so she couldn't see anything of the outside world. Even watching the television was impossible. The Fear was inside the television too. It controlled every aspect of her life.

Brooke had no friends, not anymore. There had been a time when she was on the verge of becoming a teenager that she had four of the best friends in the whole world. They had done everything together, always hung out, experimented with alcohol, shared secrets and stories. Her best girlfriend had been

Amber, but she hadn't seen her in years. She missed her very much. Sometimes she imagined that Amber would turn up at her door one day and give her a big hug, just to show her that she was not alone – no – it was better that no one came to visit because she didn't want anyone seeing her like this.

Brooke had given up on her recovery years ago. The doctors couldn't help her. Her parents had tried everything to help their daughter; medication, therapy, hypnosis, but to no avail. Ever since the disappearance of her childhood friend twenty years ago she had locked herself in her house, closed herself off from the outside world and refused to accept any responsibility. She wasn't completely alone; she had her parents of course. They would never leave her. They looked after her, cooked for her and bought her clothes. They had even tried to get her a job that she could have done at home, but Brooke had refused, barely ate and only wanted to wear her old clothes from when she was a teenager. She was living in the past and refused to believe in the present. Her father provided for the family as a manager of a local food store, but her mother no longer worked as a school nurse. Instead, she now spent her days, months and years caring for her daughter. They had barely enough money to get by, but nothing was as important to them as the well-being of their child.

Brooke was dressed in an old, loose and grey cardigan, baggy trousers and a tight black tank top, all of which she used to wear when she was a teenager. They were baggier now than they had been back then. Her weight had dramatically decreased, now she was just a skeleton with skin on.

She listened to the radio, staring straight ahead at nothing on the wall. She was vaguely aware of her mother standing in the doorway watching her. She often did this, but Brooke didn't mind because it meant someone was watching over her at all times. At thirty-two years of age Brooke was more like a child now then she had been at age twelve, depending on her parents for everything.

Her younger sister, Dorothy, had left home years ago and started a high-flying career in London as a movie producer. She had a husband and was thinking about starting a family soon. She pitied her older sister and had tried to stay home for a while to help out, but her parents had told her to go and live her life. There was nothing she could do for Brooke.

The news came on after a song and the first bulletin was:

'An old, broken watch has been found in the Beaker Ravine. Local kids found it while playing yesterday afternoon. It had splatters of dried blood on it, but otherwise was clean and in good condition.

After further investigation it has been revealed that the blood and the watch belonged to Kieran Jones, who was last seen nearly twenty years ago. The boy's parents have confirmed the watch belonged to their son due to the engraving found on the back. It is not known if he is still alive as a body has never been found. Detective Inspector Williams, who worked on the case previously, is considering reopening the case and urges anyone with information to come forward. However, without further evidence, it is likely the case will remain unsolved. Kieran Jones was last seen on the 20th of July 1998 by his parents.'

Brooke suddenly screamed louder than she had ever done in her life. Over and over and over she screamed until there was no breath left in her lungs – then she screamed again. Her mother rushed over and tried to comfort her. Nothing helped, nothing could calm the storm that was raging inside. Her memories of *that* day came flooding back, one after the other – the argument between Kieran and Tyler, Kieran falling, the thud as he exploded at the bottom of the ravine, Tyler's plan, picking up and cleaning the blood-spattered rocks, burying the mangled body, the blood oath. It was replaying in her mind like a movie. Why wouldn't it end? She cried out for her mother to make it stop.

Eventually, she begged for her sedatives, which

her mother provided. Brooke had a doctor called Doctor Perkins who would visit once a month to assess her mental state and adjust her medication if necessary. On more than one occasion he had suggested moving Brooke to a mental institution where she would be able to receive more personal help, but Brooke had declined. The house was the only place she felt safe.

Ten minutes after she had taken the sedatives they began to take effect, but the horror movie was still playing in her head. She twitched and screwed up her eyes, trying to shield herself from the awful flashbacks. Brooke tried to relax on the sofa on her side with her knees hunched up. Her eyes were wide with terror, as wide as they would open, not blinking.

'Can I get you anything darling?' asked her mother.

Brooke shook her head no. She was a woman of very few words these days. She was left to sleep off the shock on the sofa. She dreamed of dead bodies, blood-covered hands, talking corpses and a black fog of fear that followed her everywhere.

When Brooke woke up she was no longer downstairs on the sofa, but upstairs on her bed covered with her old teenage duvet, faded over years of constant use. Her father must have come home from work and carried her upstairs, knowing she would wake up and feel safer than she would if she were anywhere else. A faint beam of sunlight escaped through the drawn blackout curtains, only creating enough light to highlight a few items in the bedroom. There was her old wooden wardrobe, holding all her teenage clothes, the doors still bore the stickers she used to collect of her favourite boy band of the time – Backstreet Boys. A poster of the band also adorned the wall above her bed, faded and torn.

Brooke slowly rose to a sitting position, her head still fuzzy from the sedatives. Her eyes were brimming with tears; she had been crying in her sleep. They were a dull blue colour, but once they had sparkled like gemstones, framed by thick black lashes which batted at every cute guy they saw; now they were lifeless and full of pain. She didn't want to be on her bed, she wanted to be in her corner. Brooke crawled across her floor and sat in the far corner of the room, away from the beam of sunlight, hidden in the darkness. She pulled her knees up to her chest, her arms hugging them tight, afraid to let go. This was the spot where she felt the most safe from The Fear.

Now she was calmer and the haze from the sedatives was slowly wearing off she could focus on what she had heard earlier on the radio.

Kieran's body had been found – no, that wasn't right – his watch had been found. That's right. His watch had been found and the police were possibly going to open the case again. Did that mean that they were going to be knocking on her door soon asking her questions again?

Brooke thought back to *that* day and the moment Tyler had told her to scour the area of any evidence. She had thoroughly checked every inch of the ravine where he had fallen. She had never found a watch. She tried her best to remember if it had been attached to his wrist, but her brain just couldn't remember such a small detail.

Brooke was certain that she would be dragged off to jail, away from her house of safety. Her mind couldn't help but fixate on the most terrible outcomes. That was what The Fear did to her. It clouded her mind of any joy or positivity and instead made her focus on nothing but doom and darkness. It hadn't always been like this. As a child she had hardly ever focused on any negativity in her life, choosing instead to be happy and positive, smile at everyone and laugh. Brooke thought back to when The Fear had first come to her and she had lived through her first anxiety attack. It had all started the day after *it* had happened —

*Brooke had come home from burying her friend and gone straight upstairs to take a shower, hoping that the hot, soapy water would wash away her sins. She stood in the shower for what seemed like hours trying to get the smell of blood and dead flesh out of her skin, but it was stained – maybe forever. She scrubbed her skin so hard it went bright red and raw in places, her own tears mixed with the running water. She cried until she couldn't cry anymore.*

*Eventually, she crawled into bed and pulled her duvet up over her head, but she didn't feel safe. It felt like something was watching or stalking her or that there was a monster under the bed waiting to grab her and pull her under. She tried to ignore that awful feeling, that gnawing aching feeling, but it wouldn't go away.*

*Finally, she got out of bed and crawled across the floor into the corner of her room and huddled there. It felt safer with her back up against something solid. There was no chance of anything grabbing her because she could see across the whole room. She didn't sleep a wink. Instead, she spent the whole night with her eyes wide open, hoping that no monsters appeared to take her away.*

*The next morning, Brooke managed to pull herself away from the corner and put on some makeup to hide her tired, red eyes. She loved makeup and knew exactly how to use blusher and foundation to make her perfect facial features stand out. She hoped to have a career as a professional makeup artist, maybe doing the makeup for movie stars and for Hollywood movies. One day she would get out of this town and make something of her life.*

*Brooke looked at her young, attractive face in the mirror and smiled, knowing that this was just a blip in the road. She would get through this and would come out the other side stronger and more determined than ever. She forced a smile to hide the pain in her heart from the world and then joined her family downstairs for breakfast. Both her parents, Olivia and Frank, were young, in their early thirties. They'd had her when they were still teenagers and stayed together because of the baby. Luckily, they were perfect for each other and hopelessly in love. Brooke's younger sister Dorothy was at the table scoffing her face full of pancakes. She was quite different from her older sister, a tomboy with shorter hair. She liked dinosaurs and superheroes, but she looked up to her big sister with awe.*

*'I ate all the chocolate pancakes. Sorry.'*

*'That's okay, I'm not hungry.' Brooke took a seat opposite her eight-year-old sister, poured herself a glass of orange juice and took a sip. 'Where's Mum?'*

*'Putting washing out on the line. She's mad that you came home late yesterday. Where were you? You missed our bedtime ritual.'*

*'None of your business.'*

*'Were you with those friends of yours? I like Kieran. He's cute.' Brooke shot her sister a dirty look, telling her to be quiet – it didn't work. 'Is he going to be coming over again soon?' Brooke often had her friends round to hang out and for dinner. Dorothy always tried to join them, but she was too young so Brooke would send her away.*

*'Yeah, maybe,' said Brooke, just trying to get her to shut up.*

*'Why were you so late?'*

*'I told you it's none of your business. Leave me alone, Creep.'*

*Dorothy stuck her tongue out at her big sister and went back to eating her pancakes. Brooke returned the favour and stuck her tongue out too. They had a good relationship really, despite the constant bickering. It was what sisters did. They would often have a blazing argument and then ten minutes later it was all forgotten and they would hug and watch a film together. Every night before they went to bed, they would do a special hug and handshake, tightening their bond, but last night Brooke had not done the bedtime ritual with Dorothy.*

*Brooke got up from the table, walked to the back door and stepped outside. The sun was warm already. It was going to be another scorcher of a day. She could see her mother hanging out the laundry in the garden, her blonde hair flowing in the soft breeze. Brooke hoped that one day she would be as beautiful as her mother, but her mother always said that she was already more beautiful than anyone.*

*Brooke started walking towards her, but suddenly her vision went blurry, her head started to spin, the air looked hazy, like she was looking at it through an invisible flame. She froze on the spot. What the hell was happening? The outside was closing in around her, squeezing her. She couldn't breathe. It was a similar feeling to what she had felt last night, but worse – much worse.*

*'M-Mum.' Her voice came out as a squeaky whisper. 'M-Mum!'*

*'Brooke? Are you all right baby?' Her mother came running as Brooke collapsed to the ground, clutching her chest.*

*'I-I can't breathe.'*

*She started to panic, grabbing at her mother, begging her to help. Brooke was so frightened, more frightened than she had ever been in her life. All she knew was that she had to get back inside, or she was going to die – literally, die. Somehow, she scrambled to her feet and ran back into the house, leaving her mother looking worried and confused. As soon as Brooke stepped in the house she felt the panic, the suffocation and The Fear start to leave her body. She was safe inside. She knew that now.*

*'What on earth? Brooke, what's wrong?' Her mother had followed her into the house, still holding a wet towel that she was about to hang on the line.*

*Brooke was doubled over on the floor, catching her breath. 'I don't know,' Brooke cried.*

*'You got attacked by something called panic.'*

*Brooke looked up at the sound of her sister's voice. 'How do you know that?'*

*'A teacher at my school. The nurse said that panic attacked her.'*

*'I think you mean she had a panic attack darling,' corrected her mother. 'But why on earth would you have a panic attack?'*

*Brooke stood up and brushed herself off, determined not to be defeated. 'It's nothing. I'm fine. I don't know what came over me.' She honestly didn't know either. She had never experienced anything like that before. In movies she had seen actors portray a panic attack, but to actually live through one was the worst feeling on earth. What had caused it? A little voice inside her whispered the answer, but she refused to acknowledge it and pushed the feeling away, deep down into her subconscious. She repeated the phrase 'Fear does not control me' to herself.*

*Her mother stroked her long blonde hair. 'Are you sure you're okay? You came home late last night.*

*What happened?'*

*'N-Nothing happened. My friends and I just lost track of time.'*

*'Was Kieran with you?'*

*Brooke froze. That name sent chills up her spine. 'No ... no,' she stuttered. 'He ... never ... showed ... up.' Brooke spoke slowly, far too slowly for a normal sentence, but she was determined to get the lie they had fabricated correct.*

*'Mrs Jones called me very early this morning. He hasn't returned home. He wasn't with you?'*

*'N-no.'*

*'But you guys always hang out together,' added Dorothy.*

*'Shut up, Creep!'*

*'Brooke, there's no need to be horrible to your sister. Please do tell me if you see or hear from Kieran, won't you? I promised Mrs Jones I would call if I found out anything.'*

*'Y-yes M-mum.'*

*'Okay, well are you able to pop to the corner shop for me? We're out of bread and could do with some more milk too. Take the money from my purse.'*

*'Sure Mum.'*

*'Can you take Dorothy with you please?'*

*Brooke rolled her eyes but made no fuss. She waited impatiently as Dorothy got her shoes on. Brooke made it a hundred metres down the road before she was attacked by The Fear again and had to run back to the safety of her home. She took up her place in the corner of her room and that was where she stayed.*

There was a knock on her bedroom door. Brooke didn't even lift her head as she answered. 'Leave me alone Mum.'

'It's me.' The deep, rough voice of her father answered through the door. Her father was a gentle man of very few words, perfectly happy to let his wife do the talking and run things in the home. He was handsome though, just starting to turn a silver-grey. 'Your mum and I are worried. Should we call Doctor Perkins?'

'No!' The last thing she needed was a doctor asking questions and probing into every nook and cranny of her mind. It was bad enough he visited every month. She just wanted to be left alone. 'I'm okay. The news about Kieran just upset me.'

'Of course. Is there anything we can do to help you?'

'No. I-I just ...' What she really needed was to talk to Amber. She didn't know why she suddenly had that urge, but Amber always used to be able to make her feel better. Maybe she would be able to help her understand what was going on with the watch that had been found. 'I-I just need to be by myself for a while.'

'Okay, love.' She heard her father walk away down the corridor and the stairs, leaving her in silence once more. She thought of Amber, her best friend and the last time she had seen her or spoken to her. They had both been about to turn sixteen, three years after *it* had happened —

*Brooke stared out of the lounge window towards the driveway, looking out for her friend. Amber had said she would visit today. Her anxiety was already sky-high, but Brooke was determined to see Amber and to go for a walk through town. Her agoraphobia had stopped her from going out like she used to do, but she couldn't let it lock her inside forever.*

*For the past three years she and Amber had been drifting apart, barely a word spoken between them for months at a time, but Amber had reached out to her again recently. Brooke decided to give it one last try, to attempt to save their friendship. Immediately after it had happened she had stopped hanging out with her at school, but eventually, Brooke had stopped attending. Brooke was now home-schooled and had barely any contact with the outside world. The medication she was on was helping slightly, so she had a small hope that this visit from Amber would be the start of something good. Her friendships with Tyler and*

*Jordan had broken down completely. Jordan had become horrible to be around and Tyler was hiding away from everyone, just like she was.*

*Brooke had taken her medication today as normal and upped the dose to try and calm the rising panic within her at the thought of stepping outside the front door. Then she saw Amber walking up the driveway in her cute skirt, t-shirt and trainers, her hair flapping about in the wind. Brooke went to the front door and opened it, pausing a few seconds before doing so. It was still a challenge to open doors and windows to the outside world.*

*Amber greeted her with a big smile and a hug. 'Hey.'*

*'Hi,' replied Brooke. 'You look great.' Their friendship wasn't the same; it felt strained, forced, unnatural.*

*'So do you.' Brooke knew that was a lie. Despite the layers of makeup she had plastered on her face this morning nothing could hide the fear and tiredness in her eyes. Amber looked tired too, but she still had a small glow about her.*

*'Thank you.'*

*'Shall we?' asked Amber, stepping to the side slightly, signalling for Brooke to step out from the doorway.*

*Brooke nodded. 'Y-yes. Mum! I'm going now!'*

*she yelled.*

*Her mother suddenly appeared from the kitchen. She was making scones and was in the middle of cutting them all out into equal sizes.*

*'Are you sure you don't want me to come with you?'*

*'Thank you, Mum, but I need to do this on my own.'*

*'Okay darling. Be safe. Don't be longer than an hour.'*

*'Yes Mum.'*

*Brooke stepped outside the door and closed it behind her, feeling the warmth of the sun on her face, the cool breeze and the smell of freshly cut grass. Her father had cut it this morning. She felt a flood of happiness flow over her. What was she so afraid of? The outside was a lovely place to be, better than being stuck indoors.*

*Amber held out her hand. 'I can hold your hand if you like?'*

*Brooke extended her hand and took it, squeezing gently and the two girls walked quietly and slowly down the driveway and onto the pavement at the bottom before turning right and heading towards town.*

*'So, how have you been?' asked Amber. Brooke could tell she was apprehensive about prying too much*

*into her illness, because that's what this was – an illness. They were strangers now, no longer sharing each and every detail of their lives. Brooke barely knew the girl standing in front of her anymore.*

*'Just taking each day as it comes.'*

*'You've stopped coming to school.'*

*'I ... I can't be around lots of people. It's too hard.'*

*Amber nodded as if understanding exactly what she meant. 'Do you ever think about that day?'*

*'I never stop thinking about it. It's ruined my life. It's ruined all of our lives. Do you think things will ever go back to normal Amber?'*

*'No, I don't. Kieran's parents are still looking for him, determined to find him alive. The whole town has changed because of his disappearance. Only the four of us know the truth about what happened. Maybe if we just —'*

*'No.' Brooke cut Amber off before she could finish her sentence because she knew exactly what she had been about to say. There was no way they could tell the truth – not now, not ever. 'We took a blood oath,' she reminded Amber.*

*'But they were just words.'*

*Brooke stopped and let go of Amber's hand, backing away from her slightly. 'They were more than words. They were said so that we would be protected. I tried to tell my parents a few days afterwards. I thought I was going to die.'*

*'You tried to tell them? Why didn't you tell me?'*

*'We don't speak anymore.'*

*'I know, I'm sorry.' Amber lowered her head. 'We should have come forward with the truth there and then. We wouldn't have got in any trouble. Tyler might have got into more trouble than the rest of us, but at least we wouldn't be living a lie.'*

*'You don't know that. Besides, Tyler will kill us if we tell.'*

*'Maybe he wouldn't ... maybe ...' Amber stopped, realising that Brooke was no longer listening.*

*Brooke clutched her chest. 'Oh God,' she whispered. There it was – The Fear. It was attacking her, telling her to run and hide. Brooke started to hyperventilate. Every breath felt like burning acid in her lungs, but she needed oxygen so she continued to try and inhale.*

*Amber frowned and touched her friend on the shoulder. 'Brooke, are you okay?'*

*'I need to get home ... NOW!' Brooke screamed. 'And don't ever come near me ever again! Leave me alone! I can't deal with this!'*

*Brooke started running, leaving Amber hurt and alone on the road. She ran and ran and ran. She could hear and feel The Fear closing in on her, catching up, biting at her heels. She just needed to get home, then she would be safe. Tears blocked her vision, making the road ahead hazy, but she ran purely on instinct and soon she was racing up the driveway towards the front door. She had forgotten to take a key so it was locked. Brooke threw herself against it and banged as hard as she could, over and over with her fists.*

*'LET ME IN! MUM! DAD! LET ME IN!'*

*BANG, BANG, BANG!*

*The door immediately opened and she fell over the threshold. She collapsed onto the floor, sobbing into the hall carpet. Her mother said nothing, but just gently hugged her, allowing her daughter to scream and cry until she finally passed out.*

*That was the last time Brooke set foot outside her house. From then on, she was a prisoner and didn't feel the daylight on her skin or the breeze on her face for seventeen years.*

# Chapter Six

Amber perched on the edge of the chair, her hands clutching her coffee mug so hard they were turning white. The news story had ended now. The weatherman was saying how glorious it was going to be this week, no rain, just sunshine with highs of twenty-nine degrees. That fact did nothing to raise Amber from terrifying thoughts that spun around and around in her head. It was as if someone had pressed fast forward and everything was racing by in super quick speed.

Many questions raced in her mind: Why had Kieran's watch been found? Hadn't they got rid of all the evidence? Did the police know anything else? What if the body had been found already, but they weren't making it public knowledge until the family had been informed and made a formal identification?

None of it made sense, everything was jumbled together – she couldn't think straight. One thing she did remember was the watch. She could see it as clear as day in her mind's eye: small, blue, an average watch for a child. Kieran had shown it off to the group on his tenth birthday, pointing out the engraving on the back of the dial. Amber remembered how Tyler had rolled his eyes at that point and had tried to diminish the object as *just a stupid watch.* Amber reached out her hand and gently touched the engraving on the back of the watch. It was real and it was solid. It was ...

All of a sudden the brightly lit kitchen was clouded in shadows. They climbed the walls and began circling around Amber. She was frozen in place unable to move a muscle. It reminded her of when she woke up from one of her nightmares and the sleep paralysis took control, but this time she wasn't asleep. It was real life. A horrible, raspy breathing sound filled her ears. It was so loud she thought her head might split open. She grasped her head in her hands, willing her head not to explode. The breathing got louder, more intense, closer – it was inside her head.

'Stop it!' she screamed. 'Leave me alone!'

'Mummy?' The sound of her daughter's sweet voice dispelled the evil shadows and sounds, hurtling Amber back into the present and waking her from her daze.

'Sorry Munchkin.' Amber gasped for breath and searched the room frantically in case The Creature was nearby, but there was no sign of it. It was eerily quiet now.

'I'm going to be late for school. You said I shouldn't be late during the last week before the summer holidays. We have to leave soon.'

Sometimes Amber wondered who the adult was. Bethany was far too mature for her own good, often having to look after her mother when she was suffering one of her especially bad episodes. Amber would call it an *episode* when she lost track of time or blanked out certain memories or woke up from a nightmare. Bethany didn't understand what the cause of her episodes was, but she could sense her mother's fear and anxiety. Bethany often held her hand so Amber knew that someone was there, ready for when she returned to normality.

Amber quickly gathered her things. Bethany already had her school bag slung over her shoulder, complete with her homework and packed lunch. Amber had her appointment with Doctor Allan this morning before her shift at work so she grabbed her journal. She used it to jot down her thoughts and feelings, something she hadn't done hardly at all this last month; no doubt Doctor Allan would be disappointed in her. Right now, she didn't care. All she cared about was finding her car keys and getting Bethany to school. She couldn't handle any more disapproving looks from the other mums as she rushed her daughter through the school gates just as they were all getting into their cars after delivering their children to school on time.

'Bethany, have you seen my car keys?'

'Yes Mummy. They are in your hand.'

Amber stopped rushing around – there they were, in her hand. 'Thanks, let's go.'

They both headed out the door. The weatherman had been correct. The sun was smiling down upon the local town, basking it in a delicious warmth. Amber strapped her daughter into her booster seat in the back of the Volvo and then got behind the wheel. She listened as Bethany started listing the things she had learnt at school last week, in case they had a quiz.

It amazed her how intelligent her daughter was. Being able to list all the major cities in the United Kingdom in alphabetical order was a feat that was extremely impressive for a child of her age. Amber remembered enjoying school; she had been smart once too. She had made plans to finish school, go to university, become a doctor or a scientist, maybe discover a cure for a random disease. That hadn't happened. Amber had never finished school and didn't have any GCSE's or qualifications. She was a part time barista at a local coffee shop. Not that there was anything wrong with that, but Amber had always wanted to do more – *be* more. Becoming a mother hadn't been in her original plan either, not in her mid-twenties anyway. Now she obviously wouldn't have it any other way. Her daughter was her whole life now and the one single reason she had to smile.

Years ago, before she had Bethany, she would look at all the women with their precious babies and not understand why they were so happy, despite the exhaustion, stress and complete life change. Now, she understood. The exhaustion was nothing new though. In fact, back in the new-born days, she had enjoyed staying awake all night, just her and her tiny baby. That way she didn't have to go to sleep and see The Creature. Instead, she could stare at Bethany and watch as she slept peacefully in her arms, blissfully unaware of her mother's turmoil.

'Mummy, can we play a game?' Again, Bethany roused Amber from her dark thoughts.

'Yes, of course. What would you like to play?' Amber was grateful for the distraction.

'My friend Sarah taught me a new game yesterday. It's called I Spy. Do you know how to play?'

Amber tried to hide her panicked reaction. She felt as if an invisible sledgehammer had just hit her in the chest. Today, so far, had been a rollercoaster of emotions and feelings.

'Um, yes ... I know how to play.' She had never mentioned that game they had all played to anyone. It was a secret only they knew about. If it wasn't for *that* game, Kieran wouldn't be dead and her life wouldn't be haunted by The Creature.

'I spy with my little eye something beginning with C.'

Bethany grinned at her mother in the rear-view mirror. Amber managed to crack a smile. It was obvious the answer was *car*, but she felt obliged to play along and pretend it was a hard game.

'That's a hard one.'

Amber glanced into the rear-view mirror and saw her child smiling – something wasn't right. There was a strange shadow next to her, which slowly began to materialise, transforming into an ugly, dark creature with claw-like hands. The Creature was grabbing Bethany around the neck, but she was still smiling, her lips moving like she was talking, however Amber only heard the raspy breathing of The Creature. Then it spoke.

'I know.' It repeated those words over and over, its voice a mere whisper, but it sent shivers down her spine. Amber spun her head around to get a better look – The Creature had vanished. Had it been there at all?

'Are you okay, Mummy?'

'Yes. Are you okay? Was anyone in the back with you just now?'

'No Mummy. There's no one here. I'm fine. Are you having one of your episodes?' The question caught her off guard. She hated the fact that her daughter even knew about her *episodes*. No seven-year-old should know that her mother hallucinated.

'N-no Munchkin. I'm sorry. I-I don't really feel like playing that game at the moment. Is that okay?'

'Yes Mummy, it's fine, but you missed the turning to school.'

Amber rolled her eyes, swore in her head and made a U-turn.

Once Bethany had been dropped safely at school Amber headed towards Doctor Allan's house, a small country cottage on the outskirts of Cherry Hollow. He had transformed his garage into a professional office where he saw clients on a daily basis. She had been seeing him for about five years now. At first it had been weekly sessions, but she felt that she was no longer benefiting from them anymore. Doctor Allan advised she still touch base with him once a month, to ensure she was okay and not getting any worse. Amber had agreed but felt that therapy was a waste of time now. In therapy, the whole point was to tell the truth, open up and expose all the unpleasant details to get to the root of the problem and then slowly heal. Amber knew she couldn't tell the truth and she already knew the root of the problem. Sean had made her go to therapy originally, so she continued to go to make him happy too. Doctor Allan had only moved to the area about six years previously, so he was unaware of the sad events of twenty years ago. Amber wanted it to stay that way.

Amber was greeted by Doctor Allan at the door to his garage. He was a short, stubby man with a friendly, comforting smile that put her at ease. His hair was sticking up in random places today – maybe he had been in a rush this morning. It always fascinated Amber how even doctors could forget to brush their hair. It showed that he was human. She didn't know his age, but she guessed he was about fifty due to his grey hair and mature face which seemed to hold lots of interesting stories in those fine lines.

'Good morning Amber. Please, come in.'

Doctor Allan showed her in and she took a seat in the familiar grey armchair, its cushions faded due to the numerous visitors it received. Amber wondered how many tears and memories this chair held, how many broken people had sat upon it and how many had been healed in the process. It was a pleasant office, decorated tastefully – magnolia on three of the walls, dark brown on the fourth. Pictures of generic flowers and countryside adorned the walls, a vase of freshly cut flowers filled the room with a sweet scent as they sat upon the low table that was between her and Doctor Allan. His chair was made of leather, worn away in certain places due to years of constant use. It had been used as his therapy chair throughout his entire career.

'Thank you,' Amber said.

'So,' began Doctor Allan. 'How has the journaling been going this month?'

Amber fished into her handbag and brought out the journal, its pages and cover still brand new, proving that it had barely been opened. 'Not very well. I'm sorry. I've found it difficult to put things down on paper.'

Amber handed Doctor Allan her journal. He took it without a word and opened it onto the first page. There was only one small entry:

*Friday 1$^{st}$ of July 2018. I can't remember what I did last night.*

'Tell me about that night Amber. What *do* you remember?'

'I had dinner and put Bethany to bed as usual. Sean and I watched a film. I had some wine. Maybe too much because I fell asleep on the sofa. When I woke up, I was tucked up in bed. Sean was asleep next to me. I don't remember how I got there.'

'Is that everything?'

*No.* 'Yes.'

There was more, but Amber didn't want to expand upon the details for fear of him asking too many questions she was not prepared to answer.

When she had woken, she had not been in bed, but still on the sofa. It had been around 03:30 a.m. She'd had her shoes on which were dirty and she had been sweating, her top stuck to her body. She couldn't remember putting her shoes on. Why would she put them on during the night anyway?

'How much had you had to drink?'

'A bottle.'

Doctor Allan smiled. 'I think that may explain your blackout.'

Amber chuckled. 'Yes, you're right.'

'Why do you think you find it hard to write things down? Is it due to not having the time or because of something else?'

'I guess a bit of both. I keep forgetting and then when I do go to write something down, I don't know what to say or how to write it.'

'What is it that you would like to write down?'

Amber thought for a moment. She always hated having to explain her feelings. The frustration of not being able to tell the truth made it even harder.

'The nightmares I have. I can't form words to explain them. I had another sleep paralysis episode this morning.' She neglected to mention the bruises and contusions on her neck on purpose. She unconsciously touched her sore neck through the fabric of her top.

'I see. How many episodes have you had this month?'

*Almost every night and throughout the day.* 'About three or four.'

'Would you say they are getting worse?'

*Yes.* 'Not especially, no.'

'Have you been injured physically from any of the episodes?'

*Yes.* 'No.'

'Have you told your husband about them?'

*No.* 'Yes, most of the time.'

'And is he supportive and understanding?'

Amber paused. 'Yes.'

'Why did you pause there, Amber?'

'Did I?'

'Please correct me if I'm wrong, but I often get the impression from you that you don't tell Sean everything that's going on in your life. Is that true?'

*Yes.* 'I tell him what he needs to know.'

'And what about what he doesn't need to know? Would it upset him if you told him?'

'Yes.' Finally a word of truth.

'I see. I'd like to focus on this for a moment if I may. You say you cannot tell Sean everything that has happened or is happening in your life ... but Sean is a part of your life too. I know from previous sessions that you have a limited friendship circle, so Sean is the sole person in your life that is always around, but yet you do not trust him enough to open up. Why is that do you think?'

Amber knew she was in dangerous territory. Doctor Allan had a very annoying knack of getting directly to the point. Usually, she was on her game and could throw him off track, but today she was distracted by the news bulletin and something else – something that was clawing away at her.

'I don't know,' she replied, knowing for a fact that response was never good enough for a therapist.

'Is there anyone that you do trust?'

Now *that* was an interesting question, but what was even more interesting was the answer that popped into her head without a moment's hesitation. *Jordan.* Or, at least, it had been Jordan a long time ago. She didn't know him now.

Doctor Allan could obviously see the cogs turning in her head. 'Who is it that you trust Amber?'

'I'd rather not say their name, but twenty years ago I had a friend who I trusted more than anyone else in the world.'

'But you're not friends with this person now?'

'No.'

'Why is that?'

*How long have you got?* 'I guess we had a disagreement and we went our separate ways.'

'As is normal with most childhood friendships as we grow up, but tell me – this friend – do you miss them?'

Amber felt the familiar sting of tears. 'Every day. I feel guilty.'

'Guilty for what?'

'For not trying to stay in touch, for abandoning them.'

'Maybe you can change that. Is it perhaps worth reaching out to them now to see how they are? Whatever happened between you both all those years ago, perhaps now is the time to rekindle that friendship and gain that trust again. Maybe then you could tell this person these issues you have and it could help you overcome them. As you know a problem shared is a problem halved. That's how the old saying goes. It may help with your guilt.'

'Maybe.' Amber couldn't help but applaud Doctor Allan. He may not have understood exactly what had happened, but he had hit the nail right on the head today.

The session ended not long after. Amber was finally safe inside her car where she could breathe again. She felt as if she had been holding her breath the entirety of their therapy session. She really needed to stop her sessions. They weren't helping her and she often came far too close for comfort to revealing a secret that she shouldn't – and more importantly – couldn't tell. She couldn't risk it anymore.

Amber drove to her place of work, mentally writing out an email to Doctor Allan to cancel their sessions. She parked the car and walked the remaining one-hundred metres to the tiny coffee shop right in the centre of town. The Bean Café was ancient, as could be seen by its decrepit interior and peeling paint job, but the locals still bought their coffee from there because it was the best. Also, the home-made apple pie was pretty good too. Amber worked there most weekdays from nine in the morning till two in the afternoon, making coffee, serving it and cleaning up spills. It was a job. Not the life-changing job she had always dreamed of having, but it was enough. Luckily, Sean earned the lion's share of the income as a manager of the posh (and only) hotel in town called The Cherry Tree. He worked the usual nine to five shift, sometimes later, but usually was home for dinner at six. His income meant they could afford a decent lifestyle, a lovely big house and a new car every few years.

'Hi Amber, how was therapy?' asked Hayley, her co-worker. She was always so nosy, always wanting to know everything. Amber usually tried to keep her answers as short as possible. She had no intention of becoming friends with her. Hayley had long black hair that reached almost down to her waist, but for work she always had it tied up in a messy bun on top of her head. She was fairly plain apart from the ridiculous amount of jewellery she wore – at least six earrings in each ear, dozens of bracelets and necklaces, all different colours.

'Great, thanks,' answered Amber.

'What are you going for again?'

'Insomnia.' *Among other things.*

'Ah yeah, that's right. I had that one night. I was awake all night for no apparent reason, although it could have been because I was watching this really addictive TV show. Have you seen Game of Thrones? It's really good.' Amber wanted to laugh out loud. *One night versus twenty years – she had no idea.* 'Have you tried camomile tea?'

'Um, yeah.'

'And it didn't work?'

'No.'

'Ah, that's a shame. Anyway, it's a slow morning so I'll be in the back doing some cleaning. You okay on the till?'

'Yes, that's fine.'

'Okay, shout if you need any help.'

'Will do.'

Hayley finally disappeared and Amber was left in peace. There was no one in the shop at the moment; the morning rush had ended. It was half past ten so all the people who came in for their morning caffeine fix before work were now working. Amber reckoned she had about an hour of relative calm until the lunchtime rush began. She gazed out of the window at the business opposite – Fix It All. It was a small, family-run plumbing business. The owner, Jack Evans, had first opened it back in 1965. His son Jordan would one day take over the business – or that had been the plan twenty years ago. She wasn't sure if that plan had changed at all. Jack was a lovely man and would say hello to Amber when they crossed paths, but he knew not to bring up Jordan. Amber very rarely saw Jack, preferring to send her husband for plumbing supplies instead. There was less chance of running into Jordan that way.

Amber's heart rate suddenly increased and she felt a jolt of electricity throughout her body. Jordan had just walked out of the front door of Fix It All and was heading towards his truck, probably out running an errand. A baseball cap was pulled low over his head, his shoulders were hunched. He didn't look like the Jordan she had once known; a lot had changed in two decades. He was a different person. Despite not actually talking to him for the past fourteen years she had heard plenty about him – gossip spread fast in a small town, like a wildfire caught in a strong wind. Ever since his childhood friend had gone missing the lovely, polite young man had gone off the rails with stealing, swearing, vandalism, domestic abuse, drinking and his anger was something no one wanted to witness. He looked good though, his once skinny, adolescent frame now replaced with a strong, muscular physique. Gone was the Jordan she once knew, replaced with a stranger. She wondered if he had seen the news this morning as she had done. How had he reacted?

Amber found herself daydreaming, back to the day of their first kiss, a mere two days before *it* had happened and their lives had catapulted out of control —

*Amber and Jordan were sitting in their spot, a wooden bench in the local park next to a small, bright pink rhododendron bush. They had always called it their spot. It was where they would meet, just the two of them, to chat or hang out without the others. Amber always felt happiest when she was with Jordan. She had always trusted him and told him everything. She trusted Brooke too, but she did have a tendency to gossip to the other kids, not Jordan. They would be turning thirteen soon, no longer children, but teenagers, on the verge of becoming young adults. Amber had always had a soft spot for Jordan, had always fancied him even from a young age. It had only been recently though that her innocent crush had developed into something more.*

*Jordan reached over and took Amber's hand. His touch was soft and gentle, his skin warm and welcoming. 'Amber,' he said. 'I know we are good friends and I don't ever want that to change and I wouldn't want to do anything to jeopardise that, but ... well, I mean ... would you ever, I mean ...' Jordan couldn't seem to find the words, but he pressed on anyway. 'Would you ever consider me as more than a friend?'*

*Amber blushed bright pink to match the bushes, but she smiled. 'Yes, I think, maybe ... I mean ... yes.'*

*Jordan smiled back at her. 'Good, I mean ... me too. I like you.'*

*'I like you too.'*

*Jordan leaned in towards her; Amber followed suit. Their lips lightly touched, both of them too nervous and inexperienced to try anything other than a light kiss. They pulled away and smiled at each other. In that moment Amber's heart was full of hope for the future. She dreamt that night of what their lives would be like as they grew up; childhood sweethearts, married, have kids of their own and grow old together. That was her dream.*

Amber's attention was abruptly pulled away as the

café doors opened. A man walked in that she had never expected to see ever again – Tyler Jenkins. She was so shocked that she just froze on the spot, staring open-mouthed at him. Her heart felt like it was trying to burst out of her chest. His once charming good looks were no longer there, replaced now with a distinctly average face, greasy hair and a grubby beard. He looked tired – really tired. He was wearing a tatty high-vis vest over a dirty grey t-shirt; obviously out on a building job. She vaguely knew that he was a builder by trade, but otherwise knew nothing about the man standing in front of her, only that he had ruined her life twenty years ago by threatening to kill her if she ever told anyone that they had buried their friend at the bottom of a ravine.

Tyler walked slowly up to the counter. 'Hi Amber.' His voice was low and quiet, completely alien to her. He had the voice of a man now and not a thirteen-year-old boy. She barely recognised him.

'Hi.' It was the only word she could utter.

'Can I have a large coffee please?'

Amber suddenly remembered that she was there to serve customers, and he was a customer after all. 'Of course.'

Amber turned to the coffee machine, pressed the button and began to make the beverage, but her brain had stopped working. She realised that she suddenly had no idea how to use the machine. Her face blushed the colour of beetroot, but, luckily, she had her back to him so he could not see her embarrassment. *One step at a time Amber,* she told herself.

Seeing his face now was causing so many emotions and feelings to flood her body. Was she angry with him? Scared of him? Pleased to see him? She honestly didn't know. Whenever she had seen him in the street, he had always tried to avoid her by ducking out of sight or switching to the other side of the road. She had done the same. Amber hated to admit it, but she had made no attempt whatsoever to contact him over the years, never asked how he was or tried to make amends. He was no longer a part of her life – he was a stranger.

'How are you?' he asked timidly as she turned around holding a paper cup of steaming coffee.

'Fine.' *The biggest lie of the century.*

'You're probably wondering why I'm here.'

Amber held the coffee out to him. 'For coffee?'

He cracked the tiniest of smiles. 'Well, yes, but I ... that is, I need to speak to you.'

'What about?'

Tyler took a long drawn in breath. 'The watch.'

'The watch,' Amber repeated. She did not know why but she immediately felt relief. Her brain automatically flashed back to seeing the watch again.

'You saw the news?' he asked.

'Yes, I saw it, but Tyler I really don't think we should be talking here where we could be overheard.'

Tyler nodded in agreement. 'Okay. Yes, fair enough. You're right. Can we meet later today or tomorrow? I'm sorry this is so out of the blue. I realise we haven't spoken in —'

'Twenty years,' answered Amber, saving him from having to do the maths. Not that it was hard maths to do. Amber had spoken briefly to Brooke and Jordan a few years after *it* had happened, but not to Tyler. She had cut him out of her life completely, as had everyone else.

Tyler looked down, feeling ashamed. 'Yes. A long time.'

'Why now? Why has it taken the finding of that watch to make you come and visit me?'

'I need to fix things.'

Amber didn't reply; she didn't know how. Eventually she said. 'It's too late to fix anything. Surely you know that.'

'I know, but I have a plan.'

'And your plans always work out so well.' She couldn't hide the sarcasm in her voice.

'Can you at least give me the chance to try?'

'Can I think about it?'

'Yes, of course. Sleep on it? I live at thirty-five Hollytree, the ground floor flat. Come by tomorrow if you want to continue this conversation. Thanks for the coffee.' Tyler handed her the money and left without a backwards glance, leaving the café in silence.

Amber was left alone, the beating of her racing heart pounded in her ears. She was out of breath, as if she had just completed a hundred metre sprint. The shock of seeing Jordan across the street and then seconds later Tyler walking into the café and speaking to her was almost too much to bear. She took a few deep breaths, willing herself not to panic. She needed to think about this. On the one hand she felt relief that Tyler was actually willing to come forward and *fix things* as he put it. How did he expect to fix it? On the other hand, she was terrified of the consequences. Amber didn't know what plan Tyler had in mind, but a small part of her wanted to find out. Surely there was only one way to fix things and that was to confess. She hated to admit it, but she secretly wanted Tyler to confess. It was a selfish thought and only a brief one.

Amber did her best to push Tyler out of her mind for the remainder of her shift. Luckily, the lunchtime coffee rush kept her busy and she focused on brewing coffee, crushing beans and frothing milk.

# Chapter Seven

Amber finished her shift and headed home, still having an hour or so before Bethany needed picking up from school. She felt as if she was in a dream. Everything was floating past her in slow motion, her mind busy with questions and thoughts. She somehow managed to clean the house, prepare dinner, pick up Bethany from school and help her with her homework. These types of fazes were common for her. It was like she wasn't in control of her body, floating somewhere above herself, seeing and doing things, but not really knowing how she was doing them.

It was a similar experience to that night when she had woken up on the sofa and not remembered when she had put her shoes on or why they were filthy. It was hard to explain. Amber thought back to that moment when she opened her eyes. She had let her eyes adjust to the bright light in her lounge. She had felt woozy, hot and sweaty. Her mind had felt fuzzy and she'd had a hard time figuring out if she was dreaming or not. Her car keys had been next to her on the sofa, which was strange because they usually lived on the hook by the front door.

Sean walked in the door bang on six o'clock, just as Bethany was helping Amber set the table for dinner. He threw his jacket on the sofa, along with his keys and shoes; a bad habit that Amber hated.

She thought: *Why couldn't he hang his jacket up, put his keys in the pot and his shoes in the cupboard?*

'Daddy!'

'Hi Beth Bug!' Father and daughter embraced. Then she jumped on his back and he gave her a piggyback ride around the kitchen/diner. They laughed and played – it was a wonderful sight. He was a doting father, something that filled Amber's heart with happiness and gratitude. Her own father had not been so loving, never really showing her any affection, never playing with her or teaching her to read. He had always been too busy working. Amber didn't hold any ill will towards her own father of course. He had provided for her and her mother, but she had always wanted to ensure that if she ever had children then they would not be without a good father. Sean was the best father she could ever imagine for Bethany.

Once they had finished playing Sean came and gave his wife a quick kiss on the cheek.

'Good day?' she asked him.

'Yeah, not bad. I finally finished planning the new menu with the head chef. Should be ready to go in a couple of weeks. Fancy a night out to taste it?'

'Sounds good.'

'Cool, I'll organise it. So how was your session with Doctor Allan?'

'Yeah, it was good, but I'm thinking about stopping the sessions. I don't get anything out of them anymore and we just end up going over the same things.'

'That's a shame. They aren't helping you at all?'

Amber shook her head. 'No. I still have insomnia and nightmares.'

'I wish we could find out exactly why you suffer so badly from insomnia. There must be a reason. What age were you when it started again?'

'Um ... twelve, nearly thirteen.' Amber started feeling uneasy. She never liked talking about her past. In fact, she genuinely avoided it.

'And you can't remember *why* they started?'

'No.'

Sean sighed. 'Well, if you want to stop therapy then I can't stop you. You do whatever is best for you. Oh, by the way, did you hear the news today? Apparently, some kids found a watch in that ravine near here which belonged to that missing kid from twenty years ago. How crazy is that? I'm surprised you didn't know him.'

'Yes, we watched the news together this

morning. I mean, I knew *of* him, but you know, we weren't friends or anything.'

Sean hadn't grown up in this area (he had spent his childhood near Manchester), so he had never heard about the disappearance of Kieran and his four friends who had been so devastated over their friends' departure that they had slowly drifted apart and become strangers.

Luckily, the story was one that was rarely talked about now because it was so sad, but people often wondered. *Had the boy run away? Had he been kidnapped? Or murdered?* It seemed the whole town had suffered at the loss of that boy. Parents didn't allow their children to play outside anymore, at least not out of sight. They kept a close and watchful eye on them. Kieran's parents no longer smiled or ventured out to see people. In fact, Amber couldn't remember the last time she had seen them – it must have been at least fifteen years ago. Amber had never told Sean about her friends from that time. As far as he knew she had never had any close friends. At times she felt guilty for keeping such a big part of her life from him, but it was better if he didn't know the details. She did hate to lie to him though and felt guilty about that too.

'It's a sad story,' Sean continued. 'I read into it today. I had no idea a kid had gone missing from here. And they really don't know what happened to him?

Was there a search conducted?'

Yes, there had been a search conducted. The police had searched all over the town and surrounding areas, even getting the local community involved, but to no avail. Kieran had remained missing. The case had been closed about a year after his disappearance because there had been no evidence to keep it open. It was now one of those cold cases, locked away in a filing cabinet at the police station. That was, until today.

'Yes, there was a search, but nothing came of it.' Amber wished he would drop the subject. *Why was he so fascinated by a missing twelve-year-old boy from twenty years ago?* She assumed that to a normal outsider it was a fascinating story, one of mystery and unanswered questions, but to Amber it was an open wound and one she wished to keep closed.

'Strange. Now this watch has been found, they must have to reopen the case. It was in the ravine and it was broken, apparently it had stopped working at 15:31 p.m., but there's no way of knowing what day it stopped. Also, it was really clean apart from the dried blood. No dirt, no fingerprints at all. Isn't that weird?'

'Yeah ... weird.' Amber nodded, trying to think back to that day.

Kieran had been wearing the watch. He never took it off, but had he been wearing it when they had buried him? She couldn't remember. Her memory of the time she spent at the bottom of the ravine was so foggy. Everything was jumbled together, some parts were missing, some were intact. She found it slightly funny how a little thing like a watch was seemingly so unimportant at the time, but years later it threatened to unravel the whole true story – a story that couldn't possibly be found out because it was too terrible. Amber suddenly had a horrible thought. *What if Bethany found out that she had been involved in covering up her friend's death?* She would never understand. She would hate her own mother. Even the mere thought brought a tear to Amber's eye. She quickly turned away, back to stirring the gravy on the hob. Her whole life was on the brink of falling apart. She couldn't let that happen; she had far too much to lose. Maybe she needed to finally do something about it – maybe she already *was* doing something about it.

'You okay?' questioned Sean, noticing his wife's silence.

'Yeah, fine. I'm about to dish up. Can you call Bethany in for dinner?'

'Sure babe. Then I'll tell you about the new menu if you like.'

'Yes, that would be lovely.'

Amber heaved her injured body across the rocks,

sweating, crying, pleading with herself to move faster, but her body wouldn't co-operate. It felt a hundred times heavier than it actually was, as if she was dragging a huge rock behind her. The rock was pulling her backwards the way she had already come, back down to the bottom of the ravine. She didn't know what awaited down there, but she sure as hell didn't want to find out. Not now, she wasn't ready to face the truth. Her legs were broken, or at least, that's what they felt like. The pain was so intense she wanted to pass out just so she could no longer feel it. She grabbed a sharp rock outcrop and attempted to pull herself up; the weight was too heavy, her strength was draining from her body.

The Creature was near; she could sense it, smell it, feel it. Or was that the smell of death? She couldn't distinguish between the two. The horrible raspy breathing was so close, she could feel it on the back of her neck. Amber had reached her limit; she could no longer continue. This was the end.

'I know what you did.' The eerie voice was a gentle whisper, but it rattled the surrounding walls of the ravine so much that it sent small landslides crashing down on top of Amber, covering her in dust and small rock particles.

She coughed, spitting the dust out of her mouth. 'Leave me alone!'

'I know what you did.' The voice repeated.

Amber cried. 'What do you want from me?'

'Confess.'

'I can't! I'll lose everything! I'll die!'

'CONFESS!' The voice boomed out, louder and deeper than before. Greater amounts of dust and rocks toppled down from above. Amber feared she would be crushed, hidden forever at the bottom of the ravine, joining all the other hidden secrets that lay down there.

Suddenly she felt a forceful jolt as something landed on top of her, pinning her against the rocks, the sharp edges digging into her skin. The air was forced from her lungs as if a heavy weight were crushing her from behind. She couldn't see the recipient, but she could feel it, the cold hands against her back, the cold breath against her neck. She dared not try and turn her head to look; in fact, she didn't want to look. She was too terrified of what she might see.

Then she was dragged backwards by her hair, torn away from the rocks. She screamed a blood-curdling scream as she was thrown into the murky water of the river. It wasn't deep, but it was enough water to cushion her fall. Whatever had grabbed her was no longer there, leaving her in complete silence apart from the trickling of the river. The cool water soothed her cuts and scrapes and washed away the dirt, revealing bruised and battered pale skin. Amber lay in the river, unable to move due to her injuries. She was waiting for death – she knew that now. Her eyes closed slowly, her breath retreated to a calmer pace; in through the nose and out through the mouth.

'CONFESS!'

Her eyes sprang open and immediately The Creature screamed in her face, its eyes blood shot and wide, its teeth bared —

She was screaming and someone was shaking her violently.

'Wake up! Amber wake up!' Sean's voice brought her back to reality. Amber stopped screaming and stared into her husband's eyes. She used them as an anchor to calm herself. He repeated the phrase that her therapist had taught her to use when she had one of her episodes.

'I am in control. I am in control. Say it Amber. I am in control.'

'I ... am in ... control. I am in ... control.' With each syllable she felt the panic and nightmare lifting from her body.

Sean embraced her in a tight hug and they repeated the phrase over and over for what seemed like hours, but it was actually only a few minutes.

'I've not seen you that bad for years. You were

saying *I have to confess*. I was trying for ages to wake you up. Nothing was working. You scared the life out of me. What is it you have to confess?'

'I ... I ...' but she couldn't find the right words. 'I'm so sorry.'

Amber got up and splashed cool water on her face and took her medication, something she was allowed to do in case of a severe attack.

'Does this have anything to do with that missing boy?'

'No, why would it?'

'You said his name in your sleep. Kieran. Is there something you aren't telling me?'

'No, of course not. I must have said his name because he was on the news. It jolted my memory of when it happened, that's all.'

For a split second Amber considered telling him the truth, then she realised what a complete mistake that would be. He would never understand. It wasn't Sean she had to speak to – it was Tyler. She had finally made up her mind. He'd been right; they had to fix this or at least try. She'd never had such a clear message from The Creature before. *Confess*. It was time.

Amber didn't sleep for the remainder of the night. Instead, she waited for Sean to fall back to sleep, then got up, went downstairs and made herself a coffee. She stared blankly ahead while she sipped the hot liquid. It reached her stomach and gently warmed her. The Creature stayed with her, hovering nearby, but she ignored it, continuing to stare ahead. It seemed that The Creature was hanging around a lot more recently, possibly keeping an eye on Amber to ensure she did its bidding. She wished she could talk to it, ask it questions. It unnerved her to have it so close. She wished it would disappear into her dreams again. Real life hallucinations were never a good sign. It had been happening more and more lately. *Was she going crazy?*

Amber blinked and it was suddenly 06:30 a.m. – time to start putting her plan into action. She called in sick for work, telling them that she had food poisoning. Next, she got up from the kitchen chair, showered and got ready for work, made breakfast, said goodbye to Sean as he left for work and took Bethany to school as usual. That was where the normality ended.

Amber pointed the Volvo in the direction of Tyler's flat. It was near the centre of town, the ground floor flat he had said. Nerves were taking over her body, causing her to tremble and sweat. Tyler was the person who was responsible for destroying her life. It was *his* fault. Him and his ridiculous plan of covering up Kieran's death. If they had just owned up to the accident it wouldn't have been too bad. Surely, they wouldn't have been sentenced or blamed? It had been an accident. Yes, her memory was a bit hazy of the incident. She couldn't remember all of the exact details. One minute Kieran had been standing on the fallen tree and the next he was falling off it. There was a piece of her memory that was missing. *Maybe that's because you don't want to remember what really happened* said a raspy voice from behind her. The Creature was there in the rear-view mirror. *Had it just spoken?* Was it possible that she had blocked out a memory from her past? It could happen, especially after such a traumatic event, sometimes the mind protected itself from things that were damaging. It seemed her subconscious was protecting her from a lot of things recently.

Amber parked, got out of the car and approached the building. She knocked and waited, staring straight ahead at the door, its paint peeling, revealing worn and aged wood. The whole building was run down and not very well looked after. Even the grass either side of the front door was overgrown and looked like it hadn't been cut in years. A rattling noise could be heard from behind the door, then it creaked open and Tyler's tired, drawn-out face appeared between the gap.

'Hi Amber.'

She smiled awkwardly. 'Hi Tyler.'

'Thank you for coming.' Tyler opened the door further and stood aside to let her past. For a split second she contemplated not going in. This was a stranger who had threatened to kill her in the past; even though he had been a boy at the time. She needed to be brave, needed to see this through.

Amber nearly gagged at the sight and stench that met her upon entering his flat. She had never seen such an untidy and dirty place. *How could someone live like this?* She did her best to hide her disgust as she walked in, not knowing where to look or where to stand. The Creature followed her in and hovered in a nearby corner, sinking into the walls, almost invisible.

'Sorry about the mess. Do you want a drink?' offered Tyler.

'No! Thank you.' Amber realised she had probably answered a bit too suddenly and forcefully. There was no way she was touching anything in this place, let alone drinking from it. She watched as Tyler grabbed a bottle of beer from his mini fridge, popped the cap off and downed the entire thing in one go. He took another beer, popped the cap again and took a couple of sips, staring at her the whole time. It unnerved her slightly. His stare felt dangerous, as if he were staring straight through her into her soul. It was barely nine in the morning and he was already drinking. That was not a good sign of his mental stability. Then she saw his eyes briefly glance over to the corner where The Creature was hovering. *Could he see it?* He glanced back at her.

'What made you come?'

Amber shook off the uneasy feeling. 'Someone gave me a message.'

'Someone? Who?'

Amber paused. This was it – the first time she would ever say these words out loud to another person.

'The Creature.'

The two words felt strange to say. She felt an overwhelming amount of relief almost immediately. It surprised her that she felt so at ease telling Tyler straight away. He may have made her nervous, but there was something about him now. He was *different.*

Amber expected Tyler to look confused, but he didn't. She saw his eyes flicker over to the corner and back to her again. Her heartbeat increased, she could feel the pulse in her neck thumping hard.

'The Creature,' he repeated back to her. 'I call it The Black Shadow.'

'You see it too!' Amber gasped, completely shocked and overwhelmed by the sudden revelation. All this time she had assumed that she was the only one who was suffering with these visions and nightmares, but Tyler had been having them too. She wasn't alone anymore. That thought alone made her want to burst into tears and collapse in a heap on the floor.

Tyler nodded. 'What does it look like to you?'

'It's big, black, has red eyes, long fingers and is really scary, like something out of a nightmare.'

'Mine is just a shadow that hovers over me. It gives me an unbearable feeling of sadness.'

'Is The Black Shadow here now?' Amber glanced nervously around, searching for a glimpse. The Creature was still in the corner, but it was almost completely invisible now.

'Yes, it's always here. It never leaves me.'

'The Creature hasn't always been around all the time. It used to visit me in my sleep, my nightmares, sometimes during the day. It can pin me down, hurt me, scare me, but now it's constantly following me.' Amber knew she was spilling her deepest secrets to a complete stranger, but she didn't care. It felt amazing to be finally free of such a terrible burden.

'It hurts you physically?'

Amber pulled her top away from her neck, revealing her bruises and claw marks. Tyler stepped forward to get a better look.

'Shit,' he said and then stepped away. 'It doesn't hurt me physically, but it makes me do things to myself. A few years ago I tried to commit suicide, but it didn't work. It makes me hurt myself then pulls me back again, like it wants me to continue to suffer. It started after ... it happened.'

Amber bit her lip to stop it quivering, her eyes brimming with tears. 'Same. I thought I was the only one who ... was suffering. If only we had all stayed together, we could have helped each other all these years instead of being alone. I'm so sorry. I should have made an effort to see you, to talk to you. I know that now, but I was so angry Tyler, so lost and afraid. I didn't know what to do.'

'It's all my fault.'

Amber resisted the urge to agree with him. He wasn't wrong. It was his fault. She did blame him, but she now felt guilty for doing so. 'We all played a part.'

'My part was slightly bigger than yours, or Jordan's or Brooke's. Have you seen them or spoken to them recently?'

Amber shook her head no. 'Not at all, not in years. I saw Jordan very briefly this morning across the road.'

'I hear he has anger issues.'

'Yeah,' was all she said. It felt so surreal to be chatting to Tyler again. They had a mutual connection. They both had darkness inside themselves. It was as if no time at all had passed and they were kids again, just casually talking about their lives. She also found it odd to be talking to him calmly, usually conversations with Tyler had always been a bit highly strung or aggressive. That had just been his nature back then. The Tyler standing in front of her now was calm and controlled, but also very sad. His depression had sucked the life out of him, leaving only a hollow husk. Amber could see that the past twenty years had taken their toll, as they had on her. They had a lot to catch up on.

'Last night in a dream The Creature told me to confess. I also ... and I can't be sure about this ... but I think maybe it's him – it's Kieran. My daughter had a dream the other night that an old friend of mine was playing games with her. She said he was very scary.'

'Jesus ... you think Kieran has been haunting us and has been punishing us all these years for what we did to him ... or what *I* did to him.'

'Possibly, but I don't understand why my daughter had a dream about him.'

Tyler was silent for a moment, thinking. 'Maybe he's trying to mess with our heads, send us a message. He wants us to confess.'

'Maybe,' said Amber quietly. She was afraid for her daughter's safety. She would not allow The Creature to go after her, no matter what the cost.

There was a long, drawn-out silence, neither knowing what to say next.

'You still blame me, don't you?' Amber didn't

want to answer that question truthfully, fearing that she would hurt his feelings, so Tyler answered for her. 'You should blame me. I blame myself. Twenty years of depression and hating yourself every minute of every day is enough to make anyone regret their decisions. I'm sorry for what I did and for what I made you do, and I really do want to make things better. I need to fix it. That watch being found has given me the kick up the ass I needed. I'm finally ready to take responsibility, but I'm not prepared for you and the others to take the fall either.'

'But how can you just fix it? It's not like we can go back in time and just undo everything we did.'

'I'm going to confess.'

Amber raised her eyebrows and swallowed hard. 'Just you? But you'll go to prison if you do or worse ... you will die. We made a blood oath remember.'

'Yes, we did, but I need your help.'

'I don't understand.'

'Just hear me out, okay? I'm going to confess, but first I need to get everyone on board. We're going to undo the blood oath we took.'

'I still don't understand. How can you just undo a blood oath? I thought the whole point was that it couldn't be undone? That was the whole point,' she repeated.

'There's only one way to undo a blood oath.' Tyler paused. Amber wasn't sure whether she should press him to continue or just let him speak in his own time. Tyler finished off the bottle of beer and then took a deep breath in. 'One of us has to die ... and it's going to be me.'

'What? No! Absolutely not! Tyler, what are you thinking?' Amber shook her head over and over and almost laughed hysterically because the idea was so ludicrous. 'You can't be serious?'

'I am serious Amber. Please, just hear me out. I'm the one who started all of this. It's my fault. I'm the one to blame, so I should be the one to – you know – pay the ultimate price. It's what I want Amber and I'm doing this with or without your help, but I would prefer you to be on my side. I may need help convincing the others. Once all of this is over maybe Kieran will stop haunting us, if it is him. I need to try. Please.'

'But ...' Amber couldn't finish her sentence; words had failed her. She knew for a fact that even if she stayed here for days she wouldn't be able to change Tyler's mind. He had always been stubborn and once his mind was set on something nothing would change it. It had been that way all those years ago; today was no different.

Amber bit her lip, something she used to do when she was a little girl when she was thinking about what to do next. 'I'm not saying I agree with this. I don't want anyone else to die, but, tell me your plan. What's the first step?'

'We go and talk to Jordan and Brooke, but we don't tell them the whole plan.'

'Why not?'

'The less they know, the better. I told you because I trust you. I'm not sure I trust Jordan or Brooke. You were always the good one, the trustworthy one.'

Amber doubted that was true. She was hardly trustworthy anymore, after hiding a secret for two decades from her husband. 'Okay, but what do we tell them?'

'We just tell them that we have found a way to break the blood oath and that I'm going to confess. Leave the details to me, but we all need to go back to the place where we made it.'

'The ravine? There will be police tape and barriers all over the place.'

'Then we go at night.'

Amber furrowed her brow, unsure about how bulletproof this plan was. Too many things could go wrong. 'Okay, then I have another problem.'

'What's that?'

'Brooke hasn't left her house in seventeen years.'

Tyler looked taken aback. 'Are you serious?'

'I was with her the last time she was outside. We argued and she ran back home and hasn't left since. That was seventeen years ago. I see her mother from time to time at the coffee shop. She sometimes tells me how she is, although it's hard to hear. I should have gone back to visit her, but I never did. I feel so guilty.'

'Shit.'

There was a long silence. Amber left Tyler to think things over while she glanced around his flat, taking in the dirty clothes, piles of unwashed plates and bowls of mouldy food. The bed was unmade; a sturdy wooden box rested on it. This held her interest for a few seconds.

'Let's speak to Jordan first,' said Tyler. 'Then we'll see what we can do about Brooke.'

Amber nodded. This was it. She was actually going to see and speak to Jordan properly. The idea made her heart flip in her chest and she had butterflies in her stomach for the first time since they had shared their first kiss.

# Chapter Eight

Amber and Tyler stepped into the glorious sunshine. She was relieved to be out of his flat and able to breathe fresh air again. She felt sorry for Tyler, living all alone in there with nothing but The Black Shadow for company. At least she had Sean and Bethany to keep her going. They were the reason she was still living. At times her mind had taken her to dark places but the thought of leaving them had brought her back to her senses.

One dark instance had been a couple of years ago. Amber had almost reached breaking point; the insomnia, the hallucinations, the guilt, the loneliness. It had all got too much. She had trekked up to the top of a nearby mountain and screamed at the top of her lungs, as loud and for as long as she could. Then she thought of Bethany and she went back home and gave her a big hug. *Thank God for that child.* Tyler didn't have anyone. Amber couldn't even imagine how hard it must have been for him all these years.

'Jordan will be at work now,' said Tyler, automatically walking towards the direction of Fix It All.

'Wait, I can't go there. It's right opposite where I work. They will see me. I called in sick this morning.' Amber hated being dishonest to her employer, but desperate times caused for desperate measures.

'I'm not going in alone. He won't be happy to see me. He always liked you. I swear you two had a thing going on.'

Amber felt herself blush. She and Jordan had never told the others that they had kissed. It was their secret that only they knew about and that made it extra special. Then *it* had happened and their young romance had been forgotten; maybe not forgotten, but other things had taken over their lives. Her feelings for Jordan, whatever they had been, had still been there, were still real but over the days, weeks, months and years that followed those feelings had subsided. *Or had they?*

Amber shrugged. 'I don't know what you're talking about and besides, I'm married.'

'So is he. It doesn't change the fact that he had a crush on you once.'

'Okay fine, I'll sneak in.'

Fix It All was only a few minutes' walk. They didn't talk a lot. Tyler wasn't the chatty type anymore, preferring awkward silence. She wanted to ask him everything about his life that she had missed out on. How were his parents? They had always been nice, slightly strange and fairly strict with him, but always pleasant to his friends.

As per Amber's instructions they waited at the corner while she peered over at the coffee shop, waiting until Hayley had her back turned away from the front window. Then they scurried over to the door of the plumbing business and pushed it open.

A bell signified that they had arrived. It was a small business, but it was popular. Everyone knew Jack, the owner, and his son Jordan, but he was hardly ever at the front of the shop talking to the customers. He wasn't the friendly type. People preferred to speak to Jack who looked up at the sound of the bell. He had kind eyes, grey hair and lots of wrinkles from a long life of working hard and early mornings – maybe too much whiskey.

The recognition was instant.

'Tyler? Amber? Now there's two people I never expected to walk into my shop again. How the hell are you both?' He hadn't seen them properly since they were teenagers, yet still was as polite and kind as ever.

'Hi Mr Evans,' said Amber with a smile.

'Please, call me Jack. You're a bit too grown up now to call me Mr Evans.' They shared a laugh. 'What can I do for you?'

'Um, actually, we're here to see Jordan. Is he here?'

Jack eyed them suspiciously. 'He's here. I'm not sure he'll be happy to see you though. He has issues, I don't know if you are aware. Anger issues. He used to be such a nice boy.'

'We'd still really like to talk to him if we can, please.'

'Okay, but don't say I didn't warn you.' Jack disappeared into the back room, leaving the shop in silence.

Tyler started pacing up and down in the small area in front of the reception counter. Amber fiddled with a new set of spanners that were for sale. Her nerves were shot. She couldn't control her body; it was trembling with fear and anticipation.

Neither saw Jordan enter the room so his harsh voice made them jump; Amber dropped a spanner on the floor, the noise echoed around the room.

'What the fuck are you two doing here?'

Once Amber had composed herself after the initial shock she smiled as best she could, aware that, once again, she was blushing. He looked good – short hair, neatly trimmed beard, dark eyes. Despite now belonging to a fully-grown man she could still see the same eyes she had once stared into, the same eyes that had made her heart flip with excitement and nerves. They may have been the same eyes, but they were also *different* somehow. They were the eyes of a hurt, troubled man who had suffered more loss and sadness than joy.

'Hi Jordan. Good to see you. How are you?'

He stared at her, a blank expression across his face, his arms folded in a threatening manner. She couldn't work out if he was pleased to see her or not. Little did she know that seeing her was a shock to his system also and he was trying his best not to show his nerves. She looked good too, a little too good, despite her obvious lack of sleep.

'Aren't you going to say anything?' she asked.

'I have nothing to say to you.'

'Nothing?' Amber couldn't help but feel a little wounded.

'What do you want me to say exactly? That I'm happy to see you. That it's been *too long.'* Jordan paused, waiting for a reply, but none came, so he snapped. 'Say what you came here to say or get the fuck out.'

*Jesus. He really did have anger issues,* thought Amber. 'Okay ...' She took a step towards him. 'But can we go somewhere more ... private? We don't want people overhearing.'

Jordan gritted his teeth in frustration. He threw a sharp look at Tyler who had remained quiet and in the shadows the whole time. 'You have some nerve showing your face here. Are you going to say anything dickhead?'

'Not if you're going to continue to be an asshole.'

Amber couldn't help but hide a smile; the old Tyler was in there after all, just hidden behind the Black Shadow. Back when they were friends Tyler had always bickered and called the other boys' names, but it had usually been in a joking sort of way. It felt like they were bickering boys again, but now with the added pinch of testosterone.

'Look, this is Tyler's plan,' interjected Amber. 'So let's just —'

'Tyler's plan?' Jordan laughed sarcastically. 'I don't think so. Just look how well the last *plan* of his worked out. Both of you had better fucking leave before I get really fucking angry.' Jordan went to turn and walk away, but Amber quickly lurched forward and grabbed his arm in desperation. She could *not* let him leave.

'Please Jordan. Just hear him out. For me. It's important.'

Jordan looked down at her hand which was gripping his arm so tight her knuckles were turning white. He slowly raised his head and looked at her directly in the eyes, which seemed so much sadder than he remembered. They still had that sparkle that he had loved so much though. He felt his anger melting away at her touch, sinking down his body and into the floor.

'Fine,' he said.

Jordan stormed off into a side room; the other two followed hastily. It was a small storage room, a few boxes of supplies were piled high in one corner and some storage units held some larger items such as new sinks and taps.

Tyler was the last one in so he quietly closed the door behind him, locking them all inside away from prying eyes and ears. Now it was just them alone in a small room. Amber suddenly felt a bit scared. She had no idea how Jordan was going to react to what he was about to hear. She had heard of his anger episodes, but had never actually witnessed one – not a proper one anyway. She had a feeling that she didn't want to be on the receiving end of one either. She could almost feel his anger pulsing through his veins ready to explode.

'Talk,' he said bluntly. 'Fast.'

Amber took a deep, cleansing breath, hoping it would steady her nerves; it didn't, but she continued anyway. 'Did you see the news about the watch yesterday?'

'Yeah, I saw it. So what? What do you expect me to do about it?'

'How did it make you feel?'

'How did it make me *feel!*' Jordan snapped. 'How the fuck do you *think* it made me feel?'

Amber automatically took a step back. Jordan was terrifying. She had never expected to be afraid of him. His voice echoed around the room, causing smaller items to shake. Jordan must have seen the fear in her eyes because he suddenly looked ashamed, his eyes darted around the room, searching for something ... *anything* ... to focus his gaze on – anything other than Amber's eyes which were full of hurt.

'I'm sorry Amber.' His voice was lower now, gravelly and husky. 'It made me feel ... afraid.'

Amber took a deep breath, trying to calm her shaking body. 'We are all afraid, but we think we might know what to do.' Amber glanced over at Tyler, signalling that it was his turn to start talking. It was his plan so she knew that she should let him speak, then step in if Jordan needed further convincing.

Tyler stepped forward. 'We're going to break our blood oath and confess.'

Jordan shot Tyler a dirty look. He had hoped never to set eyes on him ever again. He hated the man with a passion.

'We?' Jordan spat. He pointed his finger at Tyler. 'There's no *we* about it. *You* have to confess. I'm not going to jail because of you.'

'Yes, and I agree. Sorry, I meant that *I'm* going

to confess, but it will take all of us to break the blood oath.' Tyler was nervous, muddling his words.

'Why now? Why not twenty years ago when it first happened? Back then we wouldn't have been charged with covering up a murder. We could have lived normal lives. The police would never have sent a bunch of twelve-year-olds to jail for fucks sake, but if we confess now we may as well kiss the rest of our lives goodbye. We're all guilty of a crime now.'

'I'm going to take all the blame.'

Jordan shook his head. 'It won't work, I promise you that. Besides, you can't break a blood oath, otherwise what was the fucking point in even making it? Trust me, I tried.'

'You did?' asked Tyler, sounding shocked.

'I think we all have at some point. Brooke told me she'd tried. I tried once. It wasn't a pleasant experience,' added Amber. 'It felt like —'

'Like you were going to die,' finished Jordan.

'Yes.' Amber didn't know what else to say.

'I can break it,' said Tyler solemnly. He glanced at Amber as a warning to not mention anything else. The fact that Tyler had to die to break it was something he didn't want anyone else knowing. Even though Amber expected that Jordan wouldn't have a problem with it right now.

Jordan gave Amber a stern look. 'You believe

this idiot? You trust him? After what he did?' His frustration was evident by the tone of his voice.

Amber nodded. 'We have to try.'

'Why? Why the hell should we try?'

'Because we have all been living with the guilt every day for twenty years. It's been eating me alive. Also ...' Amber glanced at Tyler then back to Jordan. 'We think Kieran may be haunting us.'

Jordan snorted and laughed. 'You two are fucking nuts. You think he's haunting us? Let me guess, you've seen his ghost hovering above you at night and he tells you secret messages from beyond the grave.' His sarcasm was met with serious silence. Amber was biting her lip and her eyes were trying hard not to catch his. 'You're fucking kidding me, right?'

'I have visions and nightmares of The Creature chasing me.'

'What the hell is *The Creature*?'

'It's a ... presence I feel and see. It physically hurts me in my sleep and last night it told me to *confess.* Tyler has something he calls The Black Shadow constantly following him. It can't be a coincidence. It's like we have been punished for what we did. We just never realised we were all suffering. Do you have anything like that haunting you?'

Jordan's breathing slowed, his whole demeanour changed, his shoulders relaxed. Amber could have sworn she saw a dark shadow pass over him that calmed him. His eyes flickered to the corner of the room where The Creature was hiding and then back to Amber.

'I call it The Bad Man.' Amber and Tyler's eyes met and they gave each other a knowing look. They listened intently as he continued. 'As soon as *it* happened I felt something take over me. I started getting angry all the time. The first time I properly lost my temper I blacked out. I don't remember what happened, but my mother told me that I threw things at her, called her horrible names and kicked a hole in the wall. When the anger takes over me, I can't control it until it's been released, then I start to calm down, but it builds again and again, over and over. I know it's physically me who's saying and doing things, but mentally it isn't. I feel like I've turned into this bad person, this Bad Man.'

Amber slowly reached out her hand and gently placed it on Jordan's arm. 'It's not you. You're not a bad man, something bad has happened to you ... to all of us.' Amber noticed out of the corner of her eye that Tyler was hanging his head. He appeared to wipe away a tear from his eye. She continued speaking directly to Jordan. 'It's taken twenty years, but it's time we tried to make things right again. We need to trust Tyler to get us out of this – no matter what you might think of him. I blamed him too, I did, but we have to trust him now. If it works then maybe it will all go away. My nightmares and sleep paralysis, Tyler's depression and your anger. It could all go away and Kieran will finally be laid to rest and be at peace. It's time.'

Amber stopped talking and pulled her hand away, allowing the silence that followed to fill the room. She looked over her shoulder. The Creature had emerged from the dark corner and was standing quietly behind her, not moving except for the fall and rise of its chest as it breathed. Even though she couldn't see it, standing behind Tyler was The Black Shadow, floating eerily in place, casting a dark presence over him. The Bad Man, even though it was not visible to the naked eye, was silent within Jordan, lying dormant, listening.

Jordan sighed, not quite ready to accept the plan. 'But what if it doesn't work?'

'It will.' Tyler sounded serious.

'That fills me with confidence,' he replied sarcastically. 'So what do we do, go to the ravine, dig up his body, walk into a police station and confess?'

'Not exactly, but we do need to go to the ravine in order to break the blood oath. We also need a part of him – of Kieran, so yes, we will have to dig up the body. We preferably need his blood, but that will be long gone by now, however there will be some bone or something left for sure.'

Amber gave Tyler a firm look. 'You didn't say anything about that to me! I don't want to dig him up. Haven't we done enough to him?'

'I didn't think you'd go for it if I told you straight away. I'm sorry, but if we don't have a part of him then the blood oath won't work. We made the original oath with his blood too, not just our own. We need him. We don't need to actually remove the body. We just need to dig down far enough until we find him, then just remove a part of his skeleton or a piece of clothing if it's still intact.'

'What if the police have already found his body?' asked Amber. 'There will be tape and equipment everywhere. If we dig around we'll be tampering with the crime scene. We'll be even more guilty.'

'It would have been in the news by now. It's still down there. I know it is. Look, I know the plan isn't perfect, but we need to do something now. If the body is found by the police then it's too late. If the watch was found around the same place as we buried the body then it's only a matter of time. We need to move quickly.'

Both Jordan and Amber looked uneasy. Amber was suddenly beginning to have second thoughts about trusting Tyler; he had left out the fact they had to dig up the body on purpose. The idea sent shivers down her spine. She knew it wouldn't be an actual fleshy body. By now it would be just a skeleton, stained by dirt and silt and long, lonely years under the earth.

'I've got this guys. Trust me.' Tyler seemed so sure, so confident in his plan, but unbeknown to them he hadn't even told Amber the *whole* plan. All he needed was their blood and for them to trust him. Even now there were still secrets between them – more than one.

'So what do we do when we've found the body and taken a piece of it?' asked Jordan.

'We all need to perform another blood oath, which will undo the original one. Similar to last time, but this time only I'll speak.'

'And that's it?'

'Pretty much.'

'Pretty much?' Jordan raised his eyebrows. 'Why do you only have to speak? What aren't you telling us?'

Tyler's eyes darted to Amber just as she was about to open her mouth. She closed it again, realising that he didn't want her to expand any further. Tyler decided to change the subject slightly.

'I'm the only one who's going to confess so I have to make the new oath. All you guys need to do is say your name out loud at the right time.'

'And where did you find this information about breaking blood oaths – bloodoath.com?' Jordan's sarcasm and annoyance was clear, but he made a good point. Where had Tyler got all his information from? Amber was curious too.

Tyler didn't speak and did not reply. Little did they know that he actually knew a lot about blood oaths, making his first one at age ten with his parents. They had made him do it for his own protection. Years later, when he had access to the Internet, he had conducted his own research on the history of blood oaths, but there was very limited information available on how to *break* a blood oath. The bottom line was ... *don't.*

'You don't want to know where I got the information, but we have another problem.' Tyler decided that a change of topic was needed.

'And what's that?'

'Brooke.'

'What about her?' asked Jordan, folding his arms.

Amber stepped forward. 'She has severe agoraphobia and hasn't left her house in seventeen years.'

Jordan frowned. 'Jesus, I thought she'd just moved away. You mean to tell me she's been in her house this whole time and has never left?'

Amber nodded. 'Yes, and I have a feeling that it's not just a phobia ... maybe it's Kieran keeping her locked inside, which means if he realises that we're trying to fix this, maybe he will ... let her leave.'

'This is ridiculous,' spat Jordan. 'Are you actually saying that Kieran has been keeping Brooke locked inside her house all this time?'

'As ridiculous as an angry entity that takes over your body and makes you do and say things you aren't aware of?' Tyler threw back at him.

'It could be a psychological condition. Maybe I have a split personality!'

'Yeah. Maybe. Or maybe you don't. Maybe you want to find out the truth.'

Jordan folded his arms across his chest and inhaled deeply. 'Fuck you, you fucking twat.'

'Great, glad to have you on board.' It appeared Tyler's old sense of humour was making a comeback. 'Okay,' he continued. 'Let's get the gang back together.'

'Don't push it. We may be working together now, but trust me, we are *not* friends.'

'Fair enough.'

Amber felt relief. Jordan had been the loose wire, the one that would take the most convincing, however she knew that Brooke would be difficult in a different way. Trying to convince her to leave her house after all this time was going to be no easy task, even if they explained that she would be safe. They had no idea of the severity of her condition, but it was time to find out.

# Chapter Nine

Amber didn't know how to feel about the current situation. On the one hand she was reuniting with her best friends after years of being lonely and apart from them; she felt happy, the same way she had felt on the sunny day before *it* had happened. On the other hand, she was reuniting with a bunch of complete strangers to go and dig up a dead body that she had helped bury – that made her feel sick. She was terrified that it might all go wrong and she would be taken to jail, never to see her daughter again. Maybe she was over-thinking things.

Amber tried to focus on the task ahead. If they succeeded then The Creature would no longer haunt her and she would be able to sleep at night, safely in her bed next to her husband and wake up normally, without being paralysed. The hope of that day when she was free from The Creature kept her spirits high. The fact that it was even remotely possible kept her going.

As the three of them stepped into the July heat Amber closed her eyes. For a brief moment she had gone back in time, twenty years ago to the morning of *that* day when she had been hanging out with Jordan, Tyler and Kieran. They had been about to go and pick up Brooke from her house —

*The three boys were walking in front of her, heading in the direction of Brooke's house, which was at the top of the long hill leading out of town. The four of them usually met in town, as that was where they lived, then would head to Brooke's house last as she lived slightly further out.*

*Amber watched the boys as they joked, laughed and pretended to punch each other playfully. She loved these idiots; loved the way they interacted with each other. If she hadn't known any better she would have thought they were brothers. None of them had brothers themselves so they fitted together naturally, bound forever by their bond. Amber sniggered at the way they wore their jeans too low, their baggy boxers spilling over their waistbands; every few minutes they had to keep hitching them up. Their trainers were filthy, discoloured over constant wear and tear; jumping in muddy puddles, rolling around in the grass, building dens and running up hills. She knew, just by looking at them, that they would be friends forever. One day they would be best men at each other's weddings, their wives would be friends with each other, their sons and daughters would grow up together. They would grow old, drinking beer at the pub at weekends, reminiscing about the good old days and the fun and adventures they'd had as children. Amber wished she could freeze this moment in time. Growing up meant that things would change, their responsibilities would increase, but she sensed that they would survive because they had each other and that was all that mattered.*

*Jordan turned to look over his shoulder at Amber. 'Hey Amber, you coming?' She'd been dawdling slightly, enjoying watching her friends.*

*'Yes, I'm just coming,' she called out before jogging to catch up.*

*'Where were you?'*

*'Just daydreaming.'*

*'Nothing new there then,' sniggered Tyler. 'Honestly Amber, half the time I think you don't live in the real world.'*

*'I just like to think about the future.'*

*'And what happens in the future?' asked Kieran excitedly.*

*Amber shrugged her shoulders, teasing them. 'I'm not going to tell you or it won't come true.'*

*'Isn't that what happens when you tell someone what you wished for?'*

*'Same thing.'*

*'No, it's not. Tell us.' Tyler was insistent. 'What happens in the future according to you?'*

*Amber laughed. 'Okay! Okay! I was just thinking that you three would be friends forever and you would all be at each other's weddings and grow old together.'*

*'Makes us sound like an old married couple,' laughed Jordan.*

*'Or an old threesome,' added Tyler, elbowing Jordan in the side. The three boys shared a laugh, but Amber just smiled, allowing them to have their joke. They didn't see it now. They may have joked about it, but one day they would see that she was right.*

*Later that day everything had gone wrong.*

'Amber, you coming?' Jordan's deep grown-up voice woke her from her daydream. Amber realised they had both walked on ahead of her and had turned to see where she was.

'Yes, I'm coming. Sorry. I was —'

'Daydreaming?' Jordan had read her mind, either that or he had just remembered the same memory that she had.

'Something like that,' she replied.

Amber, Jordan and Tyler walked up the hill to Brooke's house. Amber hadn't been here since she was sixteen, but it looked so familiar, as if no time at all had passed. The same pink climbing rose bushes grew majestically in the front garden; now they were massive, climbing up the fence and over the wooden archway that framed the rickety garden gate. The gate opened with the same high-pitched creaking sound.

Amber reached the front door first.

'What do we tell Mrs Willows?' she asked, suddenly realising she had no idea what she was supposed to say.

'Maybe, let's just say we are here to try and help her,' said Tyler.

'After twenty years?' asked Jordan sarcastically. 'Probably a bit late now, don't you think?'

Amber ignored his remark, took a deep, cleansing breath and then knocked on the door. A few seconds later it opened and Mrs Willows peered out. She looked too young to have a thirty-two-year-old daughter; only having just turned fifty herself earlier this year. Her hair was still blonde, thanks to some home dye to take care of her grey roots that were just beginning to peek through her re-growth.

At first when Olivia saw the three of them standing on her doorstep she didn't quite recognise them. It had been a very long time since she had seen all three together at the same time. It was Amber she recognised first.

'Oh my goodness!' she beamed. 'Amber! How lovely to see you darling!' She reached forward and pulled Amber into a tight hug. Olivia squeezed hard and started crying softly. Amber hugged her back; it felt like she needed a good hug and a cry. Brooke hadn't been very huggable lately, never wanting to be touched. Amber had always had a good, close relationship with Mrs Willows. She felt guilty for abandoning her and her daughter for so many years, especially when she lived so close by. She could have easily come to visit, but it had been too painful to think about.

'Hi Mrs Willows,' said Amber, finally pulling away. 'It's good to see you too. This is —'

'Jordan and Tyler. How could I forget? And please, call me Olivia.' She eyed them up and down, clearly too polite to mention Tyler's grubbiness and Jordan's known anger issues. She ushered them inside and quietly closed the door.

'We're here to see Brooke,' Amber continued.

'Yes, I assumed you were. I have to warn you, but ... well, Brooke is having a particularly bad time at the moment what with that watch being found. I'm sure you've heard about it. It really set off her panic attacks. She's been hiding up in her room ever since and hasn't eaten a thing. I'm really worried about her.'

'Maybe we can help. We all heard about the watch and it's brought us back together.' Amber looked to both Jordan and Tyler. They glanced back awkwardly, clearly not comfortable being so close to each other or being here. There was a clear and unspoken tension there.

'That's so lovely,' said Olivia with a kind smile. 'I fear that your appearance might actually make her worse. She just sits in her room in the corner with the lights off and the curtains drawn. I may have to call the doctor again soon.'

'Please, let us try.' Amber touched Olivia lightly on the arm, hoping it would instil some confidence in her.

Olivia thought for a moment. She was extremely protective of her daughter and often felt an overwhelming desire to shield her from anything that could upset her. Seeing Amber and the boys though had made her realise that Brooke needed someone other than herself.

'Okay.' She nodded and took a deep breath. 'Okay, you can try, but all I ask is that if she reacts badly please leave her a little while longer before coming back.'

'Of course.'

Amber prayed that Brooke would not overreact at their arrival. Their plan couldn't wait until she felt better; they were on a tight schedule. Olivia led them upstairs to Brooke's room. Amber couldn't help but notice that the décor in the house had not changed at all. It was merely faded and far too old-fashioned now. It was obvious that Olivia didn't have the time or energy to redecorate, choosing to focus on her sick daughter instead. She knocked lightly on the door and waited to see if there was a response – there was none.

'Brooke darling. It's mum. I ... I have some friends here to visit you. It's Amber, Jordan and Tyler.' Silence followed so she knocked again. 'Brooke?' she tried again.

Amber stepped forward and decided to try speaking up, hoping that the sound of her voice would help Brooke to answer the door. She remembered the last time they had spoken when Brooke had shouted at her to never come near her again. Amber hoped that was no longer the case.

'Brooke, it's me. It's Amber.' There was a very long silence. Olivia shook her head and started backing away from the door.

'I'm sorry darling, but I don't think —'

'Amber?' A small, quiet voice appeared through the door. Everyone froze. 'Amber, is that really you?'

Amber put her face up to the door. 'Yes, Brooke. It's me. It's Amber. Can you let us in? Jordan and Tyler are here too.' There was some shuffling behind the locked door.

Olivia sighed in relief, a smile spreading across her tired face. 'Thank goodness. I'll leave you all in peace. Let me know if you need anything.'

'Thank you, Mrs Willows ... Olivia.' Amber felt like she was twelve again and she and the boys had come round to hang out with Brooke. Olivia would bring them juice and biscuits; not today. Times had changed – they were all grown up now. The three of them watched as Olivia disappeared downstairs, leaving them in silence, standing in the hallway outside Brooke's room.

Then the sound of bolts being slid open could be heard and a small crack appeared, followed by a pale, scared face. Amber smiled as she glimpsed the face of her once best friend; tears filled her eyes. Brooke opened the door even further and then proceeded to fling her arms around her estranged friend's neck. Amber hugged her back, squeezing her tight, never wanting to let her go. How dearly she had needed her best friend and how silly she had been not to reach out to her. It could have made things easier on all of them if they had stuck together, to help each other through their grief and guilt, but they hadn't. They had all suffered alone.

Brooke was still crying softly as she eventually pulled away. Amber wiped the tears away from her own eyes and both girls smiled through their watery eyes. Brooke peered past Amber at Jordan and Tyler and gave them both a weak smile.

'Hi,' she whispered. She was clinging to Amber

as if she were a shield. Amber got the feeling that she didn't quite trust the men like she did herself, but nonetheless she seemed glad to see them.

Tyler smiled back at her. 'Hey Brooke. Good to see you.'

Jordan remained silent; a man of very few words when it came to displays of emotion.

'Come in,' whispered Brooke.

The group stepped inside her room. It was shrouded in darkness until she turned on a side light, which illuminated the room enough so they could see each other, but it cast a series of eerie shadows on the walls. Amber glanced around the room, taking note of the unchanged decoration in here as well. She felt like she had stepped back in time to the late nineties. The two girls had laid on Brooke's bed staring at the ceiling, talking about which one of the Backstreet Boys they were going to marry one day. That was a lifetime ago now.

The women perched on the bed while the men hovered awkwardly nearby. Amber realised that this was the first time since they had been at the bottom of the ravine burying Kieran that they had all been together – just the four of them. Not one of them could have ever imagined what was about to happen when they had left the ravine that day, how each of them would change because of what they had done.

'It's so weird,' said Brooke as she looked round at each one in turn. 'Seeing you all here in real life. We all look so —'

'Different?' offered Amber. 'Old?'

'Tired,' said Brooke. 'We all look so tired.'

'You can say that again,' said Amber with a hint of laughter in her voice.

'But we look old too,' added Brooke, touching Amber's face gently.

'Maybe we should stop with the fucking small talk and get to the point,' interjected Jordan. Amber sighed in frustration at him, whilst shooting him a stern look. The last thing she wanted was to freak Brooke out or scare her, but Brooke didn't seem to mind. She was not afraid of him.

'Jordan, I've never heard you swear before,' she said with a confused look on her face.

'Yeah well, we've all changed.'

'In more ways than one,' added Tyler.

'So why are you all here? Who initiated this?'

'Well, actually, it was Tyler who came to see me first,' said Amber, smiling at Tyler. He cracked a small one back as she continued. 'We all saw the news that Kieran's watch had been found —'

'Please!' shouted Brooke suddenly, jumping and shuddering. 'Don't say his name.' She buried her face in her hands. 'I had a full-on panic attack yesterday when I saw the news. It all came flooding back so vividly.'

'I'm sorry, but that is what we are here about.' Amber spoke calmly. 'We have to talk about it.'

Brooke's eyes started watering. 'I'm sorry. Yes, of course that's why you're here, but I don't understand ... what —'

'I have a plan,' Tyler cut her off. 'And we need all of us together in order for it to work. I ... we ... can fix this.'

Brooke shook her head back and forth slowly. 'I still don't understand.'

Amber knew this was the moment they were going to have to tell Brooke that she needed to leave the safety of her house. It was now or never.

'We need to go back to the ravine, dig up *his* body, remove a piece and take another blood oath, which will break the previous one and allow us – me – to confess and everyone else to be free.' Tyler spoke as gently as he could, aware that this sentence could send Brooke's anxiety through the roof.

'You want to go ... back ... to the ravine ... and ... dig ... No!' Brooke forcefully jumped to her feet and scurried to the corner of her bedroom, burying her face in her hands. She was crying softly. Amber heard Jordan sigh heavily in frustration, but luckily he stayed quiet and allowed Amber and Tyler to continue.

'Brooke,' said Tyler softly. He bent down next to her but didn't lay a hand on her. 'You have to trust me. I'm sorry for what I made you do and for how you have suffered. I'm trying to make things better, I promise. I just need your help and I'll do the rest. The new blood oath won't work without you. I need you. We need you.'

Brooke lifted her head slightly. 'It's not that I don't want to help you. I do. It's just ... I can't ... I haven't —'

'Left your house in seventeen years,' he finished for her.

Brooke nodded, tears filling her eyes. 'If I do then The Fear will get me.'

Tyler, Jordan and Amber all exchanged knowing looks. In a normal conversation this would have sounded odd, but this was no normal conversation and all of them by now knew exactly what she meant.

'Tell me about The Fear,' said Amber. 'What is it?'

'The day after ... *it* happened, I went outside to my garden and I had a panic attack. The air itself closed in on me. It's not a physical presence, but I can still feel something watching me, hunting me, waiting for me outside. It tries to kill me, or at least, that's what it feels like. I've tried every sort of therapy and medication there is, but nothing makes it go away. The only place I feel safe is in this house, in this room, in this corner. I can't leave. I can't. The Fear is real.'

'I believe you. We all believe you.' Amber couldn't help but think back to when they were young, before all this happened. Brooke had been so wild and carefree, full of life and flirtation. To look at her now, scared and alone, locked in her own house was heart-breaking.

She continued. 'What if I told you that if you came outside with us The Fear wouldn't hurt you? We've all suffered from similar issues. Tyler has The Black Shadow that follows him and has given him severe depression. Jordan has The Bad Man inside him that explodes with anger and takes over his body. And I have The Creature that is a physical creature that hunts me, and I have severe insomnia. We think, although we don't know for sure, that these *things* that are manifesting themselves to us ... is *him. Kieran.'* Amber flinched as she said his name, aware that it might set off Brooke's panic attacks, but it didn't. Brooke had been listening intently the whole time. 'The Fear won't hurt you. It wants you to come with us,' she finished.

Silenced followed; a long silence.

'So,' began Brooke finally, 'if we make a new blood oath and Tyler confesses ... The Fear will go away?'

'That's what we're hoping.'

Brooke was silent for a moment while she thought things over. Amber could see the never-ending turmoil inside her head. 'So I need to ... leave the house.' It was a statement rather than a question.

'We'll all be with you the entire time,' assured Amber. 'I promise I won't leave your side, not for even a second.'

Brooke nodded. 'I can't promise I'll be able to leave, but I'll try. I will try. When?'

Jordan took this question. 'It will probably be better to go under the cover of darkness. I haven't been to the ravine to check, but there may be police tape and whatnot in the area and there's less likely to be people around at night.'

Amber turned to Brooke. 'Do you have a phone? Give me your number and I'll come and get you tonight.'

'Yes, my mum got me a mobile phone to use, but I've never used it.'

'You've never used a mobile phone!' laughed Jordan. Everyone stared at him. He rolled his eyes. 'Where is it? I'll find out your number and show you how to use it.'

Brooke fished around in her bedside table for the mobile phone. She handed it to Jordan with a shy smile. 'My mum won't let me out that's for sure. If I told her I was attempting to leave the house she'd have a fit. I'll have to try and sneak out my bedroom window.'

'Just like old times,' said Amber with a laugh. 'I'll have to try and sneak out of my house too or come up with an excuse. My husband will be suspicious if I say I'm going out in the evening.'

'You're married!' exclaimed Brooke happily.

Amber smiled wearingly. 'Yes, and I have a daughter called Bethany.'

'Wow, how lovely! So what are you going to tell him?'

'If it helps, I use the old phrase *I need to do some inventory at work* when I go and cheat on my wife. Works every time.' All eyes rested on Jordan, silently judging him. 'I said *if it helps*.'

'You cheat on your wife?' Amber couldn't hide the surprise from her voice. He had always been such a perfect gentleman, but it seemed that was no longer the case.

Jordan snorted, as if it was common knowledge or it was no big deal. 'Well, yeah. No need to sound so shocked. Not everyone is a Miss Goody Two Shoes like you.'

Amber bit her lip; she didn't want to get into an argument with Jordan. His temper may have been laying quiet for now, but The Bad Man was still there and she couldn't risk baiting him.

Amber turned to Brooke. 'I'll come and get you at half past eleven tonight. Okay?'

'Okay.'

# Chapter Ten

Amber left Jordan and Tyler to go their separate ways. They had arranged to meet at midnight at the *Danger* sign near the Beaker Ravine. Amber said she would collect Brooke at the agreed time and would text the guys if there was a problem or a delay.

However, for the rest of the day, Amber was trying to come up with a good enough excuse to tell Sean as to why she was leaving the house at eleven at night. She couldn't come up with anything. He would still be awake at that time, watching television; some late-night comedy show. It would be almost impossible to sneak out without him noticing. She had to think of something and then find somewhere to lay low for a few hours.

Amber couldn't help but wonder what Sean would say and think when the truth finally came out. She feared the worst; he could divorce her and stop her from seeing Bethany. That would be the end of her life. Maybe he would understand if she told him the whole truth now, before it came out in the news and was plastered all over the television screen. Where would she even start? These thoughts and questions raced through her head during dinner, completely taking her away from the present moment. She was unaware that Sean was speaking directly to her until he touched her arm. She jumped as if she had just received an electric shock.

'Jesus babe, I was talking to you and calling your name for ages.'

'Sorry. I ...' but she didn't have an ending to the sentence.

'Are you okay?'

'Is Mummy having another episode?' Bethany asked before stuffing a fork loaded with mashed potato into her mouth.

'I'm not sure Beth Bug. Amber? Are you?'

'Um, no ... I just have a lot on my mind.'

Sean casually took a sip of wine. 'Like what?'

Amber paused briefly. It was now or never. 'I need to go somewhere tonight.'

Sean did a sarcastic chuckle. In the time he had known her she had never been out during the evening. 'Like where?'

'I ... I need to visit my mum.' It was all she could come up with in that exact moment. Her mother lived about an hour away and in all honesty, she had been thinking about visiting her soon. It had been a while; nearly six months in fact. Amber wasn't exactly close to her mother anymore, but she still liked to do the occasional visit and phone call. However, her mother didn't make a lot of effort to come and visit her either. Her mother and father had moved away from the town several years ago, leaving the seclusion and instead headed for civilisation.

'I'll leave soon and come back later tonight,' added Amber.

'You're only going to go for a few hours? Why?'

'I need to ask her something.'

'That's what a phone is for.'

Amber was losing this battle and Sean's constant questioning was starting to get her back up. He had always been like it, never in a horrible way, but always seemed to want to know *everything* and there had to be a valid reason for *everything* too. God forbid he happened to disagree with her, then she would get an exceptionally long lecture about why she was wrong and he was right.

'Oh my God Sean, I just want to visit my mum. Why is that such an issue?' Amber snapped. She hardly ever raised her voice, preferring to keep quiet and not cause an argument. Sean and Bethany looked at each other in shock.

'Mummy swore.'

'I did not swear.'

'Yes, you did. You said oh my God. That's a swear word.'

'I'm sorry, you're right. I didn't mean to swear.'

'Daddy, just let Mummy visit Granny. I wouldn't like it if my husband questioned why I wanted to see my Mummy.' Amber and Sean couldn't help but smile at each other. How was this child only seven?

'Okay,' said Sean, who was unwilling to press the matter further with his daughter present. 'Just let me know when you get there safe.'

'Thank you, I will.'

*Thank you, Bethany!* Amber made a mental note to give her daughter a piece of chocolate as a treat after dinner.

Amber started preparing to visit *her mother* by packing a few things after dinner. She quietly sneaked into the garage after she put Bethany to bed and put a shovel into the back of the car. Then she got changed into black leggings, a black shirt, along with black trainers. Sean eyed her up and down, but didn't mention her strange choice of clothing. It felt weird lying to Sean and Bethany, but now she had a more pressing problem.

It was only eight o'clock. She still had three and a half hours until she had to be at Brooke's. Bethany was fast asleep and Sean had poured himself another glass of red wine. Amber wished she could join him on the sofa, watching crap on the television and sipping wine, cuddled up next to him, feeling his heartbeat, his warm scent, maybe his hand brushing through her hair. No, she had to go and dig up a dead body and break a blood oath. What was she supposed to do for the next three and a half hours?

Then she had a thought; maybe she could go and spend some time with one of her *friends.* Brooke was no doubt still locked in her room and not exactly in a great state, probably worrying about the upcoming trip outside. To be honest Amber wasn't exactly looking forward to it either. Maybe she should give Brooke some breathing space to enable her to get her head in the right frame of mind. Then there was Tyler, but he lived in that dump that smelled like something had died in there. That left —

*Hi Jordan. It's Amber. I've come up with an excuse to leave my house, but now I have nowhere to go for the next few hours. Are you free to hang out before I go and collect Brooke?*

She finished typing, avoiding adding any kisses at the end; it didn't seem appropriate. She pressed send and waited nervously for a reply. They had all swapped numbers before leaving Brooke's.

Amber was in her car, parked a few roads over from her house, just out of sight. She was grabbing the steering wheel and leaning forwards in her seat, as if preparing for a race to start. Why was she so nervous about his reply? Maybe this wasn't such a good idea after all. Lying to her husband about where she was going and texting a man asking to hang out felt like cheating. Perhaps it *was* cheating.

Ping!

*Hang out? What are we twelve again? Meet you in our spot in ten.*

*Our spot.* He still remembered. Amber quickly fished around in her handbag for her lip gloss and applied some using the rear-view mirror. She stared at herself. Her eyes were tired, slightly hollow-looking. Sometime over the past twenty years they had lost their sparkle, their life. She didn't recognise herself a lot of the time. A single tear started forming in her left eye. She blinked and it rolled down her cheek, leaving a streak of moisture on her skin. She left it there and started driving down the road, pointing the Volvo in the direction of *their spot.* She should have been afraid about seeing Jordan, a man with a known anger problem and who had terrified her only hours before. She was nervous, yes, but not afraid.

It only took a couple of minutes to get there; a secluded bench in the local park by a small rhododendron bush, covered in brilliant pink flowers. She hadn't been there in two decades, but still remembered exactly where it was. However, the bush was no longer small. It was now massive, stretching up and wide and had grown so much it had almost hidden the bench with its foliage. The bench was older now, decrepit and falling apart in places, forgotten about and left to crumble. She perched on the edge nervously, plucked a fluorescent pink flower from the bush and twirled it between her fingers. It was a warm evening, but she was still shaking, a slight chill surrounding her. The Creature was nowhere to be seen, but she knew it was near, watching, listening.

'So, what excuse did you come up with?' Jordan's voice broke the silence and startled her.

'I told him I was going to visit my mother for a few hours.'

'Bad idea.' He shook his head. 'What if he calls her or later on he finds out that you never visited? You always need to cover your tracks – better to say you aren't visiting anyone.'

'Okay,' she sighed in frustration. 'Well, clearly you're an expert at lying to your wife. Forgive me, but this is the first proper time I've lied directly to my husband.'

Jordan took a seat next to her, rocking the bench. He was dressed in plain jeans and a black t-shirt, his muscular arms stretching the fabric at the arm holes. He had obviously showered since their last meeting, his hair still damp.

He laughed at her attempt at sarcasm. 'And

how does it feel?'

'Not great I must say.'

'It gets easier.'

'I'm sure it does.'

There was a silence.

'Why are you dressed like you're about to rob a bank?'

'Well since we're basically committing a crime I thought it made sense to dress the part,' she replied coolly.

Jordan sniggered and shook his head. 'Can't argue with that logic.'

Amber couldn't help but notice how close his body was to hers. This bench had seemed so much bigger twenty years ago; today it felt like it was squashing them together on purpose. This was the bench where they had shared their first kiss. It held memories – such wonderful memories.

'Why did you text me?' asked Jordan, suddenly sounding serious.

'Brooke has issues, Tyler's place smells horrible and I didn't want to sit in my car alone for three hours.'

'So I was your last resort?'

'No offence, but you aren't exactly pleasant to be around anymore.'

'True. Don't you have any friends you could've called?'

Amber shook her head no. She had tried to forge new friendships over the years by joining a new mum group when Bethany had been a baby, but they had all turned their noses up at her when she announced her baby was formula fed. Then she had attempted to make some friends by joining a fitness class just for women, but after seeing all the ladies in tight Lycra and crop-tops she started feeling insecure in her baggy sweats, so never went back. Making friends was not easy for Amber. It always felt forced, especially since becoming an adult. Brooke, Tyler, Jordan and Kieran – they had been real friends. Yes, they'd had their issues and arguments, but it had never felt forced. It had felt natural. They had sworn to be best friends for life when they had only been six years old; they'd even done a spit oath. It seemed obvious now that spit oaths weren't as strong as blood oaths. There wasn't the risk of death.

'Do you have any friends?' she asked, trying to turn the conversation over to him.

'I don't do friendships anymore,' came the blunt reply. 'I don't exactly like people and people don't like me. The Bad Man hates everyone.'

'Must be hard having that anger in you all the time.'

'Yeah,' was all Jordan said. 'So ... do you want to continue the small talk or do something else?'

Amber shrugged her shoulders. 'Small talk is fine.'

'What do you want to talk about?'

'Whatever you want to talk about.'

Jordan rolled his eyes as he looked at her. 'It never used to be this hard to talk to you.'

'Sorry, I guess it's been a long time since I've done any small talk. Usually, I only talk to my husband.' Jordan snorted a laugh. 'Hey, you know you didn't have to come and see me when I texted you earlier. You could have said no. If you hate talking to people and being around them so much then why did you say yes to meeting me tonight?'

Jordan sighed. 'Okay, I'll level with you. Out of all the people in the whole world if I had to hang out and talk to one of them ... it would be you.'

Amber couldn't help but crack a smile. Was the old Jordan finally making an appearance? It certainly felt like it. The old Jordan had been kind, sweet and polite. The new Jordan was sarcastic and a bit rude at times, but there was a sweetness to his demeanour that Amber could still see.

'Thank you,' she said quietly, twirling the flower around in her hands again, feeling nervous. 'I just want you to know Jordan, that even though The Bad Man may take control from time to time, I still believe you're a good person. You always have been.'

'You don't know me anymore Amber. Twenty years is a long time. A lot has changed. I've changed. We've all changed. We aren't the same people anymore.'

'Aren't we? Tyler sure has changed.'

Jordan shook his head. 'Fucking Tyler. I fucking hate that guy. He had fucking mental problems even before it all happened. Like, did you ever meet his parents? I did once. They were weird.' Jordan seemed to tail off in a daydream. He remembered how Tyler's mother had once hugged Tyler goodbye and then planted a kiss directly on his lips and stroked his hair; he had been twelve. Jordan had just found it odd and it had given him the creeps.

'At least he's trying to fix things now.'

'Yeah right. As if he could fucking fix anything. Why do you always have to see the fucking good in everyone? Not everyone is good you know. Some people are bad. Like Tyler and ... me.'

'You're not bad Jordan. You're just someone who's had something bad happen to them. The same as Tyler.'

'I hit my wife once and I cheat on her while thinking about someone else. I've robbed a grocery store and gotten away with it. I drink and smoke and swear. I've beaten up more people than I can count. I've done a bit of time in jail. Oh ... and I helped cover up a murder when I was twelve and lied about it ever since. Still think I'm not bad?'

Amber stared down at her feet, unable to look him in the eye. 'If it makes you feel any better, I also helped cover it up and have lied ever since. That also makes me bad.'

'No, you're not bad. You're like the nicest person I've ever met. You know, if that day had never happened things could have worked out differently for us in more ways than one.'

'Yes, that's true. For a start I could have finished school and become a doctor.'

'No, I meant —'

'I know what you meant.'

Amber smiled at Jordan who smiled coyly back. There was a silence between them, but it wasn't awkward, it was calm and both of them just enjoyed the moment. Amber felt her heart rate increase and her mouth go dry. She hadn't felt this way since just before they had shared their first kiss. It made her feel guilty. Here she was, a married woman, feeling things for a man that wasn't her husband. She knew for a fact that Jordan felt the same way. Out of the corner of her eye she could see his hand twitching, aching to reach across and take her own hand or place it on her knee, but he didn't.

'Ah well,' said Jordan, shrugging off the

moment. 'It probably wouldn't have worked out anyway. We were good friends; romance never works between friends.'

'You're right, it never does.'

They smiled at each other and for a split second Amber wanted to lean in and kiss him, just to know what his lips felt like again, breathe in his sweet, masculine scent. Luckily, Jordan changed the subject and started asking her about her daughter.

The remaining three hours were spent reminiscing about old times, chatting about their struggles and issues over the years and generally having a nice time. It felt amazing to be able to open up to someone finally. Doctor Allan had been right. It did feel good to talk and reconnect with an old friend, but the guilt was still there. She hoped it wouldn't be there for much longer. Amber realised how easy it was to talk to Jordan, despite his casual use of swear words in conversation. The old Jordan was in there somewhere. She felt as if they were in their own little world, away from the stresses and worries of their lives, just the two of them, the way it was when they had been children. Jordan had always been special to her; they'd always had a connection. Even though she hadn't spoken to him in many years it was like they had picked off where they left off – just now they had extra baggage. Amber couldn't have been happier in this moment. She wanted it to last forever, but it had to end sometime. Eleven o'clock arrived and Amber looked at her watch.

'I have to go and meet Brooke now.'

'I'll come with you.'

'Promise you won't be mean and scare her?'

Jordan laughed. 'I'll try.'

Amber and Jordan arrived outside Brooke's house at 11:25 p.m. All the lights were off and due to its location outside of town there were no lights around either. The area was dark, but the summer evening ensured there was enough light to be able to see. Amber sent a text to Brooke to say they were outside and a few seconds later her face appeared in her bedroom window. A wooden trellis climbed up the side of the house, covered in beautiful pink roses. It was the same trellis Brooke had used when she'd been a child to escape the house when she had been grounded, for whatever reason. Amber waved from the ground and beckoned Brooke to come down.

Brooke took a deep breath. Even opening her bedroom window had been a milestone that she never thought she would be able to do. Something had happened; something she couldn't explain. The Fear was still there, waiting for her outside, but it wasn't closing in on her or making her feel afraid. It wasn't choking the life out of her or making her want to run and hide. It was just *there.* Brooke slowly manoeuvred herself onto the windowsill and peered out at Amber and Jordan below.

'You can do it Brooke,' said Amber in as loud a whisper as she dared. 'The Fear wants you to leave, otherwise we can't fix this. I'm right here for you.'

Jordan merely gave her a thumbs up.

Brooke gave him a small smirk and nodded at Amber, understanding what was at stake if she failed. She took another cleansing breath as she angled herself onto the trellis. Her whole body was shaking, but she took her time, ensuring each foot and hand were placed securely before moving. A couple of thorns pricked her skin, but she didn't care. In a strange way it felt wonderful to feel something real, something that wasn't imaginary.

Amber watched with anticipation as Brooke descended towards the ground. Finally, what felt like hours later, Brooke's trainers hit solid earth. She immediately ran to Amber, who hugged her.

'Well done, I'm so proud of you. Are you okay?'

Brooke nodded. 'I think so. I took my medication before I left. I feel like my heart is going to jump out of my chest.'

'Just keep taking deep breaths. I'm right here,' reassured Amber again. 'Jordan is going to drive us to the edge of the field and then we are meeting Tyler by the danger sign.'

Brooke nodded again in agreement. She stayed close to Amber as they headed for Jordan's truck. Once they were all inside there was silence during the short drive. Amber could see that Brooke was focusing hard on remaining calm, reciting mantras over and over in her head.

*You can do this. You are safe.*

They reached the edge of the field where the truck couldn't go any further. Jordan got the shovels out of the back and the flashlights he had brought and handed one each to Amber and Brooke. Amber took one and switched it on to a low beam, scanning the area around her. Again, she couldn't see The Creature, but it didn't mean that it wasn't there. She neglected to mention this out loud, in case she scared Brooke. She already had enough to be afraid of, but she was doing well, even though she was gripping Amber's arm slightly too tight as they began their trek across the wide open field.

The field wasn't as big as Amber remembered or maybe she had just imagined it differently, but within minutes they were across it and standing by the *Danger* sign. Suddenly, she had a serious case of déjà vu. Her brain recalled a previous memory she had forgotten — The sign was in front of her, but it was dark; the same as tonight. However, she could clearly remember it being broad daylight the last time she had seen it; on *that* day. *Strange,* she thought. The sight of the word made her tremble slightly. The memories of that day were starting to creep back, heightening her senses. When she was twelve she'd remembered this area being exciting, welcoming, an adventure, but today it was terrifying and haunting – certainly not an adventure she wanted to be on right now. Tyler was already at the sign when they got there, holding a shovel and a flashlight of his own. The yellow beams of light caused shadows to rise and fall with every movement, creating imaginary monsters in the dark, except they weren't all imaginary. The Creature, The Black Shadow, The Bad Man and The Fear were all there somewhere, watching their prey intently.

The group walked in silence through the thick trees and undergrowth, the same path they had trodden all those years ago. It was even thicker and overgrown now which made progress slow. Jordan took the lead, breaking through the branches as best as he could to enable Amber, Brooke and Tyler to follow behind him. Tyler was at the back. Amber found it a struggle to walk with Brooke attached to her side so closely, but she didn't try and shrug her off. Her friend needed her right now and she had made a promise to not leave her.

Eventually they made it to the edge of the

ravine. Their flashlights were not strong enough to reach the bottom, but it was there somewhere, like a deep never-ending abyss. Amazingly, the fallen tree was still intact, but over the years it had been through a transformation, growing new leaves and branches even though it was horizontal rather than in its once vertical position. Amber closed her eyes and was met by a horrible vision of Kieran falling off the tree, over and over again. She opened her eyes and there was inky darkness, nothing but darkness surrounding them. It felt close, as if it were slowly squeezing them all closer together.

'There's the path,' said Tyler as he pointed to the rough path that they had scurried down so many years ago.

Jordan nodded, spotting it. 'Okay, everyone watch your footing. Go slowly. Brooke ... you good?' Brooke nodded quickly, biting her lip. 'Good girl. Let's go.'

It was slow progress again down the steep path, made harder by the blackness of the night. Even though it was the height of summer the darkness seemed extreme here, almost as if it were intentionally darker where they were standing, the cloud of shadows following them down to the abyss below.

Suddenly Amber's foot slipped out from underneath her and she crashed to the rocky ground, smashing her hand into a rock. Brooke fell with her, landing on top of her.

Jordan spun around at the noise. 'Jesus Christ! You scared the shit out of me.'

Jordan and Tyler helped the girls to their feet. There were no injuries, other than a couple of scratches. Brooke dusted herself off. The path they had landed on was very dusty.

'We're fine,' said Amber. Brooke nodded the same.

They continued to go down, down and further down. The ravine seemed deeper than twenty years ago. Amber found it strange; first, the field had seemed smaller, and now the ravine appeared deeper. Maybe, as a child, she'd seen the things around her with different eyes; how big and wide open the field had been or that the ravine had not appeared that deep because it hadn't been frightening to her then.

Finally, they reached the bottom. The river had all but dried up, leaving a damp bed of silt and mud, scattered with rocks and smaller stones. Amber shone her flashlight around to try and get her bearings. Nothing looked familiar; it was just rocks and dirt. No doubt there had been dozens of landslides over the years, transforming the ground so that it looked completely different. The only thing that stood out was the yellow police tape that was surrounding a pile of rocks nearby; no doubt the location the watch had been found.

Amber zoned in on the area. Now *that* spot *did* look familiar.

Jordan turned to Tyler. 'Right, we're here. Now what? We start digging?'

The four of them were standing in a wonky circle facing inwards. They faced Tyler. He was the leader *again,* so he had to tell them what he needed them to do.

'Um ... yeah, I guess.' The lack of confidence in his voice was unnerving. 'I think it's over there ... somewhere.' Tyler vaguely waved his hand in the direction of the police tape. There was a mound of dirt and rocks there.

'You think?' said Jordan, not sounding very amused. 'I'm not digging all night if you aren't sure.'

'It looks a bit different than it did twenty years ago.'

Jordan sighed in frustration. 'Well there's no point in standing around. Let's get going.'

They began digging and shifting rocks. It was hard work. At least this time they had shovels. Amber remembered how her hands had been so battered and cut to shreds after the last time they had dug here. She had wished her hands would heal faster so that she didn't have to be reminded of what she had done every time she glanced at them.

After an hour they hadn't found anything – not even a scrap of clothing.

'Are we sure it's in this area?' asked Amber, scratching her head. She was drenched in sweat and plastered in dirt.

'Yes, it was almost directly underneath the fallen tree.' Brooke shone the light up to the tree above and then down at the ground below. The tree was a long way up but there wasn't much room for error; there was only a few places the body could be.

'How far down did we bury it?' asked Amber.

'It was at least five feet,' answered Jordan.

Jordan stood up straight and looked over at Tyler. He was kneeling on the ground a few feet away hunched over. He could not make out what he was doing, but Tyler soon rose to his feet slowly.

'I've found something,' he said. He was holding something small and dark in his hand. He held it out as the group all shone their lights directly at the object. It was small, only an inch or so in length and stained badly by dirt.

'What is it?' asked Amber timidly. Tyler turned the object over to get a better look.

'Oh my God is that a tooth!' exclaimed Brooke, backing away and grabbing Amber tightly again for support.

'I think it's several teeth connected to part of a jawbone,' answered Jordan.

Tyler nodded in agreement. 'That's what it looks like.'

Amber and Brooke backed away. 'Can we just get this over with now?' asked Amber.

'Yeah, I'm getting a creepy feeling,' added Brooke glancing around the area. She still felt relatively calm, but The Fear was near. She really wanted to get back to the safety of her room as soon as possible.

'Yeah, now what Tyler?' asked Jordan.

Tyler dug into his pocket and pulled out a sharp rock, which looked horribly familiar. It was the same one they had used to slice their hands with for the first blood oath. He opened his hands wide, a flashlight in one and the stone in the other.

'This will all be over soon,' he said.

'Where did you get that?' asked Jordan. 'Is that the same rock we used last time?'

'I kept it.'

'You ... what? Why the fuck did you keep it?'

'Lucky I did or the new blood oath wouldn't work. We need to use the same thing to cut our hands. It still has our blood stains from last time.'

'Oh my God, that's gross,' said Brooke.

No one else said anything further on the subject.

'Remember, cut your right hand again.'

Tyler pushed the sharp edge into the palm of his hand and then sliced down, a trickle of crimson blood oozing from the open wound, covering the stone. The blood shone bright red in the light of the torches, covering the dull dark red of the blood from all those years ago. He held the stone towards Amber, who slowly reached out and took it, never breaking eye contact with him. She then glanced at Brooke, who had terror in her eyes and then slit her own palm. Amber flinched as the sharp pain tore into her body, slowly squeezing her hand into a tight fist to stem the flow of blood. Amber gave the stone to Brooke who took it with shaking hands. She cut her palm, wincing slightly at the pain and handed the stone over to Jordan, who took it and stared at it. Its surface was now covered in a mixture of their blood. He took a long breath in and then sliced his skin.

Tyler nodded. 'Okay,' he said. 'Put the stone in the middle and we all need to form a circle around it and grasp hands like we did before. I will speak the new oath, but you don't need to repeat it this time. All you need to do is say your name when I nod.'

They all agreed.

The Creature was standing behind Amber, its huge black body as still as a statue. In the darkness it was almost invisible.

The Black Shadow was hovering above Tyler, continuing to draw what little life he had left, determined to ensure he suffered until the very end. Even being with his friends again would not cause him happiness; The Black Shadow was adamant about that.

The Bad Man was lying dormant within Jordan; anger was not needed in this situation and so Jordan was safe for the time being.

The Fear was silently watching Brooke, ready to pounce and attack if she decided to not go through with the plan.

Tyler spoke, his words calm, clear and concise. He had rehearsed this.

'I, Tyler Jenkins, hereby renounce the previous blood oath made on the 20th of July 1998. I promise to uphold the payment. I release my friends —' He nodded for them to speak.

'Amber Walker.'

'Brooke Willows.'

'Jordan Evans.'

'I release them from the previous blood oath. They are free.' Tyler stopped and looked up and around at his friends as he said the remaining words. 'I promise to do what is needed to make things right.'

Amber blinked back the tears, knowing that this meant that she would lose another friend at the bottom of this ravine. This would, again, be the last time they were all together.

# Chapter Eleven

Amber and Jordan took Brooke back to her house and watched her climb up the trellis to her room to ensure she was safe. Amber promised to text her the next day to see how she was doing. Jordan offered to drive Amber home, but she declined as she still needed to go and pick up her car which she had left near their spot. She thanked him for the offer of a lift but said she wanted to walk to her car by herself. She needed time to think, to process what had just happened.

A thick fog was clouding her mind. Amber felt like she was living in one of her nightmares. She had the feeling that she was being followed, that uneasy, scared feeling you get when you can feel a hidden set of eyes watching, waiting. Her heart rate was climbing ever higher, her footsteps speeded up involuntarily. The Volvo was in sight, safely lit under a streetlight. She flung her body at the car window and into the glare of the light – she was safe now. Squeezing her eyes shut she fumbled around in her pocket for the car keys, her hands were shaking as she grabbed them and pressed the unlock button. Then she opened her eyes and looked straight at the car window pane, the clear glass reflecting the shine from the light above, but she could see something else. Amber stared at her reflection and watched as a dark shape formed next to her in the glass, its claw-like arms growing out like branches. It was behind her. She could feel its presence as one of those claws gently touched her shoulder. Amber screamed.

'Jesus Christ! Amber, it's me!'

Amber spun round and tried to hit Jordan across the head in self-defence. He grabbed her and pinned her against the car, repeating the words 'it's me' over and over. They were trying to catch their breaths; both in a state of shock. Amber kept smacking him so he had no choice but to grab her wrists and forcefully restrain her.

'Amber! Stop!'

Finally, Amber calmed down and realised what she was doing. 'Bloody hell you scared the life out of me!' she panted.

'Oh wow, you swore.'

'Well ... you scared me ... and you sound just like my daughter ... You can let go of me now.'

Jordan quickly released her wrists and moved away from her body, instantly realising that he was maybe a little *too* close. Not that he didn't enjoy it, but he knew it wasn't appropriate. Despite sometimes treating women as objects, Amber was different, special.

Amber straightened herself up.

'What the hell happened? I just wanted to make sure you got back to your car safely, but I saw you freaking out over here.'

'I saw The Creature. I thought it was you. Sorry. I'm a bit —'

'Crazy?'

'I was going to say stressed, but yeah ... Thank you for checking on me though, but I'm fine.'

'Yeah ... you seem ... fine.' The word hung in the air for a while.

Amber didn't want to admit it, but she was slightly aroused. The feeling of Jordan's body pressed against hers had awakened a feeling inside her that she didn't realise existed anymore. *Lust.*

'I better get home. I just realised I didn't message Sean to let him know I had arrived at my mother's. He's probably worried.'

'Right, well, enjoy the repercussions of that. I guess I'll ... see you.'

'Yeah ... see you,' repeated Amber awkwardly. She wasn't quite sure what had happened to their ability to hold a conversation. Maybe it was the fact they had been to the bottom of that ravine and made another blood oath or maybe it was because their bodies had been very close a few seconds ago. A mere two hours previously they had talked for ages about everything like old times. Now they were back to being awkward around each other.

Jordan turned and walked away without a backwards glance, leaving Amber shaking slightly and feeling rather confused. She immediately got into her car and drove home on autopilot.

Amber arrived home to a dark and peaceful house, her child and husband were sound asleep. She immediately stripped off her clothes and chucked them in the washing machine which was in the downstairs laundry room, making a mental note to turn it on once she got up for the day (if she turned it on now there was a chance it could wake her family). Amber traipsed upstairs naked to the main bathroom, exhausted and weary from her night's activities. She switched on the shower and ran her hand under the cool stream until it turned warm and then stepped under. There was something about running water that made her relax, its trickling sounds, its never-ending resupply of water, constantly washing away the old and dirty and revealing the new and clean. She could have stayed here forever.

Amber ran her fingers through her saturated hair, letting the hot water sting her face and run into her open mouth. Then she felt it again; that unmistakable feeling of being watched, like her privacy was not her own. She was not alone in here. Amber opened her eyes slowly and watched as the water streamed down the shower screen, making small rivers all the way down to the bottom. Behind the screen she could see a dark shape. Amber froze, her breath catching in her throat, which felt tight. She reached out her hand and slowly pulled the screen aside – the shape disappeared. Amber felt the all too familiar twinge of fear throughout her body; even after all these years The Creature still horrified her and gave her goose bumps.

Amber didn't sleep a wink that night. Sean questioned her the next morning before he left for work. She apologised and he eventually moved on. Bethany wanted to know how her grandmother was, so Amber made up a story and said that she would be visiting soon. She made another mental note to invite her mother over within the next few weeks.

Amber's mind whirled with far too many questions and worries to comprehend at one time. Before departing last night, Tyler had said that he would confess on Friday as he needed to get a few things in order first. Also, Friday was the twenty year anniversary of Kieran's death and it seemed poetic somehow to reveal the truth on that day. He had said that there was nothing else for the rest of them to do.

Amber had tried to speak to him alone before

they'd all parted ways, but he had avoided her gaze and left as soon as he could. Amber knew that he was going to kill himself, but she didn't know when or how or where. Surely there had to be another way? She realised that Tyler hadn't really told her any details about the rest of his plan, other than that he was going to confess and then kill himself. She had questions. If he went to the police station to confess then how would he be able to end his life? Amber needed to know more, but a small voice inside her head kept telling her to leave Tyler alone, that he knew what he was doing, so she tried to focus on the fact that soon The Creature would no longer haunt her. Tyler would make things right. Maybe she would just check in on him to make sure he was okay. It couldn't be easy for him right now.

Amber spent the day at work straining to hear the radio that was on as background noise, listening out for any breaking news stories about a body that may have been found. Surely the police would realise that the crime scene at the bottom of the ravine had been dug up and tampered with.

*Her footprints.*

She and the others must have left some footprints, but the thought hadn't even crossed her mind at the time. By the time she returned home and started preparing dinner there had been no mention of anything on the news. She expected that if any extra footprints or evidence had been found it would have been mentioned by now. Her and Brooke had sent a few friendly texts back and forth during the day. It was nice to be in contact with her again, but it had been radio silence from both Tyler and Jordan. She sent a text to Tyler saying she wanted to talk to him, but he had not replied. Annoyingly, she had felt her mind start to wander to inappropriate thoughts when it came to Jordan. She was standing at the sink, washing up a dirty plate.

'Babe. BABE!'

Amber stopped and turned to her husband. 'Yes?'

'You've been washing the same plate for nearly ten minutes.'

'Oh. Right.' She placed the now sparkling clean plate on the rack and picked up the next dirty one on the pile.

'What were you thinking about?'

'Nothing.' Another lie to her husband.

'Okay, well, I need to go back to work tonight. I need to do some inventory.'

Amber stopped washing the plate and froze. She suddenly had another case of déjà vu and thought back to what Jordan had said to her and the line he would use when he cheated on his wife. She didn't mean to silently judge Sean but that was where her mind went straight away. Now she thought about it he did sometimes go back to work and do inventory in the evenings. Maybe it was the best time to do it. *Or maybe he is cheating on you,* said a little voice. Then again, she had just been wondering what another man's naked torso looked like.

'Babe, did you hear me?'

'Yes, sorry ... have fun.'

'I wouldn't really call doing inventory *fun,* but thanks. I'll try.'

Amber studied her husband. He had changed his clothes since coming home from work and had a shower. Not that she thought it was proof that he was cheating, but her heart sank a little. He kissed her on her cheek. She smiled at him as she smelled a whiff of his favourite cologne. Then he left. Amber blinked back the tears as she finished the washing up.

*Amber opened her eyes. There was nothing but darkness. A faint crack of light from the full moon crept in through the gap in the curtains, but otherwise there was just black. She had been fast asleep, which was unusual in itself; it was 03:31 a.m. She hadn't been dreaming about anything, but something had woken her; a noise – a noise she was very familiar with. Slowly she rose her body into a seated position in bed, something that was easy to do for no supernatural force was pinning her down this time. There was the noise again; a raspy, creaking breathing sound, but it was very faint. Sean was snoring softly beside her (he had arrived back home just after midnight), so she quietly got out of bed, only wearing a thin blue vest top and black underwear. Even though it was July she could see her icy breath as she breathed, but she wasn't cold.*

*Amber padded quietly out into the hallway. She did a quick check on her daughter, who was also sleeping peacefully, her favourite Elsa doll clutched in her left hand and her Frozen themed duvet wrapped snugly around her. Amber smiled and backed out of the room. She needed to find out where that noise was coming from. It was here. She was sure of it – The Creature.*

*The noise led her downstairs into the lounge. The moonlight was enough to light up the room without having to turn on the light. The blue light cast eerie shadows onto random surfaces, making innocent objects look sinister. Amber scanned the room and noticed that one pair of curtains were waving slightly; she must have left a window open somewhere. The noise had ceased, leaving her standing in the middle of the lounge listening intently, watching her icy breath dance as she breathed in and out.*

*'Amber.' The soft whispering voice was crystal*

*clear. It had come from all around, not in one particular location. She spun around on the spot, expecting something to jump out at her. It didn't; there was nothing there.*

*'Please,' she whispered. 'Come out Kieran. We can talk.'*

*Surprisingly, as instructed, The Creature stepped out from out of nowhere, materializing out of the cool, thin air. For the first time, Amber could see it clearly for it wasn't hidden in the shadows, but illuminated by the moonlight. The Creature was big, twice the size of a normal man, its head grazing the ceiling. It seemed to have grown since the last time she had seen it. The body was grotesque, black, the flesh looked like it had been burned to a crisp, leaving some moist parts of muscle and skin. The smell made her stomach heave, a mixture of dead, rotting flesh and burning. Bones protruded from its limbs, sticking out in odd directions, as if they had been snapped by a sudden impact. Its face was small, the mouth open, just a hollow hole that seemed to be a vortex to another dimension, a faint blue light emanating from within. The eyes were blood red, except for the tiny pupil which was a brilliant white instead of the usual black. Its intense stare made Amber's skin crawl and develop goose bumps, the hairs on her arms standing to attention.*

*'Kieran?'*

*'Confess.'*

*'We ... we are. We changed the oath. Tyler is taking care of the rest. I'm sorry. I don't know what else to do. Please. It will all be okay soon.'*

*'Confess.' The volume of the voice was increasing, getting angrier. The Creature took a step closer to Amber, who was rooted to the spot in fear.*

*'What do you mean!' Amber cried. 'We are!'*

*Suddenly The Creature lunged forward, flew through the air, grabbed Amber by the throat and hurled her against the wall, pinning her there in suspension. She kicked her legs desperately and tried to breathe. The Creature's face was merely inches from hers, its breath making her stomach lurch due to the smell. Its lips were curled back in a snarl, revealing horrible black stained teeth. She stared into its piercing eyes, deep into its soul and suddenly she remembered everything. The Creature nodded as it slowly lowered her to the floor, the second her feet touched the floor it backed away from her.*

*'I will never leave her alone.'*

*'W-who ...' but she could not form words.*

*The Creature disappeared like a cloud of smoke, slowly breaking apart and fading into the shadows —*

Amber lurched upright in bed, jolted awake from her

dream. The digital clock read 03:31 a.m. It had felt so real, she could still feel its claws around her neck. She gently touched the area; it was sore and quite possibly bruised. Had it been real? Yes. It was the same feeling she had felt a couple of weeks ago waking up on her sofa. She had sleepwalked before. She remembered now. It came catapulting into her head all at once. *Everything.*

She looked over at Sean and had yet another moment of déjà vu. Luckily, she wasn't frozen by her usual sleep paralysis so was able to grab her glass of water and take a sip. It was painful to swallow due to her sore throat. Amber leaned back against her pillow and stared up at the ceiling. She remembered something else too; a memory she had disregarded at the time for it did not seem important or worth dwelling upon —

*It was four days after the incident; four days since her life had begun to fall apart. Amber hadn't seen any of her friends since they had parted ways once they had climbed back to the top of the ravine, but it was all over the news. Kieran was missing. He had never returned home that day and his parents were extremely worried. Basically, everyone who knew him had been brought into the local police station and questioned. They weren't in any trouble, but the police needed to gather what information they could on his possible movements leading up to that day.*

*Amber had stuck to the story that Tyler had told them to say. Kieran had never joined them in the field on the outskirts of town and when asked which field she had said the one on the south side, rather than the north side. Beaker Ravine had not even been mentioned, as it was nowhere near the south side. She knew she'd been sweating and was extremely nervous, but the kind policeman had been sweet and said to just relax and tell the truth, which was easier said than done. As far as she was aware all of their stories had been identical and no further questions were required. The police seemed to think that he may have run away, but Kieran's parents were convinced that it was something more sinister, like kidnapping. There was absolutely no evidence to suggest any foul play. A local search party had been set up by his parents, but so far they hadn't discovered anything.*

*It was a lovely Friday morning and Amber was strolling through town. It was still early so no one was up yet. She had snuck out to watch the sunrise from the top of a nearby hill and was now on her way back home, hoping to arrive before her parents realised she was gone. She didn't want them to think she had been kidnapped too. Everyone in town was on edge so she didn't want to cause any further upset. Amber liked to watch the sunrise, but usually she would watch it with Brooke or Jordan. Today, however, she had been alone and preferred it that way at the moment. The thought of seeing her friends filled her with dread. If she looked into their eyes all she would see would be the lies and the utterly horrible event of four days ago. Amber could not deal with it at the moment.*

*The sunrise had been beautiful; the sky turning yellow, orange and pink, slowly illuminating the small town, basking it in a new day. A new day meant a new start, a new beginning. Amber was certain that things would return to normal soon. They were best friends for life after all.*

*It was then that she saw him – Tyler. He was further up the road and luckily hadn't spotted her. She really didn't want to talk to him, so she hid quickly in a doorway of a local shop and watched. Amber felt guilty for avoiding him, however she was pretty certain that he wouldn't want to speak or see her either. It looked as if he was busy, on a mission. Tyler appeared to be limping slightly under the weight of a heavy backpack. She noticed there was something in his hand. Was that a shovel? Amber couldn't quite see from this distance. It may have been an axe or a broom handle. His face and hands were filthy, covered in mud and black residue. She wanted to get a closer look, but dare not risk him seeing her. He was walking back towards his house; he had come from the direction of the north side of town. He had a hard, determined look on his face. It was a look she didn't like to see on him, the same look he'd had when he was ordering them around at the bottom of the ravine. He was only visible to Amber for about ten seconds before he disappeared out of sight.*

Amber opened her eyes back in her dark bedroom next to her sleeping husband. The missing memory was there all along, but she had pushed it back into the depths of her subconscious for so long. At the time it hadn't meant anything to her, which made no sense. It *should* have meant something.

Tyler. She needed to talk to Tyler. She knew that now. There was something he wasn't telling her and before he confessed, she wanted to know the truth. Had he gone back and moved the body? It was possible and that was what it had looked like, but why? Amber rolled over and checked her phone; no new messages. She quickly typed out a message to Tyler.

*I need to talk to you. I'm coming by first thing in the morning.*

Amber replaced her phone on the nightstand and went back to staring at the black ceiling, listening to the light snores of her husband. She wasn't going to tell Jordan or Brooke that she was visiting Tyler because she expected that he wouldn't want to talk openly in front of them, Jordan especially. She decided that she was going to visit him alone.

Amber turned her head and looked at Sean in the dull light, studying his facial features, the hint of a five o'clock shadow on his chin, his hair ruffled. She wondered if Sean would actually cheat on her. He'd never given her any reason to not trust him. Amber told herself that she was just being silly. If Jordan had never said about the inventory thing then she wouldn't have given it even a second thought, but he had and she did. Now it was all she could think about, amongst all the other things going on in her life right now. Maybe she should talk to him about it. The thought crossed her mind, but then what would she say? How would she start that conversation? What if he wasn't cheating and took offence to the fact that she thought he was? It wasn't like she was perfect. She was thinking about Jordan in a very inappropriate way after all, but she would never act upon it. Never. She was faithful to her husband; she just hoped that he was faithful to her too.

Amber forced the thought of her husband cheating on her out of her mind and spent the remainder of the night thinking back to that night two weeks ago that she could now remember very clearly —

*She had fallen asleep on the sofa. Sean had gently covered her with a blanket, at which point she had woken up, but she did not let on that he had woken her. Amber waited until he went upstairs and heard him finish off in the bathroom and go to bed before sitting up, the blanket falling to the side. She was in a daze, not fully awake nor asleep; somewhere in the middle. As quietly as she could she crept upstairs and into the spare room. There was nothing remarkable about this room, more a storage room than anything else; no one ever came to visit. She was looking for something in particular that she had stored here when they had first moved in. It was here somewhere, at the back of the wardrobe behind some folded towels and in a perfectly normal storage box. Once she had found it she put on her shoes and headed outside into the night.*

# Chapter Twelve

Jordan drove home after leaving Amber at her car. She had really walloped him hard across the head and he had the beginnings of a headache, but maybe that was down to his stress levels too. He knew for a fact that Tyler was hiding something, that he wasn't telling the whole truth and it was pissing him off. It seemed suspicious that Tyler had kept the stone they had used to cut their palms. Why would someone do that? It was sick. He didn't like Tyler and he didn't trust him. He had no idea why Amber did. It infuriated him – not The Bad Man – *him.*

Jordan hated not being in control of the situation. The same thing had happened all those years ago. It had always been Tyler who had told the group what to do, not just *that* day either, even before that. On the days the group would hang out it had always been Tyler who'd decide what they would do. It had even been his idea to play that stupid *I Spy* game that had turned into a dare. Back then Jordan had just gone along with whatever Tyler had said. He had never questioned him, but now it was different. He refused to stand still and allow Tyler to walk all over him again.

Maybe he should confront him. The idea floated around in his head as he drove home. Another thing – why had it taken him twenty years to confess? Why now? Was it that stupid watch or something else? Something didn't add up in his mind.

Jordan pulled up into his driveway and turned off the engine, the lights on the truck going dim and leaving him in almost complete darkness. Without even stepping foot inside the two-bedroom house he knew something was wrong. It didn't feel right. He didn't need to see his wife's missing handbag, that was usually perched on the side of the kitchen worktop, to know that she was gone. Her shoes, normally by the back door, were also missing. The first thing he saw upon entering were the papers on the kitchen table, next to the fruit bowl, a blue pen laid neatly across the pages, a note scribbled on a scrap of paper laying next to it. He didn't need to read the papers to know what they were. He picked up his wife's note and read.

*Jordan. I'm leaving you. I can no longer be your wife. It's unfair to the both of us to keep up this charade any longer. I don't love you anymore and I know for a fact you don't love me. I did love you very much, but after we lost Alfie it all changed. I cannot keep living like this. I feel that we both need a fresh start. I deserve better and so do you. Please sign these papers and send them to my lawyer. He will be in touch. I hope you find happiness Jordan with whoever she is. I'll be staying at my mother's for the time being. Thank you. Eleanor xx*

Jordan read the note several times, taking each word in, but the only word that really stood out was *his* name – *Alfie.* It jumped out at him from the page. He had not seen the name nor said it aloud ever since it happened, ever since his son had died.

Alfie Daniel Evans.

Jordan slumped down in the kitchen chair, clutching the note with *his* name on it tightly in his left hand and stared straight ahead. Nothing was in focus, not the clock ticking on the wall opposite, not the kettle on the worktop, not even the divorce papers on the table in front of him. Those papers meant nothing to him. He would sign them no questions asked. He held nothing against Eleanor for leaving him; she was right, she deserved better. He had seen this day coming for a very long time. He was surprised that it had taken so long to arrive. He should have divorced her years ago, taking the initiative and getting the papers himself, but he hadn't. He often wondered why he hadn't. Was he afraid of being alone? It was possible, but secretly he knew the real reason – the reason why he'd stayed with her for so long. Because of *him.* Eleanor, despite her flaws and despite the fact he sometimes hated to look at her face, was the only thing left that was connected to *him*. She was a part of Alfie and he had been a part of her. Jordan wasn't strong enough to let her go, but now she had made the decision for him and it felt so much worse. She was out of his life and Jordan felt alone, like his son had left him all over again, like he had been ripped from his heart forcefully, leaving it withered and empty. Even though he tried to force the memory out of his head he could never forget *that* day, the day his son had been born and the day his son had died, both one and the same day —

*Jordan watched as his wife slept in the hospital bed. Her arms were hooked up to all sorts of machines which were quietly beeping and whirling away, doing whatever they had been designed to do; keep her healthy and alive. She had been sedated because it was the only way the doctors and nurses could calm her down. Jordan wished he could be sedated, wished he could dull the pain. Three hours ago, Jordan had rushed her into the hospital with severe abdominal pain; the onset of labour, but it was too early. Their son wasn't due to be born for another three months. Jordan already knew the outcome. He didn't need the doctor to tell him that his son was in trouble.*

*'He is very small,' they said. 'Prepare for the worst. He may not survive the night.'*

*Jordan had sat next to Alfie's plastic cot in the Neonatal Intensive Care Unit the entire time while the doctors tried their best to save him, but they had been right; he was just too small, too immature, too weak. His tiny pink body barely bigger than Jordan's hand, his skin so thin he was translucent under the bright lights. Wires and tubes entered and exited his little body, trying to breathe for him and giving him the nutrients and medication he severely needed, but his body had slowly given up as his father watched helplessly. The doctor had pulled down his mask and had shaken his head slowly.*

*'I'm sorry,' was all he said.*

*Jordan had never felt grief like it, never felt such fear and anger as what he felt in that exact moment. His little boy, who had barely even been in the world a few hours, was already gone, torn away, never to live his life. Jordan felt The Bad Man stirring within, but he didn't surface, not yet. He would, but right now Jordan beat him down. He needed to be himself right now. He didn't want The Bad Man to take over and blank out this moment.*

*'Would you like to hold him?' asked the doctor.*

*Jordan had shaken his head, never lifting his eyes from the body of his son. 'No.'*

*Jordan sat next to his dead son for over an hour before a nurse came and retrieved him; apparently his wife was awake and asking for him. Jordan took one last look at Alfie, whispered some words that were only meant for him and left the room to return to his wife. As soon as he looked in her eyes she burst into tears, already knowing the truth. He let her cry, but did nothing to comfort her except stay by her side. Even though Alfie's face had been minuscule he had looked very much like his mother. In that moment Jordan realised that his wife was the only thing that connected him to his son.*

*That night The Bad Man surfaced just as he had predicted. Jordan tried his best to hold him at bay, but he was too weak and The Bad Man was too strong. Jordan returned home alone, leaving his weak and frail wife to recover in hospital, and destroyed the living room.*

*When he awoke the next morning he surveyed the damage; broken windows, shattered ornaments, a smashed television. Half a dozen empty beer bottles lay scattered about, some broken. He had no memory of doing any of it. The anger within him had been so powerful, so raw, but it was still there and it wasn't going away like it usually did. Jordan knew that he would probably never fully recover from this and neither would Eleanor. For as long as he had known her, she had wanted a child. He had never wanted children, but she had fallen pregnant and now a child had been torn away from them. Was this his fault? Jordan could not help but blame himself for his son's death. The thought ate away at him day in and day out.*

Jordan blinked back the tears as they poured down his cheeks. He could see his son hooked up to all those wires so clearly in his mind, like he could just reach out and touch him. Jordan regretted not holding him every single day, never feeling how his body felt in his hands, never kissing him gently on the head to say goodbye. He didn't even have a picture of him. Now Eleanor was gone too, the one remaining thread that was holding him connected to his little boy. That was why he cried that night. Thoughts of Tyler and his confession were now the last things on his mind. He no longer cared what happened to Tyler, no longer cared about any of it.

The next morning Jordan woke up still at the kitchen table, his forehead resting on his arm, which was splayed out in front of him. He had no memory of falling asleep. The divorce papers were still there, unsigned. Jordan stood up, filled and switched on the kettle and popped some bread in the toaster. He checked his phone. No new messages. His head pounded, like he had a hangover, but it wasn't alcohol related. He had not touched a drop last night, even though he'd really wanted to numb the pain. The *hangover* was a mix between Amber's slap, stress and crying all night. He needed water ... or coffee. Jordan made himself a cup and then took his seat again before reaching across the table and dragging the papers towards him. He took the pen, signed his name and dated it in all the sections that were required. He then put it in the enclosed envelope and sealed it up. Done.

Alfie crossed his mind briefly, but he didn't let those feelings overwhelm him again. Last night he had let out all of his built-up emotions. It was a relief to have finally done that, but now he had to focus on the next phase of his life. Eleanor was gone; he would soon be a divorced man. Single again. He would have a fresh start, a new life, but something needed sorting first – The Bad Man. Jordan couldn't let him hang around anymore, ruining his life forever. There was only one person who could ensure he never saw the light of day again. *Tyler.* As much as Jordan hated him and didn't trust him as far as he could throw him, he needed him. Therefore, he knew that he'd have to leave Tyler to confess and do whatever it was he had to do. There was nothing left to do but wait.

Jordan looked at his watch. 'Shit,' he muttered, realising he was already late to open up the shop.

Jordan arrived at his father's business

unshaven, not showered and hungry because he'd only managed to eat half a slice of toast before rushing out the door. He completed all the usual morning opening procedures, unlocked the cash register and started the invoicing while waiting for customers to arrive. He was actually glad of the distraction. He would rather do invoicing than think of how shit his life was right now, or how shit his life had been for the past twenty years. He'd lost everything, his bond with his mother, his friends, his son, his wife, his sanity. He really had lost his sanity. A sane person wouldn't confess to having a split personality who took over him in fits of rage. He didn't know why but his mother lingered on his mind and he thought back to that awful day when she had left him and his father —

*Jordan and his father came home from locking up the shop at six in the evening. His father was not in the best of moods due to Jordan having been extremely rude to yet another customer. Jordan stormed in through the front door, almost slamming it in his father's face behind him.*

*'Fuck off Dad. The old twat was an idiot and you know it.'*

*His father, Jack, quickly stopped the door from hitting him. 'That's still no reason to call her a ... well, what you called her.' He would never say that particular word out loud.*

*'Whatever,' spat Jordan. 'I fucking hate working there.'*

*'Well by all means feel free to get yourself another job, but this was always the plan. You would take over my business one day when I retire.'*

*'Well maybe I don't want the fucking business anymore.' Jordan was twenty years old, but he had no idea what he wanted to do with his life anymore. As far as he was concerned his life was over and he was stuck in this godforsaken town forever. No one would hire him because of his temper and he had flunked all his exams at school, leaving with a fail in every GCSE he took and was unwilling to re-sit them.*

*At that moment his mother came through the kitchen door, a tatty apron around her waist. She had been preparing dinner.*

*'What's going on?' she asked. 'What's happened now?' Her relationship with her son was no longer a loving one. In fact, it had been getting worse and worse and so had her marriage. Her and Jack only ever argued, usually regarding Jordan, who was the cause of most of their stress.*

*'Our son called Mrs Thorn a ... well I can't repeat what he called her. She has raised a formal complaint and has said that she will tell everyone she knows not to shop with us anymore.'*

*'She fucking deserved it!'*

*'Jordan, you need to apologise to her. Mrs Thorn basically knows the entire town. This could ruin your father's business,' said Anne, a concerned frown on her face.*

*'I don't care. I'm not fucking apologising to that old cow.'*

*'Please Jordan, please, for me.'*

*Jordan laughed. 'Why the fuck would I do anything for you. You're as much of a fucking cunt as she is.' Anne took a sharp intake of breath, completely shocked and hurt by his use of language against her. Jack lowered his head, ashamed of his son. Anne's eyes were brimming with tears, but Jordan took no notice.*

*'Please apologise to your mother,' asked Jack quietly.*

*'No fucking way.'*

*'Then I'm leaving.' Anne choked back her tears as she spoke. 'I'm sorry Jack, but I cannot be in this house any longer with him. Jordan, you have turned into a monster. I don't even recognise you anymore. Being around you physically hurts me. I can't breathe. You aren't the boy I raised. You're not the man I wanted you to be. I have failed you as your mother. I'm sorry.' With that Anne untied her apron and tossed it aside. Jack grabbed her arm as she went to pass him.*

*'Anne please, let's talk. Give him another*

*chance.'*

*'I have Jack. I have given him as many chances as I can bear. I cannot stay. I'll be in touch to make arrangements.'*

*'Jordan, say something!' ordered Jack.*

*'Let her fucking leave. I don't need her. Fuck off Mum. I don't care if I never see you again.'*

*'Goodbye Jordan.'*

Jordan hadn't seen his mother since that day, twelve years ago. She had divorced his father a year later. Jack had been devastated and hadn't spoken to Jordan properly for weeks other than to tell him what to do at work. Their relationship remained strained to this day. The Bad Man had taken over him that day in the shop, but he had only been Jordan while speaking to his mother, which made it even worse. He couldn't blame The Bad Man for causing his mother to leave. Yet another thing that was his fault. Everyone left him eventually. He lived with that guilt every day and had often thought of contacting his mother to try and make amends, but he knew it was pointless with The Bad Man still controlling him. His mother would see he was still a monster. The word cut him like a knife.

Jordan blinked, bringing himself back to the present. He needed to think about something else, something that made him happy, or at least as happy as he was able to be.

He wasn't sure what made him look up and out the window of the shop, but he did and he saw the coffee shop opposite. He didn't see her, but he knew she was in there. He always knew she was there.

Amber. Jordan remembered how happy she used to make him feel. He may have only been a kid, but he'd loved her. In fact, he loved her to this day. He always had, but along the way she had been pushed to the back of his mind, yet here she was back in his life again. He would do anything to be able to start over with her, to rewind to that day they had kissed for the first time, press pause and then play again. He wanted to be able to feel her touch, the warmth of her skin, the taste of her lips. He'd been inexperienced, but it was a kiss he had never forgotten. Something he wished he could have the chance to repeat. A part of him had always hoped it would happen again one day, but another part knew that it would never happen. She was married, whether she was happily married was something he was yet to fully work out. She *seemed* happy.

Jordan had never spoken to her husband properly. The only interaction he had experienced with him was at his restaurant a few years ago. Jordan had got very drunk at the bar and had disrupted a private function by smashing glasses and shouting. Sean and his hired bouncers had escorted him outside and asked him to leave, however Jordan had become more irate and rowdy, shoving Sean against a wall. The police had been called and Jordan had spent the night in a local cell drying out.

Jordan expected that Sean was a decent bloke, but he didn't like him. He had what Jordan had always wanted – time with Amber. He wished he could read her mind. He wanted to know if she was really truly happy with Sean because if she wasn't then maybe there was a chance for him. He had thought there had been a moment between them in their spot yesterday evening. He was so afraid that it had only been him that had felt the spark.

For the rest of the day Jordan kept himself busy with work. His father joined him in the shop at midday and took over from then.

Jordan headed home, stopping at the local shop on the way for a crate of beer.

# Chapter Thirteen

Once Brooke had said goodbye to Amber and Jordan at her window she closed it as quietly as she could. It hadn't been opened in twenty years so the hinges were stiff and creaky. She drew the curtains across, blocking out the moonlight, plunging her room into darkness; the way it usually was. She wasn't sure how to feel at this precise moment. Brooke knew she should feel unbelievably happy because she'd left her house for the first time in seventeen years, but she felt no happiness. Instead, she felt apprehensive because she didn't know what was going to happen next. Relief also flooded her mind, but she wasn't sure why. She needed a shower because after digging for an hour she was covered in a thin layer of dust and soil was embedded in her nails. She headed for the bathroom, being as quiet as possible. She didn't want to wake her parents; a shower in the middle of the night was suspicious enough but she would never be able to convincingly explain the fact that she was covered in dirt.

After her shower Brooke crawled into bed and pulled the duvet up to her chin. She stared at the ceiling for what seemed like hours, until the sun finally started to creep in through the small gap in the curtains. Her mind had drifted from one thing to the next, never settling on anything in particular. At seven she heard her mother knock softly at the door.

'Brooke?' she called out quietly. 'Are you awake?'

'Yes Mum. Come in.'

Her mother opened the door fully and entered, cautiously perching on the end of the bed. 'How did you sleep?'

'I didn't,' answered Brooke almost immediately. 'I mean ... I couldn't sleep.'

'I see.'

There was an awkward silence for a few moments, neither women knowing what to say next.

Finally, Olivia sighed. 'We haven't spoken since before your friends arrived for their visit. Did you have a nice time with them? What did they say? I just want to make sure you're okay.' Her voice was so kind and slow. Brooke could tell she was treading carefully as if being around a wild animal, too scared to make any loud noises or sudden movements. Brooke had kept to her room once her friends had left yesterday afternoon and had not come out even for dinner. Her mother had tried to come and talk to her, but she had refused entry to anyone, instead locking them all out.

'Yes, we had a nice time. They just wanted to chat, catch up.'

Olivia didn't buy her daughter's answer, but she didn't press any further. 'Okay, well, would you like some breakfast?'

'Yes, actually I am a little hungry.'

Olivia tried to hide her surprise and joy. Her daughter very rarely said yes to eating any food. Normally she had to beg her to eat something.

'Great. Just come down when you're ready.'

Brooke arrived downstairs ten minutes later, dressed in her fluffy dressing gown despite the warm morning. She took up her usual position on the sofa. All the curtains were drawn in the house, blocking out the sunlight and the beautiful surrounding countryside. She had received a quick text from Amber already this morning asking how she was. Brooke had replied straight away saying that she was surprisingly okay. It felt strange to use her mobile phone. She had never used it properly, as she had no reason to. Her parents had bought her the phone a few years ago in the hope that she would join Facebook and make some friends online, but it didn't happen.

Olivia brought in some toast for her. 'There you are darling. By the way, I wanted to talk to you about what's happening next week.'

Brooke took the plate of toast and started

eating, her eyes fixed at a blank space on the wall the whole time.

'What's happening next week?'

'Well ... Dorothy and Eric are coming to visit. Won't that be nice?'

Brooke's nose twitched slightly as she fought the urge not to show too much emotion. 'Um, yeah, I guess.'

'Maybe you two could make amends. Dorothy really does care about you and love you very much. She didn't mean what she said last time.'

'Yes she did, that's why she said it.'

'Well, at least let's all try and be nice. Apparently she has some important news to tell us.'

'Okay, I'll try,' answered Brooke slowly. She didn't have the strength or the inclination to argue with her mother. She knew how much it hurt her to have both of her daughters on non-speaking terms with each other.

Olivia just smiled and then left her alone.

Brooke munched her toast as she glanced around the room. She sighed deeply, knowing that seeing Dorothy again would be hard work, but there was a chance that by the time she arrived The Fear may have left her. Once Tyler had done whatever it was he had to do, maybe she would be free. It was a chance she had to take. She wanted to live her life and go outside like a normal person. She wanted to not be a *freak,* as her sister had called her the last time she had visited. That had been over a year ago.

Brooke missed her little sister. They had been so close once, despite the constant bickering, but then *it* had happened and Brooke had retreated into herself, into her room and away from her sister, losing a bond with yet another person she loved dearly. Brooke couldn't help but dwell on their last encounter, wishing it hadn't turned so bitter and nasty —

*Dorothy had visited with her husband Eric. They had been married for over two years now. They were happy, or that's what Dorothy said. Brooke hadn't attended the wedding, despite wanting to go and participate in her sister's big day. Dorothy hadn't been happy about it. In fact, she'd been quite upset, but she had come to accept it eventually. She'd been there right from the start for her big sister and had watched her deteriorate throughout her teenage years into a shell of her former self. Ever since that day when she had experienced a panic attack in the garden their relationship had started to decline, piece by piece. Brooke had let her baby sister slip out of her hands and now she was all grown up. Brooke had barely noticed, never taken the time to get to know her as a grown woman. Dorothy had her own life now and a husband, who Brooke had hardly spoken to. Unfortunately, Dorothy was slightly bitter about the fact that Brooke was trapping their parents here. They never left her to go on holiday or do anything. Their lives revolved completely around Brooke. Usually during her yearly visits Brooke would sit in almost complete silence as Dorothy told her parents about her life in London. Brooke barely listened, choosing to stare ahead at nothing instead.*

*Brooke was sitting in her usual spot on the sofa staying silent as Dorothy rattled off a long list of famous landmarks she had visited in London.*

*'Oh,' she said, 'if you ever come to visit, I'll definitely have to take you to this restaurant called The Berry. You can only get in if you're on the VIP list. In order to get on the list you have to have visited twenty of the top restaurants in London, all of them have a Michelin star so of course they are very expensive, but it's totally worth it. Do you think you will be able to visit soon?'*

*The question was directed at her mother. Dorothy brushed a stray piece of hair that had fallen down out of her face. When she was younger, she had been a tomboy, but that phase of her life was well and truly over. Now she was a highly polished young woman with a pixie crop hairdo. Her jet-black hair was striking, setting off her blue eyes, which were surrounded by black eyeliner and long fake eyelashes. Her outfit of a blouse and pencil skirt looked like something straight out of a designer magazine and fitted to her slender body perfectly.*

*Olivia smiled at her daughter. 'That would be lovely darling, but ...' she glanced at Brooke, '... it's still very difficult to leave at the moment.'*

*'Mum, you haven't been anywhere in twenty years,' stated Dorothy. 'If it wasn't for Mrs Wilkins next door you wouldn't have even been able to come to my wedding. Brooke can look after herself. She's a grown woman.'*

*'I know darling, but I hate to leave her when she's so vulnerable.'*

*'But how is she ever going to get better if you don't try?'*

*At this point Brooke sighed. 'I may not speak very much but I'm not deaf.'*

*'Then why don't you ever talk to me,' answered Dorothy, turning to her sister.*

*'Because all you talk about is yourself.'*

*'Well by all means let's hear what you've been up to. Been anywhere nice lately? Eaten out at any restaurants? Travelled to any interesting countries? No? Didn't think so.' The room fell silent, no one sure what to say or do. 'Brooke, I'm sorry. I didn't mean that.'*

*'Yes, you did.'*

*'I didn't mean for it to sound so ... horrible. All I meant was that I wish you would let mum and dad come and visit me or let them go on holiday or something.'*

*'You make it sound like I'm trapping them here on purpose. I'm not keeping them here at all. They can go whenever and wherever they want.'*

*'Yes, but they don't because they are worried about you.'*

*Brooke didn't reply straight away. Olivia was looking very awkward and uncomfortable, clearly unsure which daughter she should agree with. She loved them both dearly and she hated to take sides.*

*'You don't need to worry about me.'*

*Dorothy sighed in frustration. 'We don't need to, but we still do! We love you, Brooke, but I wish you would try and help yourself once in a while. Why don't you see a therapist anymore?'*

*'Because they don't help.'*

*'Because you don't give them a chance. You are seriously ill and it's clearly going to take longer than a couple of home therapy sessions to cure you. Yes, I know, your friend disappeared twenty years ago. It was horrible. I was shocked too. I liked Kieran —' Brooke flinched at the mention of his name, '— but we all have to move on sometime.'*

*'Dorothy dear, I don't think you're helping,' added Olivia. She was worried that Dorothy was going to set Brooke off on one of her severe panic attacks. It would then take weeks until she was back to relative normality. Kieran's name was forbidden in this house.*

*'Mum, it needs to be said, maybe she needs to hear this. It's not normal to react this badly to someone going missing ... unless she knows more than we do —' At this Brooke snapped her head round so fast it made her head spin and she glared at her sister.*

*'I don't know anything! He disappeared. That's all I know!'*

*'Maybe you know more Brooke. Maybe you know what really happened to him and you just can't stand the guilt.'*

*Brooke jumped to her feet. 'Shut up!' she screamed.*

*'Brooke don't listen to your sister. Dorothy, stop this now! Apologise!' Olivia had clearly lost control of the situation; even her stern mum voice was not enough to calm things down. This moment reminded her of when they had been bickering children.*

*Eric and Frank were keeping as quiet as possible, unsure where to look in the room.*

*'No Mum, I won't apologise. Brooke needs to grow up and stop being such a ... freak!'*

*At this point Brooke screamed at the top of her*

*lungs, ran out of the room and straight upstairs, slammed her bedroom door and stayed there until Dorothy and Eric left the next day. She wouldn't answer the door and refused to eat anything.*

Brooke finished her toast and looked at the picture of her sister and her husband on their wedding day, which was hanging on the wall opposite in a sparkly silver frame. Dorothy looked so happy, so beautiful. Her wedding dress had been designed by Vera Wang and every crystal embedded in the bodice shone brilliantly whenever the light touched it. Her makeup was flawless, her smile genuine and showing off her perfectly straight, white teeth.

Brooke felt a tear come to her eye and roll down her cheek. That word *freak* echoed in her mind over and over. Dorothy had no idea how close she had been to discovering the truth that day. In fact, she knew the truth, she just didn't *know* she knew. Brooke was fearful that Dorothy could bring all that drama up again, but there was a chance that by next week Brooke could be cured, could be free from The Fear and be able to go outside with everyone. Maybe she could finally go for walks with her family, eat in the local pub (her favourite meal as a child had been the fish and chips) and watch the sunset over the hills. For the first time in a long time there was hope on the horizon.

Brooke wasn't sure what made her think of it, but she remembered the day that Dorothy had left home and how they had said goodbye. It had been one of the worst days of Brooke's life —

*Dorothy knocked quietly on Brooke's bedroom door. Brooke had been locked in here for days, only leaving to use the bathroom and to receive small amounts of food and water. It was like she was in jail. Brooke was in denial, refusing to accept that her little sister was leaving her and this small town for the big city. She felt betrayed and quite jealous of Dorothy. She was heading off for the life that Brooke had always planned.*

*'Brooke? Can I come in?' Dorothy waited for a reply which came about thirty seconds later when Brooke slowly opened the door and allowed her sister entry. They sat together on Brooke's bed in silence for a few moments.*

*'Brooke, I have to go,' said Dorothy, gently taking her sister's hand. 'I'm sorry but I can't stay here any longer. I love you, but I have to live my life.' Dorothy was now eighteen and had been accepted at one of the top universities in London to complete a film production degree.*

*Brooke started crying softly. 'Please don't leave*

*me,' she whispered. 'I know we argue and fight, but I feel lost without you.'*

*'I can't stay just for you.'*

*'But I need you,' cried Brooke.*

*Dorothy sighed deeply. 'Please just try and get better. You can't stay inside your whole life. There's a big wide world out there. Please ... just try.'*

*Brooke shook her head, knowing that she had been over and over this with Dorothy, who just didn't understand. Brooke had never told her or anyone about The Fear. Yes, she'd been diagnosed with agoraphobia, but The Fear was the reason why she stayed inside. If it wasn't for The Fear, Brooke would be perfectly normal, but no one understood so she didn't bother trying to explain anymore.*

*'I'll try,' said Brooke quietly. 'Promise me that you'll come back and visit me as often as you can.'*

*'I promise.'*

*But she hadn't. The next time Brooke saw her sister was nearly three years later. Dorothy forgot about her older sister and enjoyed her life, met new people, did wonderful things, visited amazing places and met a handsome young man who she later married.*

*Brooke felt herself crumble to pieces as Dorothy kissed her goodbye and left the room. She cried for hours, unable to pull herself together enough to even form words. Her mother had sat with her as she cried deep into the night. Brooke screamed that she hated her sister and then cried that she missed her and loved her.*

Brooke looked up as her mother entered the room again, this time holding a cup of hot tea which she passed to her daughter.

'Here you are darling.'

'Thanks Mum. I'm glad Dorothy is visiting next week. I'm looking forward to seeing her. Will you tell her that?'

'Yes, of course!' Olivia beamed a smile that lit up her entire face. 'That's wonderful darling.' She was surprised at how perky and happy her daughter seemed this morning. It was extremely unusual for Brooke to be so enthusiastic about anything.

'And I reckon I know what the news is that she wants to tell us.'

'Oh? What?'

'I'm not going to ruin the surprise Mum,' said Brooke with a half giggle. She had a feeling that her little sister was about to make her an auntie, something that she knew her mother would be overjoyed with. She would always go on and on about having a grandchild one day. Brooke had always dreamed of being able to give her one, or maybe more than one, but that, like so many other things in Brooke's life, was never going to happen unless The Fear disappeared.

# Chapter Fourteen

Tyler headed back to his flat after leaving Amber, Jordan and Brooke. He could tell that Amber wanted to speak to him, but he didn't want to talk. He had a plan to carry out and he needed to do it now. He immediately took a shower upon entering his flat; the water ran cold, but he didn't mind. He leaned against the wall and stared at his feet, watching as the dirt ran off his body and muddied the water, swirling down the drain which was clogged up with his own hair. His hand stung from the slice in his palm, the blood had clotted a while ago, but it had run down his arm and dried on his skin. He scrubbed it off and watched as it turned the water a dull red colour. He stared at the bloodied water, dark, disturbing thoughts trickling through his head. He wished they would flow out of his head, down his body and down the drain hole, like the water, but they were stuck inside with no way out. Well, there was *one* way.

It was time to put the next phase of his plan into action. The new oath had been made. There was no time to lose. He had told the others that he would confess on Friday, but that had been a lie. He was aware how untrustworthy he looked. Amber knew some but not the whole truth. It was only a matter of time before she called or showed up and wanted answers. He needed to work fast, but first he needed to get clean and somewhat presentable.

Tyler had not been surprised that there'd been questions about his knowledge of blood oaths. He couldn't tell them the reason why he knew how to make them, not yet anyway. His parents had shown him, forced him to make one when he had been ten years old. They had explained that if he broke it, he would die, or he would have to kill the person he told the lie to. His secret could never get out, his friends could never know. Tyler had agreed and he had taken the knife from his mother and sliced his palm and repeated what she had told him to say.

Once he had showered he pulled on some clean clothes, or at least the cleanest clothes he could find. Then he found his old video camera that he had owned since he was a boy and set it up so that it was facing the wooden chair. He attempted to clean and arrange the area so that it didn't look too cluttered and messy. Lastly, he pulled out the elusive wooden box that he had recently stored under his bed. He was ready to begin.

Tyler pressed record on the camera and took his seat.

'Hi,' he said to the camera. 'I feel a little self-conscious doing this so please bear with me. This recording is for Amber, Jordan and Brooke. It is for your eyes and ears only. As soon as you have watched it, I want you to destroy the recording. It will be the only copy. No one else is to watch this. That is very important. I'm not going through all this just to have you guys mess things up. Get it? Good. Now listen carefully.

'I'm going to make a second recording for you guys to watch, but that one can also be watched by the police. In fact, I want them to watch it because that's the whole point. On the second recording is a lot of information, some of it's true and some of it's not. You'll know which parts are false. The stuff about my parents, that's all true, but the stuff about what happened on the 20th of July 1998 is not true. You know that. As far as the police are concerned though it is the truth. Do you understand? I'm going to lie on tape. I'm going to confess to what I did using a lie and the police are going to buy it. They won't have any reason to suspect that you guys had anything to do with Kieran's death.

'The whole point of doing this is for me to confess and be solely responsible for what happened. It was one-hundred percent my fault and I shouldn't have dragged you guys into my mess. This is my way of fixing things for you. I won't stand by any longer as you suffer for what I made you do.

'The watch – it kick-started my brain into finally taking action. I don't know how it got there or why it was only found now, but I'm thankful it was. But I swear to God if any of you – especially you Amber – if any of you decide to tell the truth and act all noble then I will come back and haunt you for the rest of your lives —

'Yes, that means I'm going to die. That's the whole point. In order to break a blood oath, the original creator of the oath needs to make a new one with the same people again. The penalty for this is that I have to die. If any of you had broken the previous oath then you would have died. I don't know how, but I know it would've happened eventually. The fact that you kept it a secret all these years means that you took the oath seriously and I thank you for that, even if you did try and break it once or twice. You weren't only protecting yourselves, but me also.

'Now it's time for me to step up and confess. By the time you watch this it will already be too late. I've made up my mind and even if you had tried you wouldn't have been able to stop me. I've tried to commit suicide for years, but The Black Shadow has always stopped me. By confessing I believe that it will finally let me do what I have wanted to do all this time.

I believe I know what The Black Shadow is now, and, if I'm correct, the same is true for The Creature, The Bad Man and The Fear.

'The Black Shadow is a physical form of my guilty conscious. At first, I thought it was my depression or a side effect of it or even Kieran himself haunting me. After finding out that you have all suffered with your own demons over the years, I realised it must be something else. It's all connected to what happened that day. Our guilt has manifested itself as a form of a mental disorder, or an actual physical being, to torture us for what we did. I thought I was the only one. I was wrong. I originally sought you guys out to fix things for myself, so that I could kill myself and be free of The Black Shadow. After learning about The Creature, The Bad Man and The Fear, I realised that I had to do this for you guys so that you could finally be free and live normal lives. I'm not saying that our mental disorders and illnesses will go away completely. We've lived with them for two decades after all, but I'm sure they will lessen somewhat to enable you to live better lives.

'Now, I realise that what I'm asking you to do is to tell another lie, to keep another secret. Therefore, there's a chance that your guilt may not go away, but I believe it will because you should never have been guilty in the first place. I know you all blame me for what happened. It was my fault that Kieran fell off that tree to his death. If we had gone to the police straight away then you wouldn't have been guilty of anything, you would have just been mere witnesses. Yes, I probably would have gone to jail or been sentenced, but at least you guys would have been free. I forced you into a situation and turned you into guilty people. Now that I am finally taking the blame you should be free from your guilt once and for all.

'That is my plan. The rest of the information will be in my second video. My friends, I'm so sorry for what I did and for what I put you through. You deserve the last twenty years of your lives back, but I cannot give you that. I can, however, accept responsibility for my actions and finally confess, something I should have done right at the start.

'Brooke, The Fear doesn't control you nor does it define you. You're strong and confident and beautiful. Always remember that. I hope you'll be able to get out and explore the world just like you always wanted to do. Thank you for being my friend when we were children. I love you.

'Jordan, you're not The Bad Man. I am. You were always kind and loyal. I hope you'll find peace at last. We always used to joke about how we'd find and marry supermodels. I hope you'll find your one true love because you deserve her. Thank you for being my friend. I love you man ... even though you are a bit of a dick now.

'Amber ... you were always the best of us all and seeing you again recently has only reconfirmed that. You're such a good person. The Creature is only your guilt. Please don't feel guilty anymore. There was nothing you could have done or said to change my mind. Thank you for helping me finish my plan and thank you for being my friend. I hope you're happy and I hope you can sleep peacefully from now on. I love you.

'And so I come to the end ... my friends, this is where I leave you.' Tyler let the tears roll down his cheeks as he stared into the camera. 'Goodbye.'

Tyler stood up and stopped the recording before taking his seat again and sighing. He sat with the tears rolling down his face for a few moments, knowing that he would never see his friends again, but what he was doing now he was doing for them.

The first recording was finished; now onto the second. First, he needed a drink. Tyler stood and quenched his thirst with a beer from the fridge, downing it in one go. The next recording was going to be much more difficult to finish. He had a lot to say, a long story to tell. It was a story he had never told anyone. He would need to pour his heart and soul into this confession, tell the truth, but also lie and make it sound believable. However, first he needed to explain why he had done it. A truth so unbelievably awful that he had hoped he would never have to say it out loud. It was all about his parents.

Tyler couldn't help but think back to the moment he had returned home after the incident at the ravine —

*Covered in dirt, blood and sweat Tyler opened the door to his house after pausing for a few seconds on the threshold to mentally prepare himself. His head was fuzzy and he was exhausted from the hours of digging, his hands cut and bleeding. His anger was still pulsing inside of him, his heart rate still racing as if he was running at full speed. The whites of his eyes were laced with red lines. He felt like he was high and he was pretty sure a comedown was on its way. Tyler crept into the house and started creeping up the stairs, heading for the bathroom to wash away his sins.*

*'Tyler?' His mother's voice came from the main bedroom, just off the corridor of the upstairs hallway.*

*Tyler paused on the stairs. 'Yeah Mum, it's me.'*

*His mother appeared at the top of the stairs, looking down at him with a smile. Her mousy brown hair was swept back in a mum bun, wispy bits flying everywhere. Her face was attractive but well-worn for a woman of forty-two, the lines on the edges of her eyes told a thousand stories, not all pleasant.*

*'Why are you covered in dirt? Where have you been?' Her voice sounded calm, but there was a firm tone in there somewhere.*

*'Just out with my friends.'*

*His mother folded her arms in a confrontational manner and started walking down the stairs towards him, her piercing eyes staring straight through him. They sent a shiver up his spine. She moved her face to within a couple of inches of his, her warm breath on his face; she smelled of cigarettes. He held his breath, daring not to move a muscle.*

*'If I find out you have been lying to me —'*

*'I'm not lying Mum. I was with my friends. We lost track of time building dens.' He crossed his fingers in his mind's eye and pleaded to whatever Gods were out there that she bought it. He didn't want to deal with the consequences right now. Her stare made him nervous. It was like she was looking directly into his soul, searching for a reason to punish him.*

*'You're a good boy,' she said with a smirk. Then suddenly, as if she had changed her mind at the drop of a hat, she pulled away from him and smiled. 'Dinner is in the oven. Heat it up if you want.'*

*'Thanks Mum. I'll shower first.'*

*Tyler watched his mother walk past him down the stairs, the hairs on his arms standing to attention as she brushed past him. He breathed a sigh of relief and continued to his room, locking the door behind him, shutting out the demons. He knew they wouldn't stay out for long. They always had a way of sneaking and creeping back in, never giving him any peace. He wished the demons would leave him alone, but they were a part of him, always and forever.*

*An hour later he was clean and starving so he headed downstairs and started eating the dinner his mother had made for him earlier – shepherd's pie. It was hot and full of flavour. His mother was a very good cook, sometimes spending hours in the kitchen cooking and preparing meals for him. Tyler looked up as she entered, a serious frown across her face. She walked right up to him and leaned over him as he ate at the table, gently laying a hand on his shoulder and squeezing it. Tyler tried not to shudder at her touch.*

*'I love you Tyler, you know that don't you?' She kissed him gently on his cheek.*

*Tyler closed his eyes. 'Yes Mum.'*

*'You love me too, don't you Tyler.' It wasn't a question.*

*'Yes Mum.'*

*'Say it Tyler.'*

*'I love you Mum.'*

Tyler closed his eyes, remembering the soft touch of

his mother's hand on his shoulder, how she had caused his skin to crawl. He blocked out the memory and turned to the wooden box, gently lifting the lid and peering inside. He fingered the objects, another tear trickling down his cheek and into his mouth. These precious objects were sacred tokens to him, reminders to never go to that dark place again. They were special to him, but yet he knew he had to let them go, let them be free. Once they were free then he would be too. Tyler thought back to that day, several days after the incident, when he had first acquired them —

*Tyler was back at the bottom of the ravine. It was two in the morning, but there was still just enough light due to it being the height of summer that he didn't need a torch. He needed to work fast and get this done before the sun came up. He started digging. Luckily, he'd got there before another landslide had buried the body any deeper, but it was still six feet down and this time he didn't have help from his friends. He did, however, have a shovel, which made the job much easier.*

*He dug for nearly an hour before he finally hit something soft but solid; the body. Tyler scrapped around with his hands to clear some of the dirt and smaller rocks until he was able to grab the filthy clothing and drag the heavy weight out of its temporary grave. He took a moment as he stared down at his friend. His eyes were still open, but they were dirty and cloudy, lifeless and hollow. He had started to decompose quickly in the warm earth, so a foul stench of death and rotten flesh filled the air. The clothes were filthy and damp, clinging to the corpse, bloody and covered in bodily fluids.*

*'I'm sorry,' said Tyler to the corpse. 'But it was you or me.'*

*Tyler picked up the can of petrol that he'd brought with him and emptied it onto the body. The liquid soaked into the clothing, running off and onto the ground when it was drenched. Tyler reached into his pocket and pulled out a lighter, flicked it to life and without a second thought tossed it onto the body. He watched it burn – watched as the clothing dissolved, as the flesh melted away from the bones, as the bones disintegrated, until all that was left was a pile of gooey ash, a few pieces of bone and teeth.*

*It had taken longer than he had imagined, but he had never taken his eyes off the flames. Those red and yellow flickering ribbons were seared into his vision. His brain was in a slow, foggy haze, never thinking about the consequences of his actions, only the here and the now. Tyler picked up the shovel and sprinkled some loose dirt over the smouldering remains, cooling them down, snuffing out the heat.*

*Next, he picked up the second tool he had*

*brought with him – an axe. One of the pieces of leftover bone was large; a femur. He made short work of that as he chopped it up, the brittle bone easily collapsing under the sudden impact. There was not much left to chop up. He just needed it in small enough pieces to fit into his bag. The remains were still warm so the plastic bag he put them in started melting fast. He would sort it out later. The sun was coming up soon and he needed to tidy up and get the hell out of here.*

*Tyler bent down and picked up a partial piece of jawbone, a few teeth still lodged into it. He stuffed it into the bag along with every other piece of bone and piece of evidence he could find. Next, he used the shovel to scoop up the stained black earth and scattered it into the river, watching as it washed away downstream. Finally, he used some fresh, clean earth and covered the area where the fire had burned. He stood back and admired his work. If anyone happened to come down here then they would never suspect what dark and morbid thing had taken place. There was no longer a body buried down here. No one would ever know. He stuffed the black bag into his rucksack, picked it up and strapped it to his back. It was time to go.*

Tyler fingered the objects again, feeling the rough edges between his fingers. Next, he sat down and recorded the second video. Afterwards he prepared the scene and downloaded both videos onto separate hard drives before placing them inside the wooden box, closing the lid and locking it with a combination padlock. Tyler then took a piece of paper and wrote a note on it, sealing it inside a crisp white envelope and placing it on top of the box for it to be found.

This was it. It was time to go. The Black Shadow was hovering over him, casting its usual gloom over his head. It was watching him, taking in everything that he was doing, every tiny movement. It had listened to every word he had spoken on the recordings. Two blood oaths had been broken now and it was time to pay the ultimate price. For once, The Black Shadow was not doing anything to stop Tyler. This was going to work. He could feel it. He was finally going to be free. No longer would The Black Shadow have a hold over him. No longer would it make him hate himself. For once, Tyler was happy. His friends were going to be safe and he was going to die.

Tyler left his flat, leaving the door unlocked, and headed to where it had all started – Beaker Ravine.

# Chapter Fifteen

The next morning Amber got up early to get ahead of the chores. By the time Sean and Bethany appeared downstairs, both bleary eyed, she had already chucked the vacuum around the heavy traffic areas, put on some stew in the slow cooker for tonight's dinner, cleaned up from last night, made Bethany's lunch for school and made breakfast. She needed to keep herself busy because if she sat still for too long then she would start over-thinking and worrying, something she constantly did. She had today off from work so at least she didn't have to worry about that.

Once the family were out the door then she was off to visit Tyler. He was probably at work, but she hoped to catch him before he left his flat. She had sent him a text earlier, but he hadn't replied or even read it yet. In fact, he hadn't replied to any of her messages. She hadn't spoken to him since they parted ways after making the blood oath. All she wanted to do was talk to him, to ensure he was okay and what the next phase of the plan was. She knew he had to kill himself, but she was hoping to talk him out of it. There had to be another way. She didn't want to lose another friend.

Also, she needed to know if he had moved the body and, if so, why.

'Did you get up in the night?' asked Sean as he poured himself a fresh coffee from the brewing pot. 'I thought I heard you moving about downstairs.'

Amber stopped buttering Bethany's toast. 'Um, yes, I needed a glass of water.' So she *had* been sleepwalking last night. It hadn't been a dream. It had happened again. She couldn't trust her own body anymore. It was doing things without her knowing or blanking out memories that she needed to remember.

'Mummy, I had another dream last night about your friend.'

'You did?'

'Yes, he said he wanted you to find him and confess. Are you playing hide and seek?'

'Something like that sweetheart.' She took a short pause. 'Bethany ... what did he look like – my friend? Was he scary? Did he say anything else?'

'No Mummy, that was all he said. He was very nice.'

'Okay, good.' She needed to ask Tyler about the fact that her daughter was having dreams about Kieran/The Creature. She would never forgive herself if it hurt her. It needed to stop. 'Are you sure he didn't say anything else?'

Bethany furrowed her brow. 'Oh, I think he did

say something else. He said he would never leave me.'

Amber shuddered as she reached out her hand for support and grabbed hold of the back of a chair, collapsing against it.

'What the hell is going on?' Sean's tone of voice had a hint of frustration in it; he felt like he was being left out of something important. He always needed to know everything that was going on.

Amber straightened herself up and eyed her husband as she opened her mouth to speak. He was going to find out sooner or later and she would rather he hear it from her than the local town gossip or via the news. If things were going to improve between them then she needed to trust him, needed to confide in him. He was her husband and she couldn't afford to keep hiding things from him. *But is he hiding things from you?* The little voice was back. Amber blocked it out, refusing to accept that her husband was having an affair.

'Okay,' she said. 'Look, there's something you should know. I'm sorry I haven't told you before, but up until now it's been necessary to not tell you.'

'What the hell Amber? You're scaring me. What's going on?' Sean sounded like he was panicking. His heart rate sped up and his mouth went dry.

'You know that kid that went missing twenty years ago?'

Sean eyed her with a frown, clearly confused about where this conversation was going. He had assumed that she'd been about to tell him that she was cheating on him, but then that was ridiculous because she never went anywhere or saw anybody.

'Yeah. Why?'

'Well ... I knew him. In fact, I knew him very well. He was part of my closest circle of friends from when I was twelve years old.'

Sean placed his coffee cup on the counter with a loud thud. 'What? You told me you didn't really know him.'

'I know. I lied. I'm sorry.'

Sean took a long pause. 'Why would you lie about something like that?'

'Because his disappearance really upset me. I was only a kid. I lost one of my best friends. It's hard to talk about. It's not just you I never told. I didn't even tell my therapist. It's one of those things that I chose never to talk about.'

'One of those things? Why, what else have you lied about?'

'N-nothing. I didn't mean it like that. All I meant was that it upset me so much that I chose never to talk about it. It's why I have nightmares and insomnia. I've never gotten over it.'

Sean drank his coffee. Amber could see the

cogs turning in his head, round and round. He was staring at her in a way that she had never really seen before. Was that doubt in his eyes? Did he even believe her?

'So,' he said finally, 'that watch they found ... what does that mean? Has he been found?'

'No, he hasn't. I'm not sure what it means.'

'Is that why you've been weird lately? I know you didn't visit your mother.'

Amber's face dropped, all the blood drained to her feet and she felt faint.

'Yeah. Your mum called and one thing led to another and she said you didn't visit her that night. She didn't know what I was talking about. Where *did* you go the other night?'

Amber quickly searched her brain for a good excuse. She couldn't tell him the *whole* truth, but she could at least tell him half of it. 'I went to visit some old friends.'

'You don't have any friends,' replied Sean, a bit too bluntly.

'No, but I used to. Twenty years ago I had a group of friends. We grew up together. We were so close. There was me and Kieran and then Jordan, Tyler and Brooke were the other three.'

'Jordan? As in Jordan Evans who works at Fix It All?'

Amber nodded. 'Yes.'

Sean's whole demeanour changed, became defensive. 'That guy is an asshole. He once started a fight in the restaurant of my hotel. Why would you be friends with someone like that?'

'He wasn't always like that. When we were children he was really nice. Kieran's disappearance changed us. Jordan became angry. Tyler became depressed. Brooke has never left her house. It pulled us apart. I've barely spoken to any of them for years ... until a few days ago. Tyler came to visit me at work after he saw the news about the watch. He wanted to get back in contact, start afresh. I agreed and we contacted Jordan and Brooke. We all met up that night like old times and talked for hours. It was nice.' Amber stopped talking and looked at her husband. He still had that strange look in his eye. It was clear that he wanted to ask further probing questions, but Bethany's presence made him hold his tongue.

'I still wish you hadn't lied to me about where you were going that night.'

'I'm sorry, but I wasn't sure how it would work out. I didn't want to tell you in case things went badly or it made things worse.'

'Do you realise how dangerous that was? These people are strangers to you. Meeting them in the middle of the night ... if something had happened ... I wouldn't have known where you actually were.'

'You're right. I'm sorry. I just ... didn't think. It won't happen again.'

Sean nodded. 'So, do you think things will get better for you now? Your nightmares and stuff?'

'I hope so.'

'So why the hell is Bethany having weird dreams about one of your friends?'

Amber couldn't answer that question because she didn't know herself. 'I don't know.' She glanced at Bethany who hadn't been listening to a word they had been saying. Instead, she had been reading one of her school books while eating.

Sean nodded again and took a deep breath. 'Let's not talk about it around Bethany anymore.'

'Agreed.'

'Okay, well ... good, but I don't trust that Jordan guy. In fact, I'd rather you not be friends with him at all.' There it was; Sean was jealous. Amber had never experienced jealously from him before because she'd never had anyone in her life for him to be jealous of, but she knew it was jealously straight away. Could he sense that she had *feelings* for Jordan? Had she said his name differently to how she had said the others?

'He's a good guy,' said Amber, 'he just has ... issues. He's working through them.'

'I'll say,' scoffed Sean.

Neither of them said anything more on the subject. Instead, they turned their attention to their daughter, listening intently as she rattled off the list of countries in alphabetical order that she had learned at school yesterday. Amber had been married to Sean long enough to know when he was finished with a conversation. She knew that the revelation of her lie to him must have hurt his feelings. What must he have thought she was doing that night? Maybe he had thought she was cheating on him. Amber had never given him any reason to suspect her of cheating. Yes, she had weird feelings for Jordan at the moment, but she put that down to the fact that he was suddenly back in her life. They had a history. It was normal to remember that history, to think about it from time to time.

Once Bethany was safely at school and Sean had left for work Amber pointed the Volvo in the direction of Tyler's flat. He still hadn't replied to her texts or voicemail messages that she had left. She had a feeling deep down inside that was telling her to hurry, but she ignored it and drove at the speed limit. She pulled up outside, parked and headed for the door, giving it a few quick knocks and then waited. Nothing. She knocked again. Nothing. She wasn't sure what made her do it, but she reached out and used the door handle; the door opened. Her heart jumped and missed a beat. There was that feeling again – the feeling that she was too late.

'Tyler?' She called out before stepping inside.

As soon as she caught sight of the inside of the flat she knew something was wrong. The place was still a mess; dirty plates, discarded food and clothes strewn everywhere, but there was an eerie emptiness. Amber automatically shivered at the feeling. The all too familiar sense of dread crept up her whole body. *She was indeed too late.*

Then she saw it; a crisp white envelope with her name on it. It was lying on top of a wooden box that had a padlock with a four digit code keeping its lid shut. Amber frowned as she cautiously approached the box and envelope, its contents very much enticing her curiosity. She took the envelope, slit it open and read, her heart sinking further and further as she did.

*Amber. I knew you would come looking for answers. Please forgive me for using you and lying to you, but I have to make things right. There was nothing you could have done to change the outcome, please believe me. The code for the padlock is the day it happened. Inside are the answers you and the others have been looking for. The red hard drive is for you to watch along with Jordan and Brooke and no one else. Please watch this one first. The black hard drive is for you to watch and then give to the police. I'm sorry.*

*Goodbye. Tyler.*

Amber turned the paper over in case there was something on the back; there was not. Tyler was gone. She closed her eyes, a single tear escaping from each of them and trickling down her face. Despite what he said in the note she couldn't help but wonder if there was something she could have done to help him, to save him. Hadn't this always been his plan? He had made his choice, quite possibly a long time ago. It seemed The Black Shadow had finally let him go and given him what he had always wanted – peace.

Amber unlocked the box using the numbers 2.0.0.7 and peered inside. There were two small hard drives at the bottom, one red and one black. There was also another box, this one much smaller and with no lock. She picked it up and opened it cautiously. The sight of its contents made her suddenly thrust the box away from her, as if it had burned her skin.

Inside the smaller box was approximately twelve teeth, some still connected to a partial jawbone, some just on their own. They were discoloured and black, as if someone had tried to burn them and they were quite small in size, like they belonged to a child. She recognised the jawbone from the ravine a few days ago. There were also a few objects that were not immediately recognisable. They too were burned and broken. Amber guessed that they were shards of bone. A faint odour of ash escaped the confines of the box, tickling her nostrils. There was also that unmistakable smell of death; cold and unpleasant. It made her want to heave and turn away, but she stayed put, staring at the ugly, charred remains, knowing exactly who they belonged to without even having to use her brain. Seeing these teeth and bones sent a horrible tingling sensation up her spine. This was what was left of Kieran's body. These teeth once used to smile at her in their own cheeky way and had always cheered her up. The thought of his small innocent body being broken and burned and hidden away all these years gave her a tight knot in the pit of her stomach. She felt sick, disgusted at Tyler. If he had been standing in front of her now she probably would have slapped him across the face.

Then, suddenly, a disturbing thought briefly crossed her mind. *I would have done it.* The thought made her stop in her tracks. Maybe her and Tyler weren't so different after all. She wanted to hate him, but a part of her knew that there was more to this than what she was seeing right now. It was all on those hard drives. She needed to know what was on them – now.

Amber sent Jordan a text to say to meet her at Brooke's house, then sent Brooke a message to say that she was on her way over. Amber picked up the whole box and walked back to the car, placing it safely in the boot so it didn't move around during transit. She wasn't sure how they were going to react to the box of teeth and bones, but whatever was on the hard drives needed to be seen. She had the note in her pocket.

Brooke's mother opened the door. 'Hello again dear, so lovely to see you.'

'Thank you, Mrs Willows – sorry Olivia – lovely to see you too.'

Olivia's eyes focused on the box that Amber was holding. 'What on earth have you got there? It looks heavy!'

'Oh, it's nothing. Just some old stuff from childhood I found and wanted to show Brooke. Please can I see her? She's expecting me.'

'Of course! Come in!' Olivia had never had so many visitors to see Brooke since she was a child. Brooke was waiting for Amber in the living room, sitting in her usual sofa spot. Olivia showed Amber in with a smile. 'Can I get you girls anything?'

'No thanks Mum. Can you give us some privacy though?'

'Of course.'

'Oh, Jordan should be joining us in a bit too,' said Amber.

'I'll let him right in. No Tyler today?'

Amber tried not to show too much emotion

when she answered no. Brooke frowned, sensing that there was something wrong. Olivia left the room and Amber set down the box on the coffee table and took a seat next to Brooke.

'Amber, what's wrong? Are you okay?'

'I've just been to see Tyler.'

'Is he okay?' Amber answered by handing her the note. She watched as Brooke read it, her eyes wide and darting from side to side. She must have read it more than once because she didn't reply for at least a minute.

There was an empty silence hanging in the air, both of them being able to read each other's minds. They had always been able to do that as children. They had been experts at reading one another's body language, the tone of their voice, the emotion in their face.

Brooke's eyes filled with tears. 'I don't understand.'

'You will. We all will.'

At that moment Olivia returned and showed Jordan into the room. He was dressed ready for work, his beard neatly trimmed. Amber's heart did that flutter thing again as he looked at her. He looked sad; different. He thanked Olivia and she left the room, leaving the three of them in silence.

'What's going on?' he asked.

Brooke immediately handed him the note. He read it and looked at Amber. He barely reacted to what he read, turning instead to the box.

'What's in the box?'

'There are the two hard drive sticks ... and some teeth and bones.'

Brooke gasped. 'Ewww! Are you serious!'

'What the fuck,' said Jordan, opening the lid and peering inside. 'I knew he was lying to us. He must have brought the jawbone to the ravine with him the other night. He went back and dug up the body ... why?'

'I don't know, but I think there's a lot more to it than we think there is,' said Amber, bringing out the red hard drive. 'We need to watch this one first.'

'Brooke, does your television have a connection for this?' asked Jordan as he took it from Amber and approached the television.

'I don't know anything about technology.'

Jordan smiled. The girls watched as he checked the back of the television and set up the hard drive.

They watched the first recording in complete silence, no one daring to utter a single word or even a sound. Amber and Jordan were sat next to each other on the other sofa across from Brooke. Without thinking Amber grabbed Jordan's leg and squeezed it tight, her emotions threatening to overflow. He covered her hand with his own. She felt his warmth flow through her hand, up her arm and into her chest, calming her.

When the recording finished no one spoke for nearly a minute, but eventually Amber knew she had to say something.

'Let's put on the next one,' she suggested. Her voice broke at the end. She knew that whatever was on the second tape was going to be bad. It was better to just get it over with.

'I can't believe it. Why would he do this?' gasped Brooke, tears swimming in her eyes. 'I thought there was a better way.'

'I think we're about to find out,' answered Amber.

'So, The Bad Man is just my guilty conscious?' asked Jordan. He didn't sound convinced. 'I don't feel guilty.'

'I don't believe that Jordan,' said Amber, still feeling the warmth from his hand. Jordan looked down at the floor, unable to look her in the eyes. 'We all feel guilt,' she added.

Jordan shrugged. 'Maybe, but I still blame him.'

'Don't you feel guilty that he's dead because of us?' questioned Brooke.

'I don't know what the hell I feel right now.'

'Let's watch the next one before we jump to

conclusions,' said Amber as she handed Jordan the black hard drive. He got up, attached it to the television and pressed play.

# Chapter Sixteen

All eyes were on the screen, transfixed as the picture changed from black to a messy flat, with a single wooden chair in the middle. A few seconds later Tyler came into view and sat down on the chair. He looked like he had made a half-hearted attempt at smartening himself up, but it hadn't made much of a difference. His hair was still scruffy, his eyes were tired and he was slightly red in the face, like he had been crying. No one said a word while the recording played out in its entirety.

'My name is Tyler Jenkins. Today is Tuesday the 17th of July 2018 and it's about five in the morning. This is my video confession and the true story of what happened to Kieran Jones. His disappearance has shaken the entire town of Cherry Hollow over the past twenty years and has affected many lives, mine included. Unlike everyone else in the town I alone know what happened to him. No one else knows. I've been living with this heavy burden for two decades. It's time I came clean and put myself and the entire town out of its misery. Living with the truth has scarred me in many ways and has ruined my life. I'm sorry I haven't come forward sooner, but what is done is done. I believed by hiding the truth I was protecting people, protecting myself, but that was not the case. The only thing I can do now is tell you the truth, but before I do, I'd like to tell you about myself, about my background. This is another truth that I've been hiding from the world and it's going to be very difficult for me to say out loud. I need you to know this because then you will understand, at least in part, as to why I've kept everything a secret and why I did what I did.

'I was four when I was first abused by my parents. At least, that's the first time I can remember. They could have been abusing me before that. My father beat me with one of my wooden toys while my mother stood by and let it happen. This happened periodically for years. I was ten when I was first sexually assaulted by my mother while my father watched. They told me it was because they loved me and that it was normal. They filled my head with lies and stories. To the outside world they were perfectly ordinary parents, but on the inside, they were twisted and rotten. They played the doting parents very well. They took me to school, attended the school meetings, coached the football teams, yet no one knew what was going on behind closed doors. I became afraid of them, knowing the truth deep down, that their behaviour was not normal. Yet, I felt obligated to them to keep it a secret. In fact, they told me to make a blood oath so that I could never tell another living soul. If I did tell anyone then either that person would have to die, or I'd have to die. I took the oath because I wanted to make them happy. They were my parents.

'Now to go back on myself slightly. I first met my friends at the age of six. Amber, Jordan, Brooke and Kieran. They were all my best friends, but I couldn't tell them the truth. I hid my scars, my bruises and cuts from them and the rest of the world. I also hid my emotional scars and bruises. I was sad, deeply, deeply sad. I saw my friends every day. They were always so happy and full of life, smiling, laughing, so I decided that one day enough was enough. I wanted to be happy too, so I developed a new persona, a different personality than the one I truly felt. I became the funny, confident, good-looking boy. Girls always threw themselves at me. Other boys wanted to be like me. I somehow managed to convince myself that I really was a happy, carefree boy.

'I became close to Kieran around the age of ten. He'd follow me everywhere and I think we always had an unspoken bond between us. He wanted to be like me, copied me. He even copied my hairstyle, the way I walked, the way I talked. At age eleven we broke into my dad's alcohol cabinet and me and Kieran got wasted for the first time. I paid for that in more ways than one. When my dad found out he beat me to within an inch of my life. I hid away while my bruises healed, but Kieran came to visit me. Apparently, I'd told him while I was drunk that my parents abused me and he remembered all the details. I denied it straight away of course, but I warned him never to mention it to anyone or I'd kill him. I was terrified. I remembered the blood oath I'd taken and how I'd vowed to either kill the person I told or kill myself. I didn't know what to do. After that day Kieran always teased me and whenever he wanted something from me he'd use his knowledge about my parents as a bargaining tool, basically would make me do whatever he wanted in exchange for his silence. I used to get angry with him, often getting into fights in front of our other friends. They didn't know why we were always at each other's throats. Kieran didn't know the full extent of my parents' abuse towards me. At least, I don't think he did. I still can't remember exactly what I told him when I was drunk.

'I haven't gone into the full details of what my parents did to me because it's too horrible to say out loud. Just know that no child who has been through what I went through would come out the other side as a normal kid. Abuse changes you, moulds you into a person you no longer recognise. That's why I put on a different personality on the outside. On the inside I was messed up, sad, depressed and angry. I was angry at the world. Why did this have to happen to me? Did I deserve this? Was I a bad kid? No, I didn't think so. I messed around at school, swore too much and drank a bit, but I was still just a kid in pain, crying out for help. If it wasn't for my friends, I'm not sure what would have happened to me. I tried to run away once, but my parents found me. I was deeply ashamed. I never wanted my friends or anyone else to know about their abuse. It was a secret I believed I needed to take to the grave. However, I had a decision to make. It was him or me and so, my story moves on.

'Before I go on and explain what happened to Kieran please know that I'm not using the abuse I received from my parents as an excuse or condoning what I did. I'm merely giving you all the facts and explaining everything I know so that you can make up your own minds about me. You may think I'm a monster. I am – but monsters are not born. We are created. I also created my own monster.

'Now, about what happened to Kieran Jones. Everyone believes that on the 20th of July 1998 he went missing. For years, his parents and the whole town have come up with different versions of what could have happened, but no one knows the truth. Except for me. So here it is – Kieran is dead. So all those people who said he'd run away or been kidnapped then they are – unfortunately – wrong. He's dead. He has been for twenty years, ever since the day he disappeared. How do I know this? I killed him. After you hear the rest of my story you may think I murdered him. To this day I cannot say whether it was intentional or whether it was an accident. Let me just put it this way – on that day I never set out to kill him. I'd decided a few days before it happened that I was going to take my own life, but things changed. The situation changed. It happened and that is that. I'm now going to tell you exactly how I killed him. However you end up taking it, please know that I'm guilty of his death. Me. No one else. Me.

'On the 20th of July 1998 myself and my friends went to play in the south field. However, Kieran did not show up. After a while I decided to wander off by myself to the other side of town near Beaker Ravine, leaving Jordan, Brooke and Amber to hang out together. I needed some space. As I previously said I was planning on killing myself soon, but I didn't know how I was going to do it. I wandered around for a while and eventually got to Beaker Ravine where I ran into Kieran who was sitting by himself, smoking a joint. He invited me to join him, which I did. We chatted, laughed and got high while sitting on a tree that had fallen across the ravine like a bridge. I suddenly realised that this was the perfect spot in which to jump to my death. I planned to come back again later. Kieran and I somehow got on to the topic of our parents and Kieran made a crude joke about mine being kiddy-fiddlers. This immediately got my back up. He accused me of being a wimp and not standing up for myself. I said that everything was fine and he didn't know what he was talking about. I was determined to keep my confident, happy alter ego intact. He saw right through me. He said he was going to tell everyone, that my parents needed to be locked up. He was the only person in the whole world who knew my secret and he was just sitting on the tree, dangling his legs over the side. Something stirred inside me. The monster. Without really thinking about the consequences, with one swift shove I pushed him off the tree and he fell to his death.

'There you have it. I killed him because he knew too much and he threatened to tell everyone my secret. I couldn't have people seeing me as a helpless child who was abused and raped by his parents. I also killed him because it was either him or me, but I can't even explain how quickly it all happened. One moment I was sure that I'd be the one to die and the next I pushed him off the tree. I was convinced my friends would leave me if they knew the truth, that I would have no one. I didn't know if the blood oath was serious or not, but to me it was. I didn't know what would happen if Kieran had told my other friends about my parents, but I didn't want to find out. For a start, my parents would probably be locked away and I'd be put into foster care as I have no other close family who would take me in. Everything I knew would be taken away. My friends were the only good thing in my life, including Kieran, but he had threatened to take them all away. It was a split second decision that I regret every single day.

'However, after he fell, I realised I had a new problem. Kieran's body would be found if I left him there. Maybe not that day, maybe not the next, but one day someone would discover his body at the bottom of the ravine, so I came up with a plan. I did it to help myself because I knew there would be questions and I could be found out. I scrambled down to the bottom of the ravine and moved his body to a nearby landslide and buried him. I threw all the bloodied rocks into the river to wash them clean and scoured the area for any evidence. I wasn't really thinking clearly. I was twelve, nearly thirteen, I had no idea how to get rid of a dead body. I'd seen movies of course, but this was real life and I was clutching at straws. I realised a few days later that I needed a new, better plan, so I decided to go back to the ravine. I'd been questioned by the police by then, so had my friends. They all had no idea. I hid the truth from them. I didn't even tell them that I'd seen him that day. They all thought I'd just wandered on home. The police only asked me when was the last time I'd seen him. I told them it was the 19th of July. We'd hung out in town by the water fountain for a few hours, which was true.

'Anyway, as I said, a few days later I returned to the ravine with a shovel, an axe, a bag, a lighter and a can of petrol. I'd done some research and my idea was to burn the body to kill any traces of DNA and make the body disappear completely. No body, no crime. I dug up his body and burnt as much as I could of it, until only a few bone shards and teeth remained. I chopped up the bigger pieces. I scattered the ash and stained earth all over the place, in the river, in nearby river banks, until there was not a scrap of evidence that a fire had been there. The bones and teeth I put in the bag, carried it back to my house and hid it in my wooden treasure box where it still remains to this day. I hid the box under my bed until I moved out of my parents house, then, when I moved into my flat I hid it in the wall behind my bed. I never opened it, but I knew it was there, constantly reminding me of what I'd done.

'After Kieran disappeared my friends and I drifted apart. My plan had failed. I'd pushed my friends away all by myself. I could see they were overcome with grief and it changed them. We saw each other briefly over the coming years, but at school we stayed apart. Brooke never came back to school again. Amber dropped out and Jordan became an angry, bitter person, like me. I'd caused this. My friends were suffering because of what I'd done. I couldn't save myself, nor my friends. We have barely spoken in twenty years. I began to get worse. My parents eventually got fed up with me once I turned eighteen and left me alone because I was so depressed I didn't care anymore. I haven't seen or spoken to them since. I don't know where they are. I don't expect them to be arrested and jailed for abusing and raping me. There's no evidence to prove that they did it, only my word. I don't know if that's enough to convict them or not, but this is not about them. I don't care about what happens to them. I just want my story told and to tell you all that they abused me for eighteen years.

'I became clinically depressed. My doctor, Graham Davies, will confirm this as well as the long list of medication I've been on over the years. I tried to take my own life several times, but it never worked. I should have just jumped off the tree into the ravine back then. Maybe I was never one-hundred percent committed to killing myself, I don't know, but I hated myself for what I'd done. The guilt followed me everywhere, never leaving me for a single second. I didn't know what to do. I had no one. For twenty years I've lived with this depression, guilt, this Black Shadow as it were, hovering over me, never able to escape. I couldn't see a way out or how to fix it. I wanted to fix it, to make things better, but I didn't know how.

'Then, a few days ago, a watch was found at Beaker Ravine. I have no idea how it got there. The only explanation I have is that it probably broke off his wrist upon impact and was flung behind a rock where I couldn't see it. Believe me, I spent a long time searching for any evidence that could possibly be left behind. However it got there, it was found all these years later. It was a sign – a sign to tell me that it was time I confessed, but I knew I'd more than likely go to prison. I'm not afraid of going to prison, but I am afraid to live the rest of my life feeling the way I do. Depression is not something that goes away on its own. I know that by confessing I'll not magically get better. So I've decided to put my confession on tape ... and then I will jump into the ravine – the thing I should have done in the first place.

'So here it is. Listen carefully. I, Tyler Jenkins, confess to killing Kieran Jones. I did it and I'm truly sorry for the hurt that this has caused. To Mr and Mrs Jones, I'm so very sorry for what I did. Watching you suffer all this time, not knowing where your son was, whether he was dead or alive has been horrendous.

No matter how much I apologise I know you'll never forgive me, but I hope that now you know the truth you'll have some form of closure. Kieran was a good friend to me. He tried to help me in his own silly way.

'To my friends Amber, Jordan and Brooke. I'm so sorry for lying to you and hiding the truth. I should have told you the truth about my parents long ago and then none of this would ever have happened. I hope that now you know the truth about what happened to our friend Kieran you will be able to face up to your own demons and begin to repair the holes that have appeared over the years. I love you all very much and I'm sorry. I've sent Amber a message and told her where to find the wooden box with Kieran's remains. She will have brought it with her to the police station along with this hard drive.

'And so, I come to the end of my confession. I hope I have cleared everything up and you all have the answers you've been searching for. All that's left to do is finally be at peace. Thank you for watching and listening. Farewell my friends.'

The television screen turned black and the room was left in stunned silence. Amber looked at Brooke who had tears streaming down her face. Jordan was still staring at the screen, his mouth open slightly. Amber reached out and gently took his hand, squeezing it, bringing him out of his trance. He blinked several times.

'But it wasn't true, the bit about Kieran's death, it wasn't true.' Brooke sobbed.

'He did it to save us,' answered Jordan. 'If we tell the police the truth now it will ruin everything and he will have died for nothing. He admitted that it was his fault. He's finally done what we all should have done right from the start.'

'I just can't believe he would do that,' sobbed Brooke. 'I can't believe that his parents did that to him.' Brooke started crying quite hard, unable to stop the tears from flowing.

Amber was also crying, but softly, never wiping away her tears. Her heart felt like it was torn in two. The thought of Tyler suffering all those years through his parent's abuse made her feel so angry, so useless. How could she not have seen it in his face, his actions, his mannerisms? He had always been very private when it came to his parents, very rarely allowing his friends to come to his house unless they had been out. Amber had only met his parents a handful of times, but they had been pleasant, perfectly average parents. How could she have known?

'I feel like we should have known, should have realised,' said Brooke, finally bringing her sobbing under control. 'We were bad friends.'

'We weren't,' answered Jordan almost immediately. 'We were good friends to him. He said so himself. It's not our fault that we didn't know what was going on at home. We can't blame ourselves for that.'

'We can try,' muttered Amber under her breath. Jordan may have been in denial about feeling guilty, but Amber would not let this go easily.

'So now we are free. The Bad Man, The Fear, The Creature ... they're all gone now, right?' asked Jordan. He sounded confident already.

'There's a chance,' answered Amber with a shrug. 'I mean, if Tyler was right about what they are then it's possible.'

Amber, of course, knew it wasn't going to be that simple. If The Creature was a manifestation of her own guilt because of her involvement in the cover up then it wouldn't have gone suddenly. She still felt the guilt gnawing away at her insides. It would take time to heal. However, there was something else gnawing away at her, but after hearing Tyler's confession she knew she had to keep yet another secret. He had sacrificed himself for them and she couldn't let him die in vain. She knew she was doomed to carry her guilt for the rest of her life.

Jordan turned to Brooke. 'There's only one way to find out. Fancy a trip outside?'

Brooke's eyes lit up, not a tiny slither of doubt

in her mind. 'Let's try it.'

Amber envied Jordan and Brooke. The idea that their guilt was suddenly gone seemed to fill them with confidence. Could they really just forget about the fact that Tyler was dead now? Amber kept silent, unwilling to bring more drama to the situation.

# Chapter Seventeen

Amber opened the front door and she and Jordan walked a few paces down the garden path, then turned around. Brooke stood a few feet back from the door, huddled against the side wall for comfort and security. The breeze coming through from outside blew her blonde hair across her face. Even though she had made a short trip outside a few nights ago, this felt different. In fact, she hadn't stepped a foot outside her front door in seventeen years; the fact the door was even open and she was standing near it was closer than she'd been in years. The other night she could sense The Fear was near, but had trusted Amber when she'd said that it wouldn't hurt her.

Now, however, she could not sense The Fear. Usually, she could feel the tightness in her chest, the panic rising up from the soles of her feet and inside her body, the cold shiver running down her spine, but there was none of that at this moment. She felt nervous, afraid even, but not in the same way. Amber didn't pressure her, neither did Jordan. They were there for support.

Brooke inhaled deeply and then tentatively

took a step forwards, then another and another, until she was standing directly by the front door.

'Just keep looking at me Brooke,' said Amber, offering a friendly smile and a small amount of encouragement.

Brooke nodded, continuing to keep her eyes fixed on her friend. She blanked out everything else; the neighbours' houses, the road ahead, the stranger over on the other side of the road walking his dog, the tree nearby, even Jordan who was standing right beside Amber. She watched as Amber's eyes lit up and a big smile came over her face. Before she knew it she was standing in front of Amber, about ten feet from her front door, out in the big wide world. In the daylight she didn't recognise anything. It looked different than the other night when the neighbourhood had been shrouded in darkness.

'I did it!' Brooke suddenly realised where she was. Instead of being terrified and running back inside she squealed and jumped up and down several times before flinging her arms around Amber's neck. The girls hugged and started laughing, crying and jumping up and down with excitement.

'I can't believe it,' said Amber.

It had worked. Relief gushed over her in waves. She felt a heavy weight lift from her shoulders, feeling so light she could have floated away. It was over. It was truly over and they could begin to piece their lives back together. It wouldn't happen overnight, but it was a start. There was hope.

All of a sudden there was a loud shriek from the doorway, followed by a crash of glass. Olivia was standing open-mouthed at the door, a broken jug that had once held lemonade smashed to pieces at her feet. She didn't care that her shoes were covered in lemonade. She kept staring at her daughter who was slowly walking towards her.

'M-mum,' Brooke said, fighting back tears. Mother and daughter embraced in a tight hug. Olivia cried hysterically. Amber watched them with a smile, feeling so happy she could burst. Never did she think she would ever see this day. For years she had prayed for a miracle and today it had finally happened.

Jordan gently elbowed her. 'You okay?'

Amber nodded. 'Yeah. You? How will we know if your anger is gone?'

'I don't know, say something annoying to make me angry.'

Amber gave him a glare and rolled her eyes. 'I guess we'll just have to take Brooke's accomplishment as proof.'

'Yeah, for now anyway. What about you? Can you see The Creature? Do you feel any different?'

Amber looked around her. No, she couldn't see

it, but that didn't mean it wasn't there. It was very good at hiding in shadows and making itself invisible. She hoped that she would never see it again. Only time would tell, but the fact that Brooke was outside was good enough for now.

'No, I can't see it.'

'So what now?'

'I guess we take the black hard drive to the police station and destroy the red one like Tyler requested.'

'This should be fun. Maybe we better leave Brooke here. Her first proper trip outside should probably not be to a police station.'

Amber agreed and went back inside to fetch the hard drives. She pocketed the black one and held up the red one towards Jordan.

'How are we going to destroy it?'

'Let's go and see if Mrs Willows owns a blender.'

'I think she prefers that we call her Olivia now.'

'She'll always be Mrs Willows to me.'

Jordan led the way. Amber followed. They opened a few cupboards until they found a small blender. Jordan plugged it in, popped in the hard drive and turned it on. The sound of metal crunching against metal and hard plastic echoed around the kitchen. Amber watched in fascination as the hard drive disintegrated, eventually being reduced to a jumble of plastic and metal. Jordan emptied the contents into his hand.

'I'll scatter it around the town in different places later.'

Amber nodded. It was gone. No one would ever know the *real* truth. Amber couldn't help but feel a tinge of guilt that they had to keep yet another lie from surfacing, but it was what Tyler wanted. Amber knew she would have to learn to forgive herself and move on eventually.

Amber and Jordan left Brooke and her mother once they had both calmed down. Jordan drove them to the local police station, which was several miles away outside of town. Amber had the wooden box on her lap, clutching it like precious cargo.

'So we're really going to do this ... let Tyler take the blame.' Amber was still reeling from the shock of Tyler's confession tape.

'You heard him Amber. It's what he wanted. This was his plan all along. We've all suffered long enough. It's about time he owned up to what he did. I'm sorry he's dead and for what happened to him, but maybe we have to think about ourselves now. Yes, we helped him bury the body, but he was the one who knocked him off the tree. I tell you something, that watch being found was our saving grace. Thank God for those kids who found it.'

Amber shuddered. *Yeah, thank God.*

'Yeah. I remember what happened now.' Amber sighed.

Unfortunately, it was true. Along with remembering about seeing Tyler covered in ash and dirt she also recalled the scene as it had unfolded at the top of the ravine that day. Finally, her subconscious had released that awful memory, along with another —

*Amber shielded her eyes with her hand, feeling an uneasy wave of fear throughout her body. She was angry at Kieran for being so heartless towards Tyler, but also annoyed at Tyler for letting it get to him and start up a new and dangerous challenge. A part of her wanted to watch Kieran suffer for what he had said to Tyler. It seemed everyone felt the same way because no one attempted to stop him as he jumped onto the tree, its branches quivering at the sudden impact.*

*Amber quietly watched as Kieran crept along the makeshift bridge. He had a confident grin on his face as he pretended to wobble every now and then, causing Brooke to scream. He loved to tease her. Brooke had her eyes covered with her hands, barely able to watch. Amber was holding her breath.*

*Kieran got to the other end of the tree, turned*

*on the spot and held his middle finger up at Tyler, who gritted his teeth in anger.*

*'See, I'm not a big pussy like you. If you had some balls you wouldn't try and make me look weak all the time.'*

*'Shut up Kieran. I'm not a pussy. I'm not weak.'*

*'Yes you are. I dare you to tell us about your parents. Go on!'*

*Amber frowned. 'Tyler, what's he talking about?'*

*'Nothing!' he snapped. 'He doesn't know what the fuck he's talking about. He's just trying to make me look weak and pathetic, but he's the pathetic one.'*

*Jordan stepped closer to Tyler and gently placed a hand on his shoulder. 'Calm down Tyler. No need to get angry.'*

*'Fuck off!' he shrugged away from Jordan's touch.*

*'Tell them Tyler. Tell them! Tell them or I will.'*

*'Don't you fucking dare! I'll kill you!'*

*Kieran laughed. 'I'd like to see you try! TELL THEM!'*

*Tyler suddenly screamed, lunged forwards and kicked the tree, making the whole trunk shudder. Kieran wobbled, but managed to regain his balance. He stood up tall, spread his arms wide, showing that he wasn't afraid of him.*

*'Tyler stop it!' screamed Amber. 'Kieran stop it! Whatever this is we can sort it out.'*

*'No Amber, we can't. Tyler needs to tell the truth right now. Let's get this all out in the open once and for all.'*

*Tyler still had his foot resting on the tree, his eyes were glazed, directly focusing on Kieran. There was hatred in his eyes and something else Amber realised – fear. She had never seen such fear in someone's eyes before.*

*'There's nothing to tell,' he said quietly. 'The game is over. I'm going home.' Tyler turned and started walking away. He had admitted defeat at last.*

*'Fine! I'll tell them. Tyler's parents are —' But Kieran never got to finish his sentence. Within a split second of him starting to speak Tyler had picked up a nearby rock and hurled it at Kieran. It hit him square in the face. He shouted in pain, clutched his face, wobbled, lost his balance and fell off the tree, plummeting to the bottom of the ravine.*

*Brooke screamed. Jordan rushed to the edge and peered over, but Amber just stared at Tyler, watching his expression. It didn't change. The anger was still there, taking him over like a black shadow.*

Amber buried her face in her hands. 'Oh God, I remember it like it was yesterday now. I blocked it out for years. We should have realised it was something serious. We could have helped Tyler afterwards.'

'But we all barely spoke after that day. We all drifted apart because of what Tyler made us do. Things could never have been the same again Amber.'

'He was so sad and desperate.'

'The Black Shadow had him in its grasp way before that day at the ravine. He said himself that he was depressed and he put on a persona to cover it up. The Black Shadow was his real personality. There wasn't anything we could have done.'

'You don't know that.'

'No, I guess I don't, but I'm sure as hell not going to punish myself for the rest of my life. To be honest I'm not sure what I would have done had I been in his place, but he's always been depressed. Now, finally, he is at peace.'

Amber just sat and stared out of the car window, watching as the greenery of the surrounding countryside whizzed by. They would be turning onto the main road soon which would lead to the station. Her and Jordan clearly had differing opinions on the situation and she didn't want to start up an argument. Or maybe she did. It would at least test the theory to see if Jordan still had anger issues. Amber had always been the type of person to want to help people and always tried to see the best in them. Maybe that was her curse.

'I can actually hear you thinking,' said Jordan, disturbing her thoughts. 'The cogs are whirling around in your head so loudly right now.'

Amber smiled. 'I just want all this to be over. The police investigation is going to take weeks, months even. I'll have to explain to my husband what's happened. I don't know what to tell him.'

'He doesn't know the truth I assume.'

'No, although he does know now that Kieran was my friend who disappeared and his disappearance is why I have ... issues. He doesn't know about The Creature. There's a lot I haven't told him.'

'Does he know about us? I mean, that you had a crush on me?'

Amber laughed. 'And you had a crush on me! No. He doesn't. He just knows that we were childhood friends.'

Jordan nodded. 'Can you continue to hide the truth from him?'

'I've been doing it ever since we met. I guess I have no other choice. I can't tell him. What if he left me?'

'What if he did?'

Amber didn't answer right away because she had no words. She asked herself if she would actually be upset if he left her. Of course she would, but could she live without him? Yes, she could. It was Bethany she couldn't live without.

'I couldn't do that to Bethany. He's an amazing dad to her and ... I love him.'

'What was that pause for?'

'What pause?'

'You know what pause.'

'I love him.'

'Okay.' Jordan glanced at Amber out of the corner of his eye and smiled slightly. 'You're cute when you're lying.'

'I'm not lying!' Amber couldn't help but let out a frustrated giggle. He could read her so well. 'Do you love your wife?'

'Eleanor. And no.'

'Then why'd you marry her?'

'Because she was pregnant.'

Amber stopped short, suddenly realising that she had entered into uncharted territory. Jordan hadn't really opened up to her properly about his past or his relationship with his wife the other night. She could automatically tell that it was a sore subject and now she had put her foot in it.

'I'm sorry,' she whispered. 'I didn't realise you had a child.'

Jordan was silent for a few seconds. 'I don't. Not anymore.'

Amber could have kicked herself. She hadn't meant to pry or to bring up any bad memories. She didn't dare ask what had happened but she really wanted to know.

'He was born premature. He was only alive for a few hours. I was with him when he ...' Jordan didn't need to finish the sentence. 'His name was ... Alfie.'

Amber immediately started crying softly, trying to hide her tears. 'Jordan I'm so sorry. I didn't mean —' Even the mere thought of losing a child, even one so young was more than she could bear.

'It's okay,' he said with a nod as he squeezed her hand gently. 'I need to talk about it. When it happened I hid behind The Bad Man, acting out in anger all the time, never dealing with my grief. We'd got married when she was four months pregnant. It just made sense to stay married even after we lost ... him, but then things got worse. I drank and got more and more angry. Then I hit her. I knew it was over after that. She asked me for a divorce over and over but never actually went through with it. Maybe she was scared about what I would do to her. It makes me sick to think how I treated her. She didn't deserve it. We were both grieving and I made things so much worse.'

'But it wasn't you. It was The Bad Man.'

'Yes and no. It wasn't always me, but it was me at the same time.' Jordan let those words hang in the air for a moment. 'I've pushed everyone away over the years. First of all, you, Tyler and Brooke, then my mum, my dad, then Eleanor. Now I have no one.'

'You have me.'

Jordan smiled. 'It's nice to know that you've never changed. You still look for the good in everyone, always try and do the right thing.'

'The right thing would have been to tell the truth twenty years ago. I've done bad things too.'

'Maybe, but maybe not. The right thing to do now is hand this hard drive into the police and say nothing else. We need to do what Tyler wanted, what he planned.'

Amber took a deep cleansing breath. 'You're right.' She couldn't risk going to jail, ruining everything and leaving Bethany without a mother. She would never forgive herself. That hadn't been *the plan* after all.

Jordan pulled up outside the police station. It was a tiny building, only the small county branch of the bigger station, which was situated about fifty miles east. It had a small Criminal Investigation Department. The only serious crime that had been investigated was the disappearance of Kieran all those years ago, otherwise it mainly dealt with small crimes, such as theft, burglary or emergencies. They also ran a small group for the local neighbourhood watch, which did a night-time patrol on random days of the week. You never knew when they would be lurking.

Jordan and Amber entered the building and approached the small front desk. A female officer in uniform was at the desk, typing on a computer. She was a Sergeant and looked extremely bored, not even bothering to look up as the door opened. It was probably just a normal day to day walk in. This morning she'd already had an old lady walk in and ask if she could help rescue her cat which wouldn't come out from underneath a parked car.

'Hi. We need to speak to the guy in charge,' said Amber, not having a clue what the actual title of the person would be. She'd not been to this station since she had been questioned twenty years ago. She couldn't remember the name of the man who had spoken to her.

Jordan, on the other hand, had visited the station on numerous occasions and recognised the Sergeant behind the desk straight away. She was one who had turned up to the fist fight he'd caused at the restaurant where Sean worked and had tossed him in an overnight cell to sober up.

The Sergeant didn't stop typing as she replied in a bored voice. 'That would be the Detective Chief Inspector.'

'Okay, please can we speak to him.'

'He's busy.'

'Trust me, he's going to want to talk to us.'

'And why is that exactly?'

'Because we have evidence relating to the disappearance of Kieran Jones.'

The Sergeant finally stopped typing and glanced up at Amber, a single eyebrow raised. 'Oh? What evidence is that then?'

'We'd rather speak to the Chief Inspector,' added Jordan.

'Yeah well, all details have to go through me, and I decide whether it's important enough to disturb the *Detective* Chief Inspector.' She emphasised the word *detective,* like it was actually important to include the whole title.

Amber glanced at Jordan, wondering whether he was going to start shouting, but he didn't, however it was clear that he was frustrated.

'Okay, well, how about I tell you that we have a recorded confession from a local man who has admitted killing him twenty years ago, burying and then burning his body and hiding the remains in a box in his flat ever since.' Jordan raised his eyebrows at the Sergeant, as her mouth fell open and she stared blankly at him. She slowly rose to her feet as Amber and Jordan gave her the *evil* eye.

'Let me check if he's available.' She backed out

from around her desk and entered a small side room, leaving them in silence.

'Snooty bitch,' muttered Jordan. Amber muffled a giggle. 'She doesn't like me. I may have called her a few names once or twice while I was locked up, drying out.'

'May have?'

'Okay, I did.'

Two minutes later the Sergeant came out of the room. 'He's on his way.'

'I bet he is.'

A man wearing a smart white shirt and black jeans with a casual jacket arrived from the back room a few minutes later. Amber had expected a man in full police uniform, like the Sergeant, but she guessed maybe there was no need out here in the sticks to dress the part every day of the week. He was in his mid fifties she guessed, a clean-shaven face, his hair speckled with grey where once it had been jet black. He held out his hand and shook each of theirs in turn, giving them a kind smile.

'Hello. I'm Detective Chief Inspector Williams. I hear you have something for me. Please, this way. Would you like a drink?'

'Coffee please,' answered Amber.

'Same.'

'Sergeant, three coffees please.'

'Yes sir.'

Amber and Jordan followed him into the back room. They took a seat on each of the grey metal chairs, parked opposite a metal table; there weren't many luxuries in this station. The room was cool, with a single window which allowed light to enter, a blackout blind was drawn halfway down. Amber placed the box on the table with a thud.

The detective raised his eyebrows as he slowly opened the box.

'This box belongs to Tyler Jenkins. He was a friend of ours.'

'Was?'

'He's committed suicide by jumping into Beaker Ravine near where the watch belonging to Kieran Jones was found,' replied Amber.

'I see.' At that moment the Sergeant entered with the coffees. 'Sergeant, please take Price with you and go to Beaker Ravine where the watch was found. I believe you will find a body there. Please call it in.'

The Sergeant did her best to hide her surprise. 'Yes sir.' It looked like her day was about to get a lot less boring. The door closed and the detective turned his attention back to the box, pulling out the hard drive.

'And this is?'

'That's his taped confession.'

'And the bag?'

'Teeth and shards of bone.'

'I see.' The detective took a deep breath and ran his hands through his hair. 'I assume these remains belong to Kieran Jones.'

'Yes.'

'You know, twenty years ago I worked on this case. I was a Sergeant at the time. I actually remember questioning Tyler and yourselves. I'd never worked on a case like it before and haven't since to be honest. It's not every day a kid disappears in a town like this.'

Amber smiled. 'I thought you looked familiar.'

'I assume you've watched this tape?'

'Yes, we have, as has Brooke Willows.'

'Well, I guess I'd better play this thing and see what we have here.'

Amber and Jordan remained completely silent while the detective set up a computer screen and watched the recording. He made no sound during the tape, merely scribbling a few notes on his pad, otherwise he made no movement until the screen went black, signalling the end. The silence that followed was beyond tense. Amber wasn't sure what the detective was going to say or even whether he bought the story.

'Holy shit,' he said as he leaned back in his chair, running his hands through his hair again.

'Yeah, that was kind of the same reaction we had,' said Jordan.

'All this time ... all this time.' The detective was stunned, lost for words.

'So, this confession,' said Jordan, leaning forward slightly in his chair, 'is enough evidence to close the case, right?'

'Well, yes, it looks that way. We'll have to go through the evidence and reopen the case. I'll have to call yourselves and Miss Willows in for questioning again, just to go over formalities. But yes ... I believe this has solved the case. I'll need to contact Mr and Mrs Jones once we have confirmed that the remains in this box do indeed belong to Kieran.'

'What about Tyler's parents?' asked Amber.

'That, I'm afraid, is a whole new case, one that will be opened and investigated separately. We would need to find out where they are now and question them. To be honest without any evidence whatsoever apart from Tyler's word, it's highly unlikely that they will be charged with anything.'

Jordan sighed deeply. He knew he needed to do something, but he didn't know what; yet. He turned to the detective. 'Just please know that myself, Amber and Brooke will do whatever we can to help.'

'Thank you.' The detective stood up. 'Right, well, I guess we'd better get started on your statements. I'm going to need some more coffee. Refill?'

Amber and Jordan spent the next hour giving their statements and filling out paperwork. They explained that Brooke was recovering from severe agoraphobia and had been housebound for seventeen years, to which the detective agreed to get one of the Sergeants to visit her house and take her statement there. Amber couldn't help but feel a pang of guilt as she continued to not mention the fact that she had helped bury the body, cover up the murder and lie about it for the past two decades. She was only human, but a voice inside her head just kept repeating *don't do it, think of Bethany.* Also, Tyler had made it clear that only he was to take the blame. She didn't want to go against his dying wish; it seemed disrespectful somehow.

The detective confirmed that he would be in touch if he required any further information. His team were at the ravine dealing with the remains of Tyler (the call had come in while they were giving their official statements) and the detective said he would release some details to the local press once he had talked to Kieran's parents. He advised that they also keep things quiet until then. Amber agreed, although she wanted to tell Sean. Jordan advised against it. She was so scared about hiding the truth from him. Then again, she'd never been one-hundred percent truthful during their marriage about her past. How could she? The truth of what *really* happened was now only known by three people and it would stay that way forever whether she liked the idea or not. Lives were at stake if the truth got out and she wouldn't be the one responsible for destroying them. Brooke and Jordan were good people; they didn't deserve it. Brooke had barely lived; her whole adult life so far had been spent trapped inside her own house. Jordan had spent his whole adult life angry at everyone; he deserved a fresh start.

Jordan dropped Amber outside her house. They sat in silence for a while once he had turned off the engine.

'So,' said Jordan.

'So,' answered Amber. 'Now what?'

'Now you go inside, hug your daughter, kiss your husband and get on with your life ... and get some sleep.'

Amber smiled and nodded. 'I'll definitely try to do that. Will you be okay?'

'I'll be fine. I probably need to sort my life out a bit. I didn't tell you this before but ... my wife is finally divorcing me. I've signed the divorce papers already. I need to dig myself out of this hole. I may need some time to sort things out. I feel like I need to make things right with my mother again. And some other stuff.'

'Why does it sound like you're saying goodbye? Are you leaving?'

'It's not goodbye ... it's just ... goodbye for now.'

Amber felt her heart drop. All she wanted was to lean over and hug him tight and never let go. She needed him in her life, like a piece of her would be missing if he wasn't around, but it was too complicated, too risky. Amber didn't want to get out of the car. It was time she did and like Jordan said, get on with her life.

'Can I text you? Call you?' she asked with hope.

'Of course and I'll let you know where I am, where I'm going, stuff like that. You just enjoy getting to know Brooke again, do girly stuff, drink wine, bitch about men.'

'Is that what you think thirty-year-old women do?'

'Don't you?'

Amber shrugged her shoulders. 'I don't know. I haven't had a girlfriend to drink wine and bitch about men with.'

'And now you do.'

Amber smiled. 'Now I do.'

Jordan reached over and took her hand. She felt the ripple of electricity at his touch as he then used his other hand to gently tuck a stand of loose hair behind her left ear.

'See you,' she whispered.

'See you,' he repeated.

They leaned towards each other over the gear stick and hugged. Amber couldn't control her emotions as they poured out of her eyes in tear form. Jordan said nothing as he let her cry on his shoulder. Her body shook as she clung to Jordan for as long as possible, but it was time to finally let go. The thought of kissing him flashed into her mind, but she fought the urge.

Amber released him and they shared a knowing smile as she climbed out of the truck. The door closed and she looked at Jordan through the window pane. He stared back at her and gave her another small smile. She smiled back and he drove away.

'See you,' she repeated quietly.

Amber knew that Sean and Bethany would be waiting for her inside, probably desperately worried as she hadn't had a chance to message them and let them know her whereabouts. Amber walked into the house, gave Bethany a hug, kissed her husband and got on with her life.

That night she had the best sleep she'd had in twenty years. The Creature made no appearance, but she dreamed about that fateful day at the bottom of the ravine and the part she had played, the secret she had kept all these years —

*Amber was at the bottom of the ravine. Tyler and Jordan were digging the hole and Brooke was throwing blood-spattered rocks into the river. She was crouched down on the ground. She had seen something out of the corner of her eye, a glint of something in the light; it was Kieran's watch. It was just lying there in the dirt, smashed and with a few spatters of blood on it.*

*Amber reached out and picked it up. It must have broken off his wrist upon impact. The dial read 15:31 p.m. She blinked back the tears as she ran her fingers over the engraving – We will love you till the end of time.*

*Without a second thought she quietly slipped the watch into her pocket.*

# Chapter Eighteen

*One year later.*

Amber and Brooke stood next to each other, their arms encircling each other's waist, looking down at the gravestone in front of them. The stone itself was brand new, not yet scarred and weathered by age and the elements. The grass around the gravestone was neatly cut, the edges trimmed, a black vase stood at the top of the grave filled with beautiful flowers, some shone like gold in the sun, others were the colour of rubies. Dozens of other bouquets of flowers were placed neatly all around the gravestone, along with messages, toys and gifts. The engraving read:

*Kieran Jones.*
*Born 17 September 1985. Died 20 July 1998.*
*Gone too soon.*
*His memory will live on in our hearts forever.*
*We will love you till the end of time.*

The funeral had been a week ago and almost the entire town had attended, all dressed in their best black clothes, laden with flowers, cards, gifts and messages for him and his family. The remains hadn't been released to the family until the initial investigation had been finalised. His parents had said a short speech for him. The fact he had been killed had not been mentioned, which was appropriate because Mr and Mrs Jones were still heartbroken at the shocking revelation.

The whole town had been horrified. There had been rumours and suspicions for years that he had been murdered, but there had never been a main suspect. Everyone had secretly lived in hope that he would be found alive one day. Now that they knew the truth, the town was in mourning and everyone was devastated by the news. All the adults of Amber's age were affected the most because they had known Kieran at school. As soon as the news had been released a memorial site was set up for him in the centre of town; a simple wooden bench with a plaque where people could sit and remember him. They would talk about how he had been such a lovely, innocent young boy. Everyone appeared to forget that he had actually been a bit of a troublemaker and wasn't always pleasant.

Amber and Brooke had become best friends again, as if nothing had ever happened. They chatted almost every day and gossiped like school girls, just as Jordan had said they would. Brooke's first proper trip outside her house had been a week after she had stepped outside the front door. Amber had taken her for a coffee where she worked, on the house of course. Brooke had done amazingly well and now, a year later, she was almost completely cured. However, there were times when she started to get anxious, especially at night, but she had started seeing a therapist again and was sticking with it this time, which helped her a great deal. There were still a lot of underlying issues to work through, yet Brooke was optimistic and excited about the future.

Amber was so happy that she had her best friend back. Even Sean was glad to see her socialising for the first time. Brooke often came round to Amber's house for dinner and wine. Bethany adored her. They chatted about makeup and beauty stuff while Bethany painted her nails. Brooke had rediscovered her love for makeup and fashion and now looked the complete opposite of her former tired, pale and worn out self. She was back to being the bright, bubbly and beautiful Brooke that Amber had known all those years ago. She had also, finally, ditched her old wardrobe and now dressed in a very sophisticated, yet stylish way, emphasising her slim build. Brooke had started to eat properly and had put on an appropriate amount of weight, no longer looking like a sick child, but a healthy woman.

Amber, however, had not bounced back as

quickly as Brooke. She still had the odd sleepless night. The only issue was Bethany's dreams. They were becoming more and more vivid and she had started having nightmares, something that had never happened before. Although Amber had not had the opportunity to ask Tyler about her daughter's dreams, she had worked out on her own the reason for them; and it was not comforting, but she had a plan.

Amber bent down and placed a fresh bouquet of flowers by the grave and went back to stand next to Brooke. It was the twenty-first anniversary of Kieran's death. They wanted to commemorate the day by all coming together, but there was still someone missing.

'Do you think he'll show up?' asked Brooke, checking her watch.

Amber shrugged. 'I said we would be here at half past three.' It was 15:25 p.m. at the moment.

'Then I'm right on time.' Jordan's voice from behind made the girls spin on the spot in fright. They both squealed with delight when they realised who it was and ran and hugged him at the same time. He hugged them back, one arm around each of them, managing to lift them both off their feet effortlessly.

'You girls don't weigh a thing!' he joked.

'You came!' exclaimed Brooke.

He set them down. 'Sorry I missed the funeral. I was caught up. I'll explain in a bit, but I wanted to get back for today.'

'I'm glad,' said Amber with a smile. 'It's good to see you.'

Jordan looked good too. There was a softness to his face, something she had not seen since he was young. The Bad Man had once given him such a hard expression, but now he was just Jordan. He had let his hair grow an extra few inches, so it was thick and luscious, making Amber want to run her fingers through it. She immediately realised that her feelings, or whatever they were, had not gone after all. Jordan had been away for a whole year, so she had taken that time to try and convince herself that she was not in love with him, that he was just an old crush from her childhood, but it had been difficult. They had texted or spoken on the phone as often as they could, but Jordan had always been busy or unable to speak for long, which made her wonder what he had been up to for all this time. She did not want to pry.

'It's nearly time.'

Jordan, without saying anything else, took Amber's hand and the three friends stood together in silence for two minutes, commemorating the moment with their heads bowed. Jordan and Brooke had their eyes closed, but Amber kept hers open, focusing her gaze on a fat bumblebee that was buzzing around the entrance to a flower. It was 15:31pm, the approximate time that Kieran had fallen to his death. She thought of that exact moment and despite her best efforts she could not remove one single thought from her head: *Could I have done something to stop it?*

The two minutes ended. Without a word they walked together through the graveyard a few metres and stopped beside another gravestone. This one had no flowers adorning the slab, no gifts or messages, just a plain stone with simple writing. This one read:

*Tyler Jenkins.*

*Born 02 August 1985. Died 20 July 2018.*

*Now he is at peace.*

The funeral for Tyler had been a few months ago, but only Amber and Brooke had attended as guests. His old work colleagues had sent some flowers, but otherwise there had been no other mention of him, not even in the local paper. Jordan had sent his apologises along with flowers and a few words which Amber had read aloud. It seemed the entire town was still reeling from his confession when it finally hit the news headlines. No one was willing to put aside their grief over Kieran and acknowledge the fact that Tyler had been in pain and had suffered too. No one, that is, apart from his three remaining friends. They alone knew Tyler's true sacrifice.

They spent another two minutes in silence, after which Brooke placed another bouquet of flowers on Tyler's grave. She kissed her own fingers and then pressed them gently against his name carved into the stone. Their heads were bowed in respect the whole time.

Amber felt like there was an empty space in her heart, a void that all four of her friends used to fill. It was only half full now, but it was more than what it had been a year ago. She may have lost all her friends once, but now she had two of them back. The past year had been life-changing for all of them and she had a feeling the next year would be just as challenging, especially for her.

Brooke stood up and her and Amber hugged each other, then turned to Jordan.

'And then there were three,' said Jordan solemnly.

Brooke took a deep breath. She treasured the scent of the warm summer air now and spent as much time outside as possible. Her skin was tanned and healthy-looking.

'It feels strange now, doesn't it?' she said. 'We're all here, back together, yet still broken somehow. It was always the five of us. I thought we told each other everything back then.'

'If we'd all been honest and open with each other then none of this would have happened,' added Amber.

'We should promise to tell each other everything from now on,' said Brooke, lightening the mood slightly. 'Like ... how about you tell us why you've been away for a whole year. And it better be a damn good reason,' she warned Jordan.

Jordan shrugged his shoulders. 'Well, I'm not sure if this is what you'd class as a *good* reason, but my divorce is finally final. Eleanor has left me with the house and gone to live with her mother. She holds no ill will towards me for how I treated her over the years. I think she's just happy to be finally free of me.'

'You mean The Bad Man?' corrected Amber.

'I sometimes think The Bad Man and me were the same person, but she's happy, I think.'

'And you?'

'I'm happy too, although I will miss her. We may not have gotten on all the time, but at least I wasn't alone. Living by myself in that house will be strange. However, I've already planned ahead and got myself a new housemate to keep me company.'

'Oh?' said both girls at once, raising their eyebrows.

Jordan laughed. 'Not like that. I got a puppy two days ago. A black Labrador called Morgan.'

Both girls squealed in delight.

'Oh my God, where is he!' said Brooke jumping up and down in excitement.

'In the truck, I'll go and get him so he doesn't think I've abandoned him and then we can talk some more.'

Jordan returned a couple of minutes later with a beautiful, excitable Labrador puppy. Brooke immediately crouched on the ground and greeted the puppy, who licked and rolled on the grass, lapping up all the fuss. His jet black fur glistened in the sun, his paws seemed too big for his fourteen-week-old frame. His pink tongue was darting in and out of his mouth, trying to lick everyone in sight.

'Hello gorgeous,' said Amber, bending to stroke Morgan, feeling his soft, velvety ears between her fingers. He licked her, but continued to jump all over Brooke who was making lots of high-pitched sounds and rubbing his pink tummy. Amber had always wanted to get a puppy for Bethany who adored dogs, but Sean didn't like dogs and used the excuse that he was allergic just to reiterate the point even more.

Amber stood. 'Jordan and Morgan?'

'It's got a good ring to it, don't you think?'

'Yeah totally!' she laughed. 'What made you get a puppy?'

'Well to be honest I've always wanted a dog, but I was afraid that I'd get angry and mistreat it. I haven't had a severe anger outburst in over a year so I thought I'd give it a go now that I'm moving back here.

The house feels empty with just me in it.'

'So you aren't moving away after all?' asked Brooke, still stroking and playing with the puppy. 'Amber mentioned once after you spoke that you weren't sure whether you were coming back.'

'After much consideration I've decided to stay here and help my dad with the business. I never put much effort into helping him. He wants to hand it over to me when he retires so I need to actually start learning the ropes properly rather than just causing him a hard time. I owe him a great deal. So yeah, I'm staying.' He smiled at Amber.

'I'm glad,' she said. 'So did you make amends with your mother?' Jordan had told her a little about what he had been up to, but not all of it and she didn't want to question him too much just yet.

Jordan grinned and nodded. 'Yes. As you know I was staying with her for a while. I explained as best as I could about how Kieran's disappearance had affected me, but to be honest there was no excuse for the way I treated her and what I said to her. I apologised and she accepted. She told me that the monster in me was gone. She could somehow tell. You remember my mum, always forgiving. It was me that was making her stay away. Her and dad are now on speaking terms, but obviously still apart. So yeah, things are good with her. She's coming to visit in a few weeks and I'll be visiting her as often as I can.'

'That's great,' said Amber. 'I'm so pleased you were able to make amends.'

'Yeah, me too. Actually, there's more. I was gone for so long because of something else. Another reason.' Both girls turned their attention away from the puppy and focused on Jordan, afraid of what he was about to say in case it was something bad. 'I found Tyler's parents.'

They both gasped at once. Tyler's parents had not been able to be tracked down by the police. No one knew where they had gone. It was as if they'd disappeared off the face of the earth, but Jordan had refused to give up even when the police had. That was why he had been away for so long, searching, tracking, questioning people. He felt he owed it to Tyler to see them brought to justice.

'You found them! Where? How?' Amber had no idea that was what he'd been doing all this time. He had never mentioned it, not even once.

'They'd changed their names and moved up north into the countryside in Scotland. Literally in the middle of nowhere. Mr and Mrs Jenkins ceased to exist over ten years ago. They are now Mr and Mrs Warner. Anyway, I found them and spoke to them.'

Amber gasped loudly again. 'What did you say?'

'Well, I won't repeat the exact language I used,

but it wasn't a pleasant conversation. I told them that I knew everything they had done to their son. Obviously, they denied it at first, but eventually when I told them that he was dead they began to talk. It felt like they were almost relieved that he was dead. Little did they know that I was wearing a wire. I'd set it up with Detective Williams before I left and I said if I found them then I'd try and get a confession because it was the only way to ensure they were convicted.'

'S-So ...' stuttered Brooke, 'did it work? Will they be jailed for life?'

'I've given the recording to Detective Williams. He's going to do his best and take it from there. I've given the police their address and names, so I've done all I can. Obviously when the time arises, I'll testify in court and do whatever it takes. I owe Tyler that much.'

Amber's eyes brimmed with tears. 'I can't believe you did that for him. I thought you hated him. I thought you didn't care.'

Jordan shrugged, but didn't answer. He and Amber shared a knowing look. Amber could have hugged and kissed him, but she held back. There would be time for that.

'Wow, I can't believe it,' said Brooke, still kneeling on the ground with Morgan. 'It's so great to see you Jordan, but you have ridiculously bad timing. You come back here just as I'm about to leave.'

'You got the job?'

Brooke nodded, grinning from ear to ear. 'Yeah, with a little help from my sister. Amber's probably told you, but I've been studying and practising my makeup skills. I even took a course. I start next week as a makeup assistant for this little drama company. I'll be staying with Dorothy and Eric for a while until I can afford my own place. I don't want to impose on them for too long because Patrick is six months old now.'

'You're an auntie!'

'Yep! I love him to bits, but he's a handful, so I've offered to baby sit so Dorothy and Eric can go to one of those fancy restaurants once and a while.' Brooke had taken to her role of auntie extremely well and her and Dorothy had formed a close bond again. Brooke and her parents had been to visit them in the city when Patrick had been born and everyone had cried with happiness.

'Wow, that's great. Congratulations.' Jordan gave her a hug.

'Thanks,' said Brooke with a giggle. 'I won't lie, I'm so nervous about leaving, yet I'm also determined. The Fear doesn't control me anymore.'

'Nor does The Bad Man control me.' They both looked at Amber, expecting her to repeat the same answer for herself, but she didn't. She just smiled.

'So it looks like it's just me that's still stuck in

the same rut as before. I still work at that damn coffee shop.'

Jordan noted her change of subject, but decided to question her later. 'My dad is expanding the business. Maybe I can ask him if he has anything that's suitable for you.'

'You don't have to do that.'

'No, but I will.'

'Thank you.' There was a brief silence while Amber and Jordan looked into each other's eyes. At that moment Brooke happened to glance up and notice.

'As much as I'd love to stay and play with this little angel, I have to get back home and start packing and sorting out my room. I still have a lot of crap in there that I haven't thrown out yet.'

Brooke gave Morgan one last tickle and kiss and rose to her feet. She hugged Amber and then Jordan. Amber knew what she was doing; giving her and Jordan some alone time. They had spoken on several occasions about Jordan. In fact, they'd spent one night getting very drunk on wine and somehow ended up talking solely about Jordan. Amber had accidentally let slip that they had shared their first kiss all those years ago before Kieran's death. Brooke had been beside herself with excitement and then had started talking about what could have happened had

Kieran not died that day. Maybe Amber and Jordan would have been together, married and had kids. They had discussed his anger issues, his stint in jail, his battery on his wife. He had grown into such a bitter, hate-filled man, but today he was back to being the old Jordan, the one she had kissed, the one she had loved.

'Bye Brooke. Let's all go for dinner before you leave and get wasted.'

Brooke laughed. 'That sounds great. I'll set it up. Amber, I'll text you later.' She winked before walking away, clearly letting Amber know that she expected all the juicy details.

Amber and Jordan were left standing by Tyler's grave, along with Morgan who was watching his favourite playmate walk away back to her car. He let out a little whimper before being distracted by a fly.

'Fancy going for a walk?' asked Jordan.

'Sure.'

They started walking in the opposite direction of where Brooke had disappeared, through a gap in an old stone wall and towards town. They chatted about nothing in particular; the weather, their jobs, Morgan (who was enthusiastically scurrying everywhere, sniffing and loving life), Bethany. Amber realised that they were heading towards *their spot,* the bench by the rhododendron bush. They sat and fell silent while they watched Morgan dig a hole next to the bench.

Then Jordan spoke in a solemn, serious voice. 'Tell me the truth.'

'About what?'

'You still see The Creature, don't you?'

Amber looked away from his gaze and down at her feet. She didn't want to tell him. In fact, she had hoped to keep it a secret from him and Brooke, but it seemed that Jordan could read her mind. Amber lifted her head and stared over the road at a big oak tree, its branches and leaves forming a massive shady canopy over the grass below. There was a dark recess next to the tree, in amongst some others smaller trees and bushes.

Jordan noticed her staring and looked over at the spot, but there was nothing there.

'Amber?'

'Yes,' she answered. 'It doesn't hurt me or talk to me or do anything. I don't see it in my dreams anymore, but ... Bethany has seen it.'

'What?' Jordan stuttered, unsure if he had heard her correctly.

Amber continued, a shaky note to her voice, like she was on the verge of tears. 'The day the watch was found Bethany had a dream about Kieran, then she had another a few days later. They were harmless enough, but then she started having nightmares a few months ago. The first time she woke up screaming. I've never heard her scream like that before. It frightened me. She started crying to me that something was standing over her bed. I tried to get her to explain what it was she saw, but she couldn't explain it. The next time it happened she said the same thing again, that there was a *thing* standing over her. She told me it didn't hurt her or talk to her. It was just there watching her. Then one night when I went to check on her before I went to bed I saw it ... The Creature. It was standing over her and stroking her hair while she slept. I told it to leave her alone, that it was me it wanted, but it wouldn't leave her. It said that it would never leave her.' Amber finished and blinked as the tears streamed down her cheeks.

'Shit,' said Jordan. 'Amber I'm so sorry. What do you think it means? Why is The Creature still here?'

'I think I know why. Do you still feel any guilt over what happened, over the fact that Tyler had to take his own life to set us free, but we haven't confessed?'

Jordan took a few seconds to answer. 'No. Why do you think I tracked his parents down? I needed to clear the last bit of guilt within me and now it's gone. Amber, you need to stop blaming yourself and feeling guilty for what we did, then The Creature will go away for good and will leave Bethany alone.'

Amber shook her head. 'I can't. I can never

forgive myself. My guilt is a part of me and so is Bethany. For as long as I feel guilty then she will suffer the consequences. I tried to fix it ... I tried.'

Jordan took her hand. 'What do you mean?'

'Jordan ... I have to tell you something. Something I'm not sure you will want to hear. I planted the watch in the ravine.'

Jordan's grip on her hand slowly loosened until he let it go completely.

'You ... you planted it?' He couldn't seem to find his words. Part of him wanted to shout out in anger, the way he used to do, but he remained calm as she continued to explain.

'When we were clearing up all the evidence from the bottom of the ravine, I found his watch and I kept it. I don't know what made me do it at the time. I didn't take it for any particular reason. I never even looked at it over the years. I just kept it locked away, like Tyler did with Kieran's remains, until ... well, a couple of weeks before it was found I took it out of its hiding place and went to the ravine and left it there to be found. I was in a haze, like I was sleepwalking because I woke up on the sofa with my shoes on and I didn't remember what had happened. I think my own subconscious wanted me to do something and once it was found it kick-started everything into gear. Tyler came to see me and told me his plan and I went along with it because that had been my plan all along. It was what I wanted, that Tyler would finally confess and I hoped that everything would get better, but it hasn't. Not for me anyway. I still feel guilty.'

Jordan had been listening quietly. Amber was terrified of his reaction, that he would think she was a monster.

'Please say something, anything. If you're mad at me just tell me, shout at me, I deserve it.'

Jordan did nothing of the sort. He leaned across and wrapped his strong arms around her. Amber embraced him back, crying softly into his chest.

'I think that makes you the bravest of all of us,' he said quietly. 'I wish I could make things right for you. Please don't blame yourself for Tyler's death.'

'But I knew something like that would have to happen. I let it happen! Just for my own selfish reasons. I should have come forward myself and confessed. In fact ... I'm going to do it.'

Jordan released his arms from around her and looked her straight in the eyes. 'Do what?'

'I'm going to confess. It's the only way to be completely free from The Creature and for it to leave Bethany alone. I can't put my child at risk over something I did and can easily fix.'

Jordan sighed. 'There's nothing I can say or do to change your mind is there?' Amber shook her head no. 'Then I support your decision.'

'Thank you.'

'I feel like I'm losing you all over again.'

'You'll never lose me Jordan. Whatever happens I'm ready to face the consequences. If it was just me that my guilt was affecting then I would keep it a secret until the day I died, but I can't risk Bethany's life.'

'I understand. I would do the same thing if she were my child.'

They shared a smile. Amber wiped away her tears. 'I'm just glad you're back now. I've really missed you.'

'I've missed you too. Actually —' Jordan stopped, glanced at the dark spot beside the tree and then turned his whole body to face Amber. 'I need to tell you something.'

'Actually ... I need to tell you something too.'

'There's more!'

Amber laughed and then took a deep breath. She had kept this piece of news from him during the times they had spoken on the phone. She hadn't wanted to distract him or cause him to worry about her. It was something she had wanted to tell him to his face.

'I've left Sean.'

In the silence that followed you could have

heard a pin drop. Jordan opened his mouth to speak, but no words came out. He was stunned, utterly speechless. It had been the last thing he had expected her to say.

Amber continued. 'Sean was cheating on me. I had a suspicion that I just couldn't shake, so with Brooke's help we spied on him. He was seeing someone called Rachel, a girl who works for him – pretty, blonde, young. I confronted him about it and he couldn't deny it. At first, I tried to see things through, hear him out, but I just couldn't do it. I thought about Bethany, about what it might do to her, but I realised that even if Sean and I split up she would still have a loving father. He loves her so much and she loves him. So at the moment we're separated, but we're starting the divorce proceedings in the next couple of weeks.'

The whole time Amber had been talking Jordan's heart was doing back-flips in his chest, his mouth had turned to sandpaper. She had stopped talking and he suddenly realised he needed to say something.

'I ... I don't know what to say. Why didn't you tell me when we spoke on the phone?'

'Why didn't you tell me about Tyler's parents? I guess I wanted to tell you in person along with everything else.'

Jordan nodded, accepting her response. 'Are

you happy? Sorry, that's probably the wrong thing to say ... what I mean is ... how are you?'

Amber smiled, sensing his nervousness. 'I'm really ... okay. I didn't think I would be. I mean, when I found out he was cheating on me I was devastated, obviously. I felt betrayed, but I recovered. Brooke was amazing. Sean moved out for a few days and she moved in to help me. I realised that even though I was upset I wasn't heartbroken. I felt alive. I did love him, but I wasn't in love with him.' She knew that she had been happy once, very happy indeed. She remembered those days when her and Sean would just glide through life with smiles on their faces and not a care in the world. She would gaze into his dark eyes and he would smile back. It had been bliss, but somewhere along the way, somehow, that happiness had slowly faded into just acceptance.

'I'm so sorry Amber. I wish I'd been here for you. He's an asshole for doing that to you. I kind of want to punch him in the face right now.'

Amber laughed. 'Thanks, but I'd rather you didn't. We're on civil speaking terms. I'm still in the house for now, but I expect we will sell and split the money, but I don't know what will happen when I confess. If I go to jail then he will have Bethany and if I don't then he may stop me from seeing her. I just don't know and that scares me.'

Jordan smiled. 'Whatever happens I'm on your side and will fight for you.'

'Thank you. That means a lot. Are you going to tell me your thing now?'

Jordan suddenly looked nervous and glanced away to try and hide it. 'I don't think now is exactly the right time.'

Amber felt her heart sink. A part of her had hoped that Jordan had been about to tell her that he had feelings for her. She knew she loved him, but as Jordan had said, now wasn't the right time. Her heart was thumping so loudly in her chest she thought that Jordan must be able to hear it. Her mouth was dry and even though it was a warm day she was shivering, but not because she was cold. Amber placed her hand gently over his, which was resting on his own knee and squeezed. There were a lot of things that she needed to sort out in her own head and her life. She knew she couldn't just go and jump about ten steps ahead. It wasn't right to rush things. The last thing she wanted to do was ruin it.

'Will you promise to tell me one day?'

'Yes. I promise. One day soon I'll shout it from the rooftops.'

They shared another knowing look. Then, without really thinking, they both moved towards each other, wanting to be as close to each other as they could, but then stopped, simultaneously realising that it would be a mistake. There was time. There would always be time. Amber resisted the urge to kiss him, fought it with all her might.

'So,' said Jordan, snapping out of his haze. 'Can I meet Bethany?'

'Of course you can. I've already told her a lot about you.'

'All good things I hope. So ... now what?'

'Now we tell Brooke my plan,' answered Amber.

'She won't be happy.'

'No, but she will understand. Then I guess ... I need to speak to Detective Williams. Whatever happens next is out of my control, but I'm ready. Tyler will just have to forgive me.'

'I'm sure he would if he knew you were confessing to save your daughter.'

'I know he would. He was a good guy really.'

'Yes, he was.'

Amber and Jordan rose to their feet and faced each other. He reached out and drew her towards him and planted a gentle kiss on her forehead, lingering for a few seconds before pulling away. In that moment Amber felt like everything was going to be okay. She was transported back to her childhood when he used to kiss her on her forehead. It was such a perfect moment.

In the dark recess by the tree The Creature stirred. It was not finished with Amber yet.

# Epilogue

Guilt; we enter the world completely innocent and guilt-free, void of bad thoughts, evil doings and have a totally clean slate. Somewhere along the way, somehow, we develop into guilty beings, have bad thoughts and do evil deeds and dirty that slate. Sometimes this is through no fault of our own. It happens because of something that happens to us or is done to us and is out of our control. Other times we make bad choices and decisions and we grow further and further away from the innocent child we once were. Only we know our true feelings and thoughts and see into the dark recesses of our minds. People can get close, can maybe peek into those shadowy corners, but only we, truly, know the darkness that lies within ourselves.

## Did you like this book?

I really hope you enjoyed reading my debut novel - The Darkness Within Ourselves.

If you liked this book please feel free to leave a review on my Amazon page, Facebook page, Goodreads or Instagram.

Leave me a review on Facebook - Jessica Huntley - Author @jessicah.novel.author
Follow and tag me on Instagram -
@jessicah_novel_author with a picture of the book!
Follow and tag me on Twitter - @new_author_jess
Review my book on Goodreads - Jessica Huntley - The Darkness Within Ourselves

To receive emails about my new novels and author blogs please feel free to sign up via my website and click on the Sign Up Icon.

Website - www.jessicahuntleyauthor.com

## Connect With Jessica

Find and connect with Jessica online via the following platforms.

Website: www.jessicahuntleyauthor.com

Facebook: Jessica Huntley - Author - @jessicah.novel.author

Instagram: @jessicah_novel_author

Twitter: @new_author_jess

Goodreads: Search for Jessica Huntley

Keep an eye out for her future novels and ensure you sign up to her email list to be notified of future releases.

Printed in Great Britain
by Amazon

60162896R00203